DEATH WATCH

Also by Jack Cavanaugh
Beyond the Sacred Page

Jack Cavanaugh
Jerry Kuiper

DEATH WATCH

ZONDERVAN™

GRAND RAPIDS, MICHIGAN 49530 USA

ZONDERVAN™

Death Watch
Copyright © 2005 by Jack Cavanaugh and Jerry Kuiper

Requests for information should be addressed to:
Zondervan, *Grand Rapids, Michigan 49530*

Library of Congress Cataloging-in-Publication Data

Cavanaugh, Jack.
    Death watch / by Jack Cavanaugh and Jerry Kuiper.
       p. cm.
    ISBN-10: 0-310-21576-5 (pbk.)
    ISBN-13: 978-0-310-21576-9 (pbk.)
    I. Kuiper, Jerry, 1944– II. Title.
  PS3553.A965D43 2005
  813'.54—dc22

                                             2005000372

Interior design by Michelle Espinoza

Printed in the United States of America

---

05 06 07 08 09 10 11 12 /❖ DCI/ 10 9 8 7 6 5 4 3 2 1

To our fathers,
William H. Kuiper
and
William J. Cavanaugh

ACKNOWLEDGMENTS

Our heartfelt thanks—

To Frances Cavanaugh, Shirley Strong, and Fred B. Kinne for their insightful comments on an early draft of the story.

To the staff and radio guests at Save a Friend ministries, whose prayers and encouragement were felt each step of the journey.

To Steve Laube, constant friend and advisor.

To our wives, Sheri and Marni, who have been a loving support through the years, especially during this project.

To the staff at Zondervan, particularly Karen Ball and Diane Noble, two talented women and faithful friends.

DEATH WATCH

PROLOGUE

Delta Flight 1565, the red-eye from Atlanta to Los Angeles, was uncharacteristically on time as it descended from thirty thousand feet over a scrub-brush-dotted California desert.

The man in seat 4A opened his ultrathin laptop and connected his cell phone to the modem port. A mouse click initiated the sequence of dial tone, keypad tones, and connection static common to accessing the Internet.

"I swear those things are gonna be the death of us," the man seated next to him said. "Between laptops and cell phones, a guy can't get a moment's peace anymore. Time was a business trip meant a nap and drinks on the plane and a girlie revue at night. Now it's spreadsheets and reports in the hotel room and email in flight." He grinned. "Not this time, pal. My hard drive crashed just before takeoff." The grin widened. "Took three 'Oops!' to crash it, too."

"What business?" 4A asked.

"Auditor. IRS." He laughed. "Yeah, that's the expression I usually get."

"Sorry. I've never met an IRS auditor."

"Lucky you."

It was the first exchange between the two men since takeoff four and a half hours earlier.

The IRS auditor sat in the aisle seat. His rumpled gray suit coat was unbuttoned, his tie loosened. He leaned back and gazed at 4A's computer screen, interested in how another man did his email.

A high-resolution image of a rotating earth filled the screen. A tiny envelope seemed to rise out of Europe. It got larger as it circled the globe. After a single orbit it filled the screen with the software company's familiar triangular logo. A female voice said, "You have thirteen new messages."

The auditor leaned closer.

"Do you mind?" 4A said.

"Oh, sorry . . ." Straightening himself in his seat, the auditor signaled to the flight attendant. "Another scotch and soda."

4A clicked on the envelope graphic. A column of file folders appeared. A digit in brackets beside each folder indicated the number of messages that had been routed into each one.

```
OFFICE      [3] UNREAD MESSAGES
PERSONAL    [2] UNREAD MESSAGES
ADS / SPAM [7] UNREAD MESSAGES
```

That left one message the program was unable to route. The email's routing data was displayed.

```
From:       <blocked by sender>
To:         Seat 4A
Sent:       Wednesday, 11:47 a.m. EST
Subject:    Death Watch
```

Beneath it were three options:

```
Read
Save to folder
Delete
```

The man in seat 4A stared at the subject line. For a full minute he didn't breathe, neither did his heart beat. Then, pointer icon shaking, he clicked on the Read option.

A new window opened with the text of the message.

```
You have been selected for death. Precisely
forty-eight hours from the time of this
transmission you will die.

This is an official death watch notice.
```

Seat 4A glanced nervously at the man next to him, who was busy eyeballing the flight attendant as she handed him his drink.

As casually as he could, 4A clicked the program closed and eased shut his laptop with the same slow, deliberate motion a mortician would use to lower the lid of a coffin. 4A's breathing came in short, shallow gulps.

The auditor didn't seem to notice his distress. Taking a sip of his drink, the man reached for the phone that was embedded in the headrest of the seat in front of him. Balancing his drink, a phone card, and the handset, the auditor's freckled finger punched in a number. He stopped after three digits.

"What in blue blazes . . . ?" Pulling the phone away from his ear, he looked at it, then listened again. To 4A, he said, "There's an incoming call! That's not possible, is it?"

Heads in the first-class section turned his direction.

The man across the aisle frowned. "Those phones can't take incoming calls."

"That's what I thought," said the auditor. "But I got an operator telling me to hold for an incoming call."

"That's impossible."

"I swear, that's what she said!"

The auditor put the phone to his ear, slowly, almost as though he expected something to jump out at him. "He . . . Hello?"

He listened for a moment.

His eyes grew wide.

He held the phone out to 4A. "It's for you."

"Me? You don't know who I am."

The IRS auditor spoke with a queer tone of voice. "She told me to hand the phone to the man in seat 4A. That's you, isn't it?"

The handset was shaking. The auditor seemed desperate to get rid of the phone. He handed it over. "It's bad news, I tell you. Believe me, I know. I've delivered it often enough."

"What did they say?"

"This woman just said to hand the phone to 4A. But she had a really weird voice. Eerie, you know? It echoed like it was coming from the bottom of a well."

"Probably just a bad connection."

A perky blonde flight attendant appeared. She spoke to 4A with a smile. "I'm sorry, sir, you'll have to hang up. We're beginning final approach."

Seat 4A held up a finger. "One moment, please." He placed the phone to his ear.

The voice offered no greeting.

You have forty-eight hours. Your Death Watch begins now. This is your second and final notification.

Then the line went dead.

Outside the double-paned window, an endless patchwork of LA streets, frame houses, strip malls, and palm trees slid beneath Delta Flight 1565 in a dizzying blur.

CHAPTER ONE

"Not today! Oh, please, not today!"

Sydney St. James punctuated each syllable with the heel of her hand against the steering wheel of her stationary Volvo.

A black Cadillac SUV rose up in front of her like a cliff. Behind her, an ancient white van with rust spots that looked like some form of car cancer appeared to be wedged up against her. With parked cars to the right and a stalled lane of cars to the left, she was boxed in. No one had moved in the last ten minutes.

"I can't be late. Not today!"

Her destination, KSMJ-TV, Channel 2, was within sight, so tantalizingly close it was maddening.

The worst part was, she allowed for this. She'd given herself an extra thirty minutes to make the commute from Glendale just in case traffic was bad. But predicting LA traffic was like predicting the weather. Patterns and forecasts were useless.

The Hollywood Freeway gobbled up the extra time and more. In a word, it was clogged. The morning radio newscasters referred to it as *congestion*. For Sydney, the word was not descriptive enough. She'd seen film footage of faster-moving lava flows. She preferred *clogged*. Like a drain. Ugly, smelly, and always inconvenient.

When she finally reached her off-ramp, she checked the time. It would be close, but she had a chance. At first, traffic on Sunset Boulevard was like any other morning. Sydney managed the go-and-slow with a practiced two-step on the brake and accelerator. Then she saw red, the color of every commuter's nightmare. Brake lights as far as the eye could see. Sydney's stomach twisted into a double knot.

"Why today?" she moaned. She banged the steering wheel a couple more times.

Her father had warned her it would be like this. "There's nothing out in Los Angeles but gridlock and wackos shooting at each other. Take the job in Tulsa. It's better suited to a Midwestern girl."

But her father didn't understand news broadcasting. LA's television market share dwarfed Tulsa's. If she could make it as a newscaster in LA, she could have her pick of stations anywhere in the nation. Assuming, of course, she could actually get to work.

Sydney cranked down the driver-side window of her ten-year-old beige station wagon and stuck her head out to see what was causing the delay. The SUV in front of her was too wide. All she got for her effort was a lungful of exhaust and a handful of stares, first at her, then at her Volvo.

It was a Southern California thing.

The Volvo seemed like a good idea when she bought it used two years ago in Iowa. She'd remembered hearing someone say Volvos were good, reliable cars. Solid. Safe. What really attracted her to it was the number of heaters—front, back, under the seats. Now, with Canadian cold fronts several state lines away, it didn't seem like such a big deal. She'd only used the heater twice since moving to California. Out here, people equated style with status, and a beige Volvo station wagon was better suited to a retired Swedish farmer than an ambitious young female reporter for a major television station.

She checked her watch.

The meeting would start in five minutes. Even if traffic started moving right now, by the time she parked the car and walked back to the station she'd still be late.

Helen would save the assignment for her, wouldn't she? How could she fault her for gridlock?

A voice played in Sydney's head.

"There are no excuses in journalism."

Professor Puckett. Journalism 101.

"When you're handed an assignment, you get it done. Period. No excuses. If it's getting a statement, you dog the source until you get the quote. If it's on location, you get there even if you have to grow wings and fly."

Puckett was old school, tough as leather, with an impressive broadcasting pedigree.

He told his class of journalist wannabes, "The word *deadline* was coined at Andersonville, a notorious Confederate prisoner-of-war camp. A peripheral wire stretched around the entire facility. Any prisoner crossing that wire was shot on sight. In journalism, time is the wire. Cross it and you're dead."

Sydney glanced anxiously around. In the movies this was where the hero jumps out of the car and makes a run for it. But then, the films where that happened were usually shot in New York. This was LA, where *everyone* owned a car. Jumping out and making a run for it wasn't an option.

So what were her options?

She threw the transmission into park. With the engine still running, she climbed out of the car in search of options. A number of other drivers were doing the same thing. They didn't venture far, ready to jump back behind the wheel if traffic started moving. Some drivers stood in the open door, using the floorboard as a stepping stool to get a better look.

With a mountainous black Cadillac SUV blocking her view, Sydney had no choice but to venture away from her vehicle. What she saw wasn't encouraging.

The cause of the traffic tangle was a hazy blue Ford Taurus. Its hood mangled, facing oncoming traffic, it blocked the intersection of Sunset and Vine. Steam rose from under its hood as the car gave up the ghost. The back half of a policeman protruded from the driver-side window as he assisted the victim or victims. In the distance an approaching siren wailed.

Three black-and-white cruisers surrounded the wreck at odd angles, their driver-side doors standing open. Police milled about the scene, thumbs hooked in their belts, showing no concern for the long line of stranded commuters. It was obvious Sydney wasn't going anywhere anytime soon. Nobody was.

A smile surprised Sydney, prompted by the first happy thought she'd had all morning. Nobody was going anywhere! Nobody. If she was stuck in traffic, so was everyone else at the station. *Nobody* was going to make it to the meeting on time.

Then, as quickly as the smile appeared, it faded.

Standing on the far side of the intersection, preparing to cross the street, was Helen Gordon. An attractive middle-aged African American woman, impeccably dressed in a stylish gray business suit, Helen surveyed the accident scene with a seasoned eye, then checked her watch.

Sydney didn't have to be clairvoyant to know what Helen was thinking. Five minutes to make it to the meeting. Plenty of time.

Sydney slapped the top of a white Acura in frustration.

The driver-side window of the Acura rolled down. A balding man stuck his head out. "Hey, lady! It's a car, not a drum."

"Sorry."

The man looked Sydney up and down. His anger gave way to a wolfish grin. "No problem, sweetheart. How 'bout if you join me? We can discuss payment for damages."

Without comment, Sydney retreated to her car, more desperate than ever. How was she going to convince Helen she had what it took to be a professional political correspondent if she couldn't even make it to a morning meeting?

For the last year and a half Sydney had been paying her dues, which meant taking assignments that ran the gamut from cute to sensational. Her first west coast on-the-air report was about a mother cat that suckled an orphan puppy along with her litter of seven kittens. Sydney's second story covered the birth of a baby hippopotamus at the Los Angeles Zoo.

The station liked her coverage of the stories well enough. Sol Rosenthal, the station producer, complimented her, saying she had a knack for cute—hardly the kind of comment a serious reporter wants to hear from a producer.

Part businessman, part carnival barker, Rosenthal was a corporate suit in his late twenties. Industry execs considered him to be a real comer. This was his third television station and from all appearances, he wouldn't be with KSMJ for long. Sol Rosenthal was network bound. Thin, energetic, a fast talker, there was no newsman in him. For Sol Rosenthal, exposure was king, and the way to court success was through increased ratings.

"This'll make a splash!" he cried at one assignment meeting. Sol was always looking for ways to make a splash. "How about a story on all those impotence ads? You know, the ones with that coach and the other one with that Red Cross woman's husband."

"Mike Ditka. Former Chicago Bears coach," Grant Forsythe said. "Ditka advertises Levitra. Former Senator Bob Dole does the Viagra commercials."

Forsythe was the prime-time evening news coanchor, the face of KSMJ for fifteen years. He loved nothing better than to show off his fifteen years of accumulated news trivia.

Rosenthal leaned forward, elbows on the table. "Isn't there one more?"

"Cialis," Grant said, his tone smug.

"Yeah, that's it. And they don't call it impotence anymore, do they? What's it called now?"

"Erectile dysfunction." Grant beamed like a sixth-grade schoolboy.

"Here's my idea. We have Sydney do the story."

Helen Gordon frowned. "Why Sydney?"

"Because it's sweeps week, Helen. A hot blonde doing a story on erectile dysfunction? It'll make a splash."

During sweeps week broadcasters used the viewership numbers to set local advertising rates for the rest of the year. Competition between stations was fierce.

Sweeps or no sweeps, Sydney didn't want to do the story. She thought Rosenthal's idea was in bad taste. Privately she told Helen as much and tried to back out of the assignment.

Helen didn't buy it.

"We all get assignments we don't like," the veteran newswoman snapped. "So stop whining and just do your job."

Helen liked Sydney.

Helen Gordon had risen through the ranks from intern to reporter to newscaster to assignment editor and knew firsthand broadcasting was a tough business, especially for a woman. It was obvious she liked Sydney too much to coddle her.

Sydney took the assignment. Once she started researching it and realized erectile dysfunction was a serious health issue, she saw its potential.

On camera, she said, "Between fifteen and thirty million men suffer from erectile dysfunction. That's nearly 10 percent of the American male population. Yet, tragically, only one man in twenty will seek treatment."

Her report explored the causes of the problem: fatigue, high blood pressure, diabetes, prostate cancer surgery, and wounds that were often the result of combat. She described how the problem affected both men and their wives. She interviewed couples, keeping their identity hidden with backlighting. She encouraged viewers suffering from erectile dysfunction to seek treatment, giving them contact information for local hospitals and counselors.

Her report didn't come off as hot as Sol Rosenthal envisioned it, but the station switchboard received a surge of phone calls from community leaders, health organizations, and others who said they appreciated the professional and tactful way the station handled the sensitive topic.

Sydney's report was a sweeps success.

Rosenthal took credit for his idea paying off. The next time sweeps week rolled around, he had another idea.

"How hot would it be for Sydney to do a story on Hollywood hookers? A hot blonde interviewing hookers. It'll make a splash!"

This time Sydney didn't complain, though she did grit her teeth when Helen readily agreed Sydney was the best reporter for the job.

Sydney turned the assignment into a family issue. As the story aired, Sydney reunited a sixteen-year-old Colorado runaway, now living on the streets, with her parents.

The switchboard flooded with calls.

While Sydney was pleased with the response, she feared her success would be her undoing. Rosenthal would never see her as anything other than a feature-story reporter.

Her hope lay with Helen Gordon. Helen knew her heart and yesterday had stopped shy of promising her an assignment to interview the governor of California, who was coming to LA to announce a get-tough-on-gangs bill. The assignment would be handed out at this morning's meeting.

All Sydney had to do was get there.

From the middle of clogged Sunset Boulevard, she shouted at the sky, "Why is this happening to me?"

An instant later, Sydney's darkening morning turned black.

Strolling up behind Helen Gordon was Cori Zinn, the station's evening coanchor and Sydney's self-appointed nemesis. Like Helen, somehow Cori Zinn had managed to escape the traffic.

"How? How? How?" Sydney groaned. "Is there a secret underground boulevard I don't know about?"

A brunette, Cori was a competent newscaster, attractive but not beautiful. And in an industry that worships physical appearance even above talent, she would always be threatened by beautiful young talent. That made Sydney the enemy.

Standing beside her beige Volvo in the middle of Sunset Boulevard, Sydney watched helplessly as Helen Gordon reached the front door of KSMJ with Cori Zinn right behind her.

Cori caught up. The women exchanged pleasantries. Apparently Cori said something about the accident, because both women turned toward the intersection.

Sydney saw her chance. Raising both hands over her head, she waved and shouted, hoping to catch Helen's attention. Instead, she caught Cori's.

The two rivals exchanged glances. Just as Helen turned to see what Cori was looking at, Cori distracted her and held open the station door.

Helen entered the building. Cori followed, but not without first turning to Sydney and grinning.

With a frustrated yelp, Sydney fell back into the Volvo. She grabbed her purse and plunged her hand into it, searching for her cell phone. A moment later, she was connected to the station. Helen didn't always go to her office before the morning meeting, so Sydney left a message with the receptionist, leaving explicit instructions for the girl to see that Helen Gordon received it.

That done, Sydney slumped behind the wheel. She'd done all she could do, hadn't she?

There are no excuses. Get there if you have to grow wings.

Sydney jumped out of the car. She looked around for a pair of wings. Something. Anything that would get her into that meeting.

She spotted a couple standing on the sidewalk, gawking at the tall buildings. Pointing.

Sydney grabbed her keys from the ignition switch. This wasn't New York, but it was time to get out and run.

CHAPTER TWO

Helen Gordon sat at the head of a table that seated twelve. It was situated in a central open area flanked by a row of office doors on one side, and on the other, a wall lined with wire service printers and computer terminals. Telephones and monitors were poised to order up anything from unedited video clips to fully prepared segments to competitor's newscasts. Dubbed Command Central, it was here KSMJ's news broadcasts were planned and choreographed.

Helen looked up as Sydney hurried into the room. "Sydney! We were just getting started."

Out of breath, Sydney approached the table. There were several empty chairs, including the one next to Helen where the producer sat. It was unusual for him not to be in attendance. Maybe he was stuck in traffic.

She remained standing.

"I see you escaped the mess outside," Helen said.

Her comment surprised Sydney. "Didn't you get my message?"

"No message."

"I called the receptionist and specifically told her to make sure you got it."

Cori Zinn sat up in her chair as though she just remembered something. "Oh! I must have it here." She fumbled through her papers. "With all that was going on this morning, I picked up your messages for you, Helen." She slid a pink telephone slip across the desk to Helen.

Sydney fumed. Intercepting Helen's messages was low, even for Cori.

Helen read the note. "Says here you're stuck in traffic. Has it cleared already?"

"No. I . . . um, made arrangements."

Helen looked intrigued. "Arrangements?" She waved the note. "You say you're stuck in traffic, yet minutes later here you stand. Could it be that Sydney St. James has solved the problem that has plagued Southern Californian commuters for decades?"

Sydney felt the heat rise in her cheeks. Everyone was staring at her—coanchor Grant Forsythe, who always sat next to the producer; Cori Zinn; Josh Leven, sports; Phil Sanders, weather; as well as a sampling of the station's other reporters, studio personnel, and interns. They all wanted to hear Sydney's secret.

"Um . . . I spotted a Midwestern couple on the sidewalk," she said. "And I paid them to park my car for me."

"Ho! You can kiss that baby good-bye." Grant Forsythe laughed. "What kind of car was it?"

"Sydney drives a beige Volvo station wagon," Cori said, as if it was something to be ashamed of. Her comment got some laughs.

"Ah! No great loss then," Grant said. "Not like it was a Jaguar." Everybody at the station knew Grant Forsythe drove a Jaguar.

"Sydney, you handed your car keys to total strangers?" Helen asked. "Do you think that's wise?"

"They can be trusted." It had seemed like a good idea at the time, but the reaction in the room made Sydney doubt her decision.

"You've never met these people before in your life?" Helen arched her eyebrows.

"No."

"Yet you trust them with your car."

Sydney nodded. "They looked like an honest couple."

"You said they were Midwesterners."

"Well, I didn't know that for sure until I talked to them. I mean, they dressed like Midwesterners, and they were looking up at all the tall buildings, pointing in awe." She shrugged. "They looked like tourists."

Grant Forsythe sat back with an amused look. "And you really think you'll see your car again?"

"I paid them twenty dollars."

Grant howled. "You gave them your car *and* gas money?" He turned to a pretty intern seated behind him. "There's one born every minute."

The intern wrinkled her nose at him and sniggered.

"All right, everybody, let's get down to business," Helen said.

Sydney took a seat at the foot of the table, trying to ignore the subtle and not-too-subtle glances that said she was some kind of country hick.

Helen took charge. She presented a quick overview of the news items that had come across her desk from the network, various news agencies, phone calls, and emails. Ten minutes into the meeting she came to the item Sydney was waiting for.

"Next on the docket," Helen said, "the governor will be at city hall today to announce his anti-gang bill." She paused. "Cori, I want you to take this one. Take Bihn with you. Tell him we want footage of the governor's announcement and your interview."

Cori nodded, a little too smugly.

Sydney slumped in her chair. The effort to get here, all the anxiety, for nothing.

Moving on to the next item of business, Helen looked up and saw Sydney's disappointment. Then the assignment editor did something she rarely ever did. She explained herself. "Cori has a contact in the governor's office," she said. "I just learned about it last night. She thinks she can get an exclusive."

Grant turned to Cori. "Who?"

"Milt Abrams, the press secretary."

"You sleep with him?" Grant said with a smirk.

Cori spat an off-color reply.

"That's enough, you two," Helen said. "Moving on . . ."

They worked their way through the agenda, doling out assignment after assignment to fill the thirty-minute newscast. Sydney barely heard any of it. She bit her lip. Cori Zinn had stolen her story. Sydney wondered if she really knew the governor's press secretary. She wouldn't put it past Cori to make up something like that.

"Sydney," Helen said, breaking into her funk. "Why don't you go with Cori. Mill about city hall. See if you can dig up anything interesting."

Sydney nodded. She wondered if the morning could get any worse.

"You know," Cori said, "you could send Sydney out front. There might be a story in that car accident."

"Better yet," Grant Forsythe said, "have her do a story on tracking stolen automobiles. She can color her report with personal anecdotes."

Grant was just being insufferable, as always. Sydney could live with that. Cori Zinn was a different matter altogether. Sydney tried not to hate her, but some days Cori made that next to impossible to do.

To Sydney's horror, Helen said, "Cori may have something there. Sydney, see if there's anything about that accident we can use." Helen stood, indicating the meeting was over. "And people," she said, "remember, we have Hunz Vonner from EuroNet arriving at eleven. Let's behave ourselves."

As the others dispersed to their various work areas, Sydney lagged behind, absorbing the amused smiles and sympathetic pats on her shoulder.

"A car crash, Helen?" she said when they were alone. "That's about as newsworthy as the sunrise."

Helen disagreed. "There's something going on down there," she said. "Call it a hunch."

Scattered laughter and applause interrupted them from a short distance away. Helen and Sydney turned to see what was causing it.

A security guard approached them. With him was a young couple, wide-eyed at everything around them. The woman wore tan slacks with an understated blouse; he wore jeans and a button-up short-sleeve shirt. What was remarkable about them was the lack of piercings, tattoos, beer logos, or cartoon character images on their clothing.

"Miss St. James?" the guard said. "These people say they have a delivery for you."

The young man held out a set of Volvo car keys.

The scene at Sunset Boulevard and Vine Street had changed only slightly when Sydney approached with her cameraman. A single lane of traffic had been opened. Police were funneling cars through it. The signal lights overhead flashed red in all four directions. Paramedics had arrived.

The Ford Taurus had not been moved. Its driver-side door stood open. It was unattended while paramedics and police loaded a gurney into the back of an ambulance. They were in no hurry. There was no life left in the body they had come to save.

Sydney motioned to her cameraman. "Zappa, get some shots of the car with the ambulance in the background."

Cameraman Fred "The Assassin" Zappa was an oafish pile of unwashed laundry with legs. He had a full beard and a head of hair that looked like a greasy brown fireworks display. But he was a competent cameraman and a pleasant enough guy, as long as you didn't have to ride with him anywhere with the windows rolled up and didn't mind nonstop narration of "Doom," a violent video game Zappa claimed was a classic. While some thought his screen nickname came from his gaming, it actually referred to his camerawork. "I get it done on the first shot," he told anyone who asked.

While Zappa maneuvered himself into position, Sydney took advantage of the unattended car, first checking to make sure the police were occupied. She approached the car from the driver's side.

For the most part, the interior was clean. It was dusty, but there wasn't any clutter. No cup holders. No stick-on crucifixes or compasses. No CD or audiocassette cases. No trash on the floor. Nothing like her Volvo, which had empty Starbucks cups and breakfast bar wrappers scattered about. In this way the Taurus was not a typical Southern California car. From all appearances, the driver used the car for transportation. He didn't live in it.

The windshield was intact, no cracks or shatters from heads slamming against it. There was no blood, which was somewhat unusual for an accident. Even in minor incidents there was often a cut head or smashed nose, something that would leave blood. Not in this case.

The glove compartment hung open. Someone—probably the police—had retrieved the owner's registration, which was face up on the driver's seat. Sydney wrote down the information. The owner was a man named Jeffrey Conley of West Groverdale Avenue, Covina.

There was another slip of paper on the passenger seat, larger than the registration. Yellow. Sydney leaned into the car to get a better look. Western Union was printed across the top. A telegram, dated two days ago and addressed to Jeffrey Conley.

Sydney's breath caught in her throat when she read it.

```
You have been selected for death stop pre-
cisely forty-eight hours from the time of
     this transmission you will die stop

This is an official death watch notice stop
```

She turned to signal Zappa.

"Hey! What do you think you're doing? Get outta there!"

Through the passenger-side window Sydney saw an officer striding toward her. She backed out of the Taurus.

"Stand right where you are," the policeman shouted.

Several others turned to see what was going on, even the officer directing traffic, though he kept his right arm twirling like a windmill.

The approaching officer was of average size with a round face and close-cropped hair. His chest appeared huge for his size, probably from a bulletproof vest beneath his uniform.

He grabbed Sydney by the arm. "You've got a lot of nerve, lady! Just what do you think you're doing?"

Sydney identified herself and Zappa. His camera carried the station number and logo on it and they were right in front of the station. There was no reason for the officer to doubt her.

Right about then, the policeman took a good look at her. Then a second good look. He signaled to the other officers that he had everything under control. Then he half pulled, half led Sydney away from the car to the sidewalk. He demanded to see identification.

Sydney produced a press card and driver's license.

"Want to see mine too, Officer?" Zappa asked.

The officer winced, either from the sight of Zappa or the smell of Zappa.

"Yeah," the officer said, but he didn't sound all that eager.

Zappa dug into his back pocket, nearly losing his already sagging pants in the process. He pulled a limp driver's license and a stained press card from a wallet that had once been brown, but was now covered with some kind of black goo.

The policeman held Zappa's ID by the edges. The picture on the driver's license showed a clean-shaved, short-haired happy-looking guy. The officer squinted at the cameraman as though he was trying to locate something recognizable beneath all the facial hair. Apparently he did, because he handed Zappa's ID back to him.

"What did you take pictures of?"

"Panorama of the intersection. Then you busted us."

The policeman looked at Zappa, then the distance Zappa was from the car when he'd first seen him.

"All right. You can go," he said.

Zappa looked to Sydney.

"I'll be all right," she said.

Zappa shrugged and walked away, pulling an unwrapped piece of beef jerky from his pants pocket.

The officer turned his attention to Sydney's ID. "Glendale, huh?" he said. He looked at her, at the ID, then back at her. "Best driver's license photo I think I've ever seen."

"Why are the police taking so long to clear this accident?"

The officer handed her ID back. "I should arrest you."

"For what? Stealing loose change from the floorboard? It's an accident, not a crime scene."

"You shouldn't have been nosing around."

"That's my job, Officer Pollard." She'd read his name from the badge above his shield.

"Did you touch anything?"

Sydney smiled. "What an interesting question, Officer."

Why would he be concerned if she touched anything? He could easily see she didn't take anything. There were two pieces of paper still on the seat, and the keys still in the ignition. There was nothing else to take. But there was something to leave. Fingerprints. Police didn't dust traffic accidents for prints; they dusted crime scenes for prints.

"Why haven't you taped off the scene?"

A worried look clouded Pollard's face. He'd tipped his hand and he knew it. "This is just what it looks like," he said. "A car crash. Nothing more."

"With a telegram on the front seat that threatens a man's life?"

Officer Pollard cursed. "You shouldn't have seen that."

"Why the ruse?"

Pollard looked past her to the other officers. There was worry in his eyes, the kind of worry that's a close cousin to fear. He didn't want to tell his superiors that he'd messed up.

"Look, Officer Pollard," Sydney said, "you know all this is going to come out eventually."

"I'm going to let you go this time," Pollard said, trying to make it sound like he was doing her a favor. "Get outta here."

"You know I have to report what I saw," Sydney said.

He stared at her, the long-standing animosity between law enforcement and journalism flaring up one more time.

Sydney said, "Look, I can speculate as to the reason why the police want this to appear to be something other than a crime scene, but I'd rather report the facts."

Pollard started to walk away.

"I won't use your name," she called after him.

He kept walking.

Sydney stared at his back. Her source was getting away. She could follow up at the police substation, but all she'd get would be an official, carefully worded statement, devoid of any newsworthy copy. Pollard knew what was going on here. Somehow, she had to get him back.

An approach came to mind. She rejected it. She'd promised herself long ago she'd never resort to that tactic. But she had to do something! If she allowed Pollard to reach the other policemen, she'd never get him back.

"Officer Pollard," Sydney called. There was a story here, and she was going to get it. She caught up with him. "Officer Pollard," she said, placing a hand on his arm.

Pollard swung around and looked at her hand. His gaze followed it up her arm to friendly eyes.

Sydney hated doing this. She hated it when women used their sexuality to get what they wanted.

Pollard didn't seem to mind.

"Give a girl a break, will you?" Sydney pleaded. "My assignment editor sent me out here. She sensed immediately something was odd about this accident. I know you have your job to do, but I have a job to do too. And if I go back there empty-handed, I'm going to be stuck reporting the birth of kittens for the rest of my career."

Her hand was still on his arm. She gave it a squeeze. Pollard didn't seem to mind.

"Look, Miss ..."

"Sydney. Sydney St. James."

"Look, Miss St. James, I'd like to help you, but ..."

He wanted to help her. His goofy grin gave him away. He just needed a little nudge.

"This is more than just the death of a Covina man, isn't it?"

Pollard reacted visibly when she mentioned Covina.

"The registration on the front seat. It was there when I arrived. Honest." She gave him a small smile.

Pollard stared at her. Evaluating. Thinking.

Thinking is good, Sydney told herself. *A minute ago, he was walking. Now he's thinking.*

Pollard glanced over his shoulder. Behind him a police photographer was shooting stills of the vehicle. A sergeant looked on. Pollard turned back to Sydney. He sighed.

A sigh is good. From walking, to thinking, now sighing. That's good, isn't it?

Pollard walked her back to the sidewalk.

"That telegram?" he said in a low voice.

"Yes?"

"It's the seventh one this morning."

"Seven telegrams informing people they're going to die?"

"The form varies, but there have been seven transmissions, all with identical wording. All found at a death scene."

Sydney reached for her notepad.

Pollard became agitated. "What are you doing? If my sergeant sees you . . ."

"Oh, sorry."

Simultaneously, they checked on the sergeant. He was instructing the photographer, leaning over and pointing at the steering wheel.

"Sorry," Sydney said again. "You have seven notices tied to seven murders all this morning?"

"That's not the strangest part," Pollard said. "As best as we can determine, the deaths occur exactly at the announced time. I mean *exactly.*"

"According to the telegram in the Taurus, the victims are given forty-eight hours' notice. Surely, they contacted you that their lives had been threatened."

"Five did. Mr. Conley was one of them."

"So he was under police protection?"

Pollard shook his head. "We're not a bodyguard service."

"The deaths. All car accidents?"

"I'm not at liberty to elaborate, but I can tell you, from what I've heard, they're all different."

"Have you been able to establish any link between the victims? Did they all work at the same place, belong to the same union, members of the same bowling league?"

"As far as I know, nothing links the deaths other than the notices."

"Has anyone called to take credit for the deaths?"

Pollard was feeling increasingly nervous. He kept glancing over his shoulder. "I've gotta go," he said.

"One more question, Officer Pollard."

But he was walking away. His sergeant met him. Sydney couldn't hear what was being said, but by the way the sergeant was looking at her, it was obvious she was the topic of discussion.

Sydney decided now would be a good time to leave.

Billy Peppers pushed the dreadlocks out of his face as he leaned against the corner of Bennett's Mattress Warehouse and watched the activity that surrounded the crumpled car in the intersection.

He was wearing all the clothing he owned in layers: three shirts, two pair of pants. His shoes were the newest addition to his wardrobe, a pair of black Converse tennis shoes. They were tattered, the tread was worn, and the left shoe had string for a shoelace, but they were better than his old pair of Nikes that had holes in the soles. Billy had traded for the Converse with Harold, the guy who slept on the back step of Ray's Electronics. The shoes cost him a blanket and a crumpled Cup O Noodles that still had its cellophane wrapper.

As he watched the police photograph the accident scene, Billy rubbed a wooden cross he wore on a leather strap around his neck. The ambulance momentarily cut off his view, passing in front of him. Its emergency lights were dark, its siren silent.

"Ordained to die," Billy mused. "Whatcha gonna do when you're ordained to die?"

Billy's attention returned to the leggy blonde who had been talking to one of the policemen. He watched her stride back to the television station, pull open the door, and disappear. She was the reason Billy was here.

He was told she'd be here. He'd watched her since she emerged from the station. He'd watched her give instructions to the big guy toting the camera. He'd watched her poke her head into the car. He'd watched as the policeman confronted her and escorted her out of the intersection. He'd watched as she placed a hand on his arm. He'd watched her return to the building.

"You didn't tell me she was an angel," Billy muttered to thin air, turning away now that there was nothing left to watch.

"You there!"

The side door to the mattress warehouse stood open. A skinny man in a suit with a skinny tie glared at Billy.

Billy had been chased away by him before. He was an employee of the store, the guardian of the parking lot. He came out here half-a-dozen times a day to smoke and drive off the undesirables.

"I thought I told you to stay away. Shoo! Shoo! Shoo!" The man flicked his hands at Billy with the same gesture he'd use to chase away a dog. "Go on, git! Git!"

Billy put a hand to his shopping cart that was packed with cardboard, a blanket, a jug of water, a Nike shoe box, and some pastries he'd found in a dumpster. He made his way across the mattress store parking lot to the alley.

He whistled as he walked.

CHAPTER THREE

Sol Rosenthal waved his hands over his head. He looked like he was gathering armloads of air. Responding to the sound of his voice, station personnel migrated from offices and the news set. They congregated in front of him in a loose half circle several layers deep.

Standing next to Rosenthal watching them gather was a man in his midthirties sporting an expensive haircut and wearing a flashy European suit.

Sydney's first impression of the international newscaster was how the appearance of television personalities obviously transcended culture. He looked like every other news anchor in America. After that, she didn't give him another thought. She was looking for Helen.

As Sol began his introduction, Sydney located Helen. She was on the far side of the room.

"If you will recall," Sol Rosenthal began, using his professional speaking voice, the one the station purchased for him for three thousand dollars at a two-week public speaking seminar for CEOs. Now, instead of sounding like a squeaky clarinet, Rosenthal sounded like a loud squeaky clarinet.

Sol coughed, cleared his throat, and began again.

"If you will recall, last year it was my privilege to travel to Europe to observe the fastest-growing news station in the international market, the EuroNet Broadcasting System. You'll also recall I came home quite impressed."

"Helen!" Sydney whispered when she was within earshot of the assignment editor. "I think I've got something."

Helen Gordon cut Sydney off with an upraised hand. "I want to hear this."

"For those of you who don't know," Rosenthal squeaked, "EuroNet dominates the European market. Within five years of their inception, EuroNet attained their stated objective of establishing themselves as the number one source of news from a European perspective. They broadcast in seven languages—English, French, Italian, German, Portuguese, Spanish, and Russian. Launched in 1996, EuroNet provides their viewers the widest perspective of any news agency in the world."

Sydney leaned close to Helen. "Your instincts were on target about that accident," she whispered. "It's a crime scene."

Helen shushed her.

Sydney wouldn't be shushed. She couldn't hold it in. She had a real news story, one that didn't involve animals or sex.

"While I was in Germany," Rosenthal continued, "it was my privilege to observe EuroNet's top newscaster. Having begun his broadcasting career at a small radio station in Munich, he has risen to anchor the number one newscast in Europe. And wait until you hear him speak! His English is better than mine, with no trace of accent."

"I give full credit to video clips of American newscasters," Vonner said with a chuckle. "I watched Walter Cronkite so much, I started sounding like him."

Sol laughed the loudest. Then he said, "Please give a warm welcome to EuroNet's brightest star, Hunz Vonner."

The television crew's response was cordial. Most of them were industry veterans, no longer awestruck at the sight of television personalities, especially one they'd never actually seen on the air.

When the clapping started, Sydney politely joined in. She thought Vonner looked like a men's store mannequin, stiff and attractive in a cardboard cutout way.

"Hunz will be observing our operation here at KSMJ for a week," Rosenthal said. "He will meet in turn with anchors, reporters, production personnel, and advertising. My secretary will coordinate with your schedules. Let's do everything we can to make his stay in America a memorable one. I'm confident you will give Mr. Vonner every courtesy. Treat him as you would treat me."

There was a smattering of laughter. Sol looked puzzled. He thought everyone loved and admired him.

The assembly dispersed. Everyone returned to work, but not too quickly.

"Helen, it's a crime scene!" Sydney said, louder now.

Sol Rosenthal interrupted her. He horseshoed his way between her and Helen. "Hunz, I'd like you to meet our assignment editor, Helen Gordon."

Helen offered her hand. Vonner gave it a quick pump and turned to Rosenthal with a *what's next* expression.

"Helen will be joining us and the coanchors for lunch; you two can talk then," Rosenthal said. He took Vonner by the arm, directing him toward Grant and Cori, who were standing nearby. "And over here we have . . ."

Vonner broke away. He turned to Sydney. "And you are?" He raised an eyebrow and gave her a smooth, easy smile.

Maybe it was because Hunz Vonner shared nationalities with the famous brothers Grimm, but Sydney got the distinct impression she knew how Little Red Riding Hood felt when greeted by the wolf.

Helen made the introduction. "Mr. Vonner, this is Sydney St. James, one of our reporters."

"Miss St. James," Vonner said, taking her hand with a slight bow.

Sydney had seen the bedroom-eyes expression on a hundred different men. The European version was no different from the American version. His voice, however, was impressive. Rich, smooth, confident, it was an instrument uniquely suited to news broadcasting. It could deliver stories of graphic violence while assuring viewers that despite what they'd just heard, everything would be all right. And his English was impeccable, not a trace of an accent.

"Yes, well," Sol said. He was ready to move on. "Over here we have . . ."

"Helen, did you hear me? It's a crime scene!" Sydney said the instant he was gone.

"Our guest seems quite taken with you," Helen said, looking amused.

Sydney dismissed the comment. She wasn't interested in Hunz Vonner of EuroNet. She wanted to tell Helen about her news story.

"The accident outside?" she said for the third time. "Not an accident. It's a crime scene, though the police are trying to keep it under wraps."

Finally, Helen was listening. Sydney told her about the unattended vehicle, the telegram, getting caught, Officer Pollard's blunder, and the resulting disclosure.

"Exactly what did the telegram say?" The newshound within Helen Gordon stirred. Sydney had seen it happen before, but this was the first time she was the one poking it to life. It was exciting.

"I wrote it down." Sydney flipped open her notepad. "It said, 'You have been selected for death. Stop. Precisely forty-eight hours from the time of this transmission you will die. Stop. This is an official death watch notice. Stop.'"

A voice came from behind her. "What did you say?"

Sydney looked up to see Hunz Vonner turning his back on Cori Zinn, who was in the middle of telling him there was a vacancy in the prime-time broadcast and how she was being considered for the slot. Vonner wasn't listening.

"What was that you said?" he said again to Sydney.

He looked at her notepad. Reached for it. She pulled it away, pressing it flat against her chest.

"Did you pick that up off the wires?" Vonner's eyes were sharp, demanding. His voice had an edge to it that a television audience would never be allowed to hear.

Conversations around them stopped. Everyone was looking at him. At them.

Sol Rosenthal jumped between them. "What is this all about?" He glared at Sydney as if she'd done something wrong.

Helen said, "How about if we take this into my office?"

Hunz and Sydney stood face-to-face. He, insisting on an answer; she, protecting her story.

"What did you say to him?" Rosenthal demanded.

"In my office," Helen said again, this time with authority.

Helen led the way. Sydney was right behind her. Hunz Vonner and Sol Rosenthal trailed, with Sol attempting to smooth over any ruffled feathers.

Sydney didn't hear everything the producer said, but she did hear Rosenthal say, "If she's offended you in any way, she'll apologize. You have my word on that."

Entering Helen Gordon's office, the producer stepped past Sydney, shooting her a murderous glare.

Sol Rosenthal began speaking the instant the door was closed. His intentions were obvious: Exert his authority, and smooth everything over with Hunz Vonner.

He turned first to Vonner. "I apologize if our staff has done or said anything to offend you." Then he frowned at Sydney. "I think an apology is in order."

Sydney and Hunz stood in front of Helen's desk like children in the principal's office. Helen took her seat at the desk.

"It's not what you think, Sol," Helen said.

"I'll take care of this, Helen," Rosenthal barked. "Hunz? What did this woman say to you?"

"She has a death watch notice," Hunz said.

Sol Rosenthal didn't know what to do with that. Perched on the edge of Helen's desk, he raised his hand to his chin, nodded gravely. "Is this true, Sydney? Did you threaten Mr. Vonner's life?"

"Oh, for crying out loud, Sol," Helen said. "You're making a fool of yourself. Mr. Vonner, do you know about this?"

"If it's what I think it is, yes."

"Know about what?" Sol asked.

"Sydney, let him see it," Helen said.

Had Sol Rosenthal asked her to show this foreigner her notepad, she would have refused. Had he threatened to fire her, she would have walked out and started looking for another job. Helen, on the other hand, had been a reporter and had, as an assignment editor, when needed, fiercely protected her reporters.

Sydney handed her notepad to Hunz.

The room fell silent as he read it, then read it again.

"What? What is it?" Sol craned his neck to see what was on the pad.

"Is it what you think it is?" Helen said to Hunz.

"Where did you get this?" Hunz asked Sydney.

Sydney shot a questioning look to Helen, who nodded her consent.

"What's going on here?" Sol shouted.

"Shut up and listen, Sol," Helen said. "Sydney's stumbled on a news story that apparently has farther-reaching implications than we thought."

At Helen's request, Sydney told the story of how she came across the telegram notice of death. Hunz Vonner listened intently.

"Officer Pollard said it was the seventh death in LA this morning linked to notices like this one."

Sol Rosenthal demanded to see the notepad. His eyebrows rose as he read it.

"Mr. Vonner, do you know something about this?" Helen had let him in on their story; now she expected the favor to be returned.

He took a moment before answering. "Just before I left Germany, a story was breaking about an alarming number of people who had received death threats. The wording in every one of the threats was identical."

"Identical to this notice?" Sydney asked.

Hunz nodded. "That was two days ago. This is the first I've heard of a death that's related to the notices. We thought it might be a hoax. If people are dying here as a result of these notices, there are probably reports hitting the wires all across Europe."

Sol Rosenthal went to the door. He shouted at a passing intern to get him the most recent printouts from the major international news services.

Minutes later, with Hunz looking over his shoulder, producer Sol Rosenthal read aloud the names of cities that were reporting deaths associated with similar notices: "Berlin, Paris, Rome, Madrid, Brussels, Warsaw, London, Moscow, Beijing, Cairo, Jerusalem, Sydney, Tokyo." He went to another sheet. "Here in the United States, Associated Press is reporting deaths in Phoenix, Austin, Cleveland, New York, Philadelphia, Miami, Nashville, Tulsa, Bismarck, Denver, Portland, San Francisco . . ."

"Good Lord," Sol Rosenthal breathed, "we've stumbled upon the mother of all news stories!"

CHAPTER FOUR

Sydney, write up what you have for the noon newscast," Helen said. "Incorporate the information we have from the wires."

"We'll lead with it," Sol Rosenthal added. "Better yet, we'll break into programming with a teaser. This is going to make a splash. Sydney, get a quote from Hunz, something about the European angle on this, and make sure you mention he's working with us on the story. Hunz, of course you won't actually be working on the story. We'll keep to our schedule."

"Forget the schedule," Hunz said. "This story is too important to pass up."

With his best diplomatic smile, Sol said, "No can do, big fella. Your week is pretty much booked. Did I tell you you're meeting the mayor on Wednesday?"

"Cancel it. Cancel everything," Hunz said. "I'm not going to sit around spreading jam on biscuits while the biggest news story of the millennia is breaking. Either I cover the story here, or I cover it in Germany."

"You know," Sol said, not missing a beat, "this could be good for ratings!"

When it came to bootlicking, no one ever accused Sol Rosenthal of being inflexible. He had the backbone of a wet noodle.

"All right then. You're in!" Sol slapped Hunz on the back.

"Who will I be working with?" Hunz said. "I'll need someone who knows their way around."

"Grant Forsythe, naturally," Rosenthal said. "He's our senior news—"

"It's my story," Sydney said.

Sol Rosenthal scowled at her, one of those parental scowls, the kind that said, *I'll deal with you later.*

Sydney ignored it. "I was assigned the story this morning. I did the initial investigation. I found the death telegram. I should be the one to follow up."

"I'm not working with some inexperienced Barbie doll," Hunz said.

Sol was quick to agree with him. He turned to Helen. "This story is much bigger than we originally thought. I'm sure you'll agree, we have to go with a veteran."

"First of all, Mr. Vonner," Sydney said, emphasizing his name, "I resent the implication that my appearance has anything to do with my ability as a reporter. And secondly, this is my story. I should be the one choosing who I'm going to work with."

"And I'm the one who decides who works at this station and who doesn't," Sol shouted. "Any more from you and not only will you not have a story, you won't have a job."

Sydney shot a pleading look at Helen.

"We could put you with Cori Zinn," Sol said to Hunz. "She's our evening coanchor. You just met her. A real fireball."

"It's Sydney's story," Helen said.

Stunned, Sol took a moment to recover. "Helen, this has already been settled."

"You're right. It *is* settled," Helen said. "I gave Sydney the assignment, and I see no reason to take it away from her. It's Sydney's story."

"I won't work with a cupcake," Hunz said. "This is a serious news story." He turned to Sydney. "Have you ever done a major news story?"

"One of my stories was picked up by the network," she said. It was a weak answer, but it was all she had.

"Let me guess," Hunz said. "Children, pets, and sex stories, right?"

Sol said, "She did one on erectile dysfunction that really made a—"

"This is Sydney's story," Helen said. "I'm the assignment editor and this is my call. Or are you going to fire me too, Sol?"

Rosenthal frowned and made an obvious effort to stare her down. But he was no match for Helen Gordon. To his credit, he seemed to realize that pressing the matter any further would get messy.

"All right, Helen," he said, "it's your call."

"That's what I just said. Sydney, are you willing to allow Mr. Vonner to assist you in this investigation?"

Sydney could have kissed her. For a moment, she considered saying, *I might be able to use an assistant on this story*, but she thought that might be pressing her luck. "I would welcome the chance to work with Mr. Vonner," she said, though she wasn't sure she meant it.

"Mr. Vonner," Helen said. "I never want to hear you refer to any of my reporters as cupcake, sweetie, baby doll, or anything like that again. Is that understood? If you want to investigate this story, you'll work with Sydney. Otherwise, I'm sure we can find someone to drive you to the airport."

Hunz Vonner didn't respond immediately. Clearly, this was a man who was accustomed to getting his way. But he wasn't in Germany now and this wasn't his station. With obvious difficulty, he said, "I'll work with Miss St. James."

"Very well," Helen said.

The two men left the room with Sol Rosenthal talking fast and soothingly to his guest. Sydney hung back.

"Helen, thanks for sticking up for me."

Already working on her next project, Helen didn't look up. She scribbled comments in the margins of a report, then said, "I believe you have copy to write for the noon edition."

The newsroom monitor displayed a montage of California scenes. Children at the beach. Hang gliders. The HOLLYWOOD sign.

Mission San Juan Capistrano. Symphonic music swelled. The station's call letters swooped in and filled the screen. A deep baritone announcer said, "KSMJ: News for a New Millennia."

The call letters gave way to friendly, smiling portraits of the noon newscasters as each one was introduced by the announcer.

"With Robin Hernandez, Gary Johnson, and Phil Sanders with the weather."

The opening camera shot was of Robin and Gary seated behind the anchor desk.

Sydney stood beside camera two, watching both the monitor and the flesh-and-blood newscasters.

"Good afternoon, I'm Gary Johnson."

"And I'm Robin Hernandez. Our top story at noon—seven fatalities have been reported in Los Angeles, with reports of similar deaths coming from every major city in the world, all of them linked to bizarre death notices. Here in LA . . ."

"You've hit the big time."

Sydney recognized the voice behind her. She turned with a smile. "Thanks, Josh," she said.

Joshua Leven was the station's evening sportscaster. At twenty-nine years, tall and muscular, he still had a boyish look to him. A former all-American tight end at Northwestern University, he was drafted by the National Football League in the second round by the San Diego Chargers. His professional football career proved to be a short one. Five games into the first season a linebacker hit him low on a crossing pattern, blowing out his knee. It was a career-ending injury.

As a player, Josh's infectious smile, exuberant passion for the game, and emerging superstar status made him a media darling. Being an eligible bachelor was icing on the cake. His career cut short, Josh followed up industry contacts. With a degree in journalism— which he'd thought he'd use much later in life—he secured work at a local radio station doing color for college football games. When KSMJ lost their evening sportscaster to a sister station in Phoenix, a local headhunter lined Josh up for an audition. He'd been with the station three years when Sydney was hired.

Josh and Sydney became friends, lunching together, swapping nostalgic stories about their Midwestern roots and humorous anecdotes about adapting to the West Coast lifestyle.

Sydney could talk to Josh about anything. Well, almost anything. There was one topic that was a sore point between them, one that led to an argument whenever either of them brought it up. The only way they could deal with it was to agree not to talk about it. Or, more correctly, *her*.

Cori Zinn.

Josh was head over heels for her. He couldn't explain it himself, but anytime anyone hinted that Cori was less than a goddess, Josh charged to her defense with armor and sword flashing.

What really infuriated Sydney was the way Cori treated Josh. Fully aware of Josh's feelings for her, Cori made it clear to everyone with ears that she didn't feel the same for him. But that didn't stop her from exploiting him. For Cori, attention was a one-way street leading to an altar made in her image. She openly joked of Josh's feelings for her, reveling in all the menial things she could get him to do for her.

What made Sydney even more furious was that Josh knew this and didn't care. When it came to Cori Zinn, he was a lovesick zombie. Convinced she would come around some day, he lived for her smile, her pout, the brush of her fingers.

Rendered powerless by their agreement not to discuss the relationship, Sydney toyed with the idea of hiring a priest to exorcise the demon Cori from him.

"They're reading your copy, aren't they?" Josh brought Sydney back to the noon broadcast.

"Yeah." Sydney smiled. It was nice to hear someone acknowledge it.

"Someday that'll be you behind the desk, reading your own copy."

"That's the dream."

"It'll happen. Just a matter of time."

They listened as Robin Hernandez read the text of the telegram Sydney found on the front seat of Jeffrey Conley's Ford Taurus. Josh knew to keep quiet so Sydney could enjoy her moment of triumph.

"Had lunch yet?"

"I've been busy writing copy."

"Artie's?"

"Sure. Give me five minutes."

Another voice interrupted them.

"There you are! I've been looking all over for you." Cori Zinn approached with a swagger. Ignoring Sydney, she linked arms with Josh and whispered something in his ear. Laughing, she tried pulling him away.

"I can't," he said. "Syd and I are doing lunch."

Cori shot Sydney a dismissive look. "I'm sure she won't mind. I was counting on you for a ride."

"I thought you were going with Grant in his Jaguar."

Squeezing Josh's arm, Cori wrinkled her nose at him. "I'd rather ride with you."

"Sorry," Josh said. "I already made plans. How about if I make it up to you with dinner tonight?"

"I'm busy tonight," Cori said with a pout.

She didn't like Josh anywhere near Sydney St. James. To Josh's credit, that was one place where he drew the line with Cori, which infuriated her and made Sydney love him all the more.

Cori released Josh's arm. "If you'd rather be with her than me . . . ," she said, walking away.

Sydney whispered to Josh, "Are you supposed to be at the luncheon with Hunz Vonner?"

"Nah. Cori just wants me to drive her there."

"And what? Wait in the parking lot while they eat?"

Cori swung around. "Sydney, I hear you're going to be working with Vonner on this mass killing thing. Can't wait to see how you'll dress up this time to get the story. Have you considered going as the angel of death?"

CHAPTER FIVE

"Y̶ou have to forgive Cori," Josh said. "She gets a little possessive at times."

Sydney absorbed the comment by pretending to look at the menu, even though she ordered the same thing every time. If she said something, Josh would get defensive and angry, and Cori would have succeeded in ruining their lunch. Sydney refused to give her that victory.

The lunch crowd showed no signs of thinning. People queued to the take-out counter a dozen deep to order from a long menu of specialty sandwiches, soups, knishes, and salads. Behind the counter, an array of salamis dangled on string, frankfurters rotated on a grill, and employees kept the salad display fresh.

A waiter appeared, notepad in hand. "What'll you have?" He glanced at Sydney.

"Chicken salad sandwich."

"That all?"

"And a glass of water."

"You?" He turned to Josh, who was still deciding.

"He'll have a number four with fries and Coke," Sydney said.

"You got it." The waiter grabbed the menus and was gone.

"I might have wanted a hot dog," Josh said.

"You always order a number four," Sydney said.

They spent the next couple of minutes people watching. Sydney couldn't help but wonder how many had heard about the alarming number of unexplained deaths. Everybody in line seemed focused on ordering. And from the conversations drifting from nearby tables, no one seemed overly concerned. But then, the news just broke. How many people listen to the noon news on their lunch break?

"What Cori said back at the station," Josh said. "I think she was out of line, but since I didn't understand what she was referring to, it was hard to tell. What did she mean about you dressing up as the angel of death?"

Sydney grinned. "She was just being Cori."

"I still don't get it. Why would you dress up like the angel of death to get a story?"

The grin widened. "You haven't heard about the fat suit."

"Um, no, can't say that I have."

"It got me the job at KSMJ. It was a feature story I did back in Davenport. Helen saw it and offered me a job."

"You did a feature story on extra-large suits?"

Sydney laughed. "No. I wore a fat suit to get the story."

"Really?" Josh was intrigued. "You're talking about a theater costume, right?"

"Makeup and everything. Made me look like I was three hundred pounds."

Josh howled. "I've got to see this tape!"

"The network picked up the story."

"Why would you do such a thing? A dare?"

"More like a bet. Scott Hurlihy, one of the reporters at the station, was giving me a hard time about my looks. He said everything came easy to me because I was female and pretty, that I had an advantage over male reporters. Well, it ticked me off."

"He's right, you know," Josh said.

Sydney leveled a finger at him. "Don't get me started."

"You don't think your looks give you an edge?"

"Do you want to hear this story or not?"

Josh motioned her to go ahead.

"I told him that nobody takes me seriously. One look and people think *blonde bimbo*. Scott refused to give ground. He said that if I had to spend one day without my looks, I'd see that he was right."

"And a bet was born," Josh said.

"No money was exchanged, but I was determined to prove Scott Hurlihy wrong. Actually, we came up with the idea of the fat suit together. The University of Iowa's drama department had just done a production of *Falstaff*, so we knew where to find one. We talked a couple of the makeup guys into fitting my face with latex jowls. I died my hair mousy brown with gray streaks and wore faded, pale green sweats and a pair of grungy tennis shoes."

"I've got to see this tape!" Josh said. "So how did it go?"

Sydney sobered. "It was a real eye-opener. Of course, I'd thought about what it would be like carrying around the extra weight, climbing in and out of the car, walking down narrow aisles, falling into and climbing out of chairs. I knew it would be physically taxing.

"What I wasn't prepared for was how mean people suddenly became. All I did that day was run errands. I went to the usual places: the grocery store, the post office, I put gas in the car. A film crew recorded me from a distance."

Even now, remembering it, tears came to Sydney's eyes. "People were openly rude to me for no reason. Strangers called me names in passing. They stared at me and made faces like I disgusted them. I used to think salesmen were so friendly, that the stores trained them that way. At the film counter of a drugstore, I waited thirty minutes to be waited on while the man behind the counter finished stacking shelves, took phone calls, and assisted a couple of cute high school girls who came in after me. In a restaurant, four grown men made pig noises in the booth behind me. A woman who looked like a grandmother pulled me aside and told me that if I lost weight I'd feel better about myself. I'd never met this woman before!"

"It really shook you," Josh said.

"How was I to know that anyone took me seriously after that? How was I to know that teachers didn't give me a grade better than I deserved just because I was pretty? Or that I was hired for my looks instead of my talent?"

"Your good looks open doors for you."

"I hate that," Sydney said. "I don't want to be treated differently just because my hair is blonde."

"But they do."

"They shouldn't."

Their order came. Sydney picked at her sandwich. Josh attacked his fries.

"So Scott won the bet," Josh said.

"I swore to myself I'd never knowingly use my feminine wiles to my advantage," Sydney said.

"Your what? Feminine wiles?" Josh laughed.

"It means—"

"I know what it means, it's just that I haven't heard anyone use that term. Not in this century, at least."

Sydney sniffed. "Well, it's a perfectly good expression."

"So how's that going? That abstaining-from-using-your-feminine-wiles thing."

Josh had a sly grin on his face. There was something behind it, more than just being amused over her choice of words. Did he know something?

"Were you watching me today?"

Josh laughed. "No more than usual. Why?"

"Because I backslid this morning with a police officer."

"To get out of a ticket?"

"To get a story."

"Good, you should do it more often," Josh said. He stretched his mouth around a mountain of deli meat and took a hearty bite.

"Good? What do you mean, good? I told you I didn't want to use my looks to my advantage."

"I know," Josh said, chewing. "You're wrong."

"No, I'm not," Sydney said stubbornly.

"All right, have it your way."

Sydney fumed. Sometimes Josh could be too agreeable. "No, you said I was wrong. I want to hear your reasoning."

"You won't like it."

"Try me."

Josh shrugged as though it made no difference to him either way. He took a sip of drink and leaned forward. "You were born beautiful."

"That's it? That's your reasoning?"

"Yeah, pretty much." He picked up his sandwich and took another bite.

"Not a very strong argument," Sydney said.

Josh shot her a grin. "Wilt Chamberlain was born tall."

"So?"

"What do you mean, so? Wilt Chamberlain. Basketball player. Seven foot one inch. Four-time Most Valuable Player in the NBA. Scored seventy-eight points in a single game. And never once did he apologize to his opponents because he was taller than them."

Sydney sat back, not wanting to admit he might have a point.

"All I'm saying is you're the Wilt Chamberlain of good looks. We work in a competitive business. Stop feeling guilty about being beautiful and use what you have to do the best job you can."

"You're quite a philosopher, Josh Leven."

"It's the pastrami. I always wax eloquent when I eat pastrami."

CHAPTER SIX

What do we know about these death notices?" Helen Gordon said, getting the afternoon meeting started.

Sydney picked up from snippets of conversation that Sol Rosenthal had managed to salvage one item on his itinerary—lunch at Ago's, actor Robert de Niro's elegant, open-kitchen restaurant with its specialty, fettuccine with shaved white truffles. But Hunz Vonner cut the lunch short by insisting they get started on the death watch story. It had been his idea for Helen to call the staff together.

Seated around Command Central were producer Sol Rosenthal, coanchor Grant Forsythe, interim coanchor Cori Zinn, Hunz Vonner, Sydney, and news director Brad Miller, whose job it was to oversee the news operations and maintain consistency among the various newscasts.

Brad was a gruff man who hid behind a full beard. Plainspoken and direct, he made decisions quickly and decisively. He'd missed the early morning meeting because of traffic.

"So what do we know?" Helen said.

"I've been in contact with my sources at EuroNet," Hunz said. "They project the number of deaths in the thousands and it's accelerating."

Helen leaned forward intently. "Does EuroNet have any idea who's behind it?"

"Not yet," Hunz said. "They have a couple of leads. They're working around the clock. I should have something tonight. Tomorrow morning at the latest."

"I have something," Grant Forsythe said. "The Department of Homeland Security is raising the awareness system to Level Three for the entire nation. Secretary Perkins is scheduled to hold a news briefing in an hour."

"Does station programming know about this?" Helen asked.

"They do now," Brad Miller said.

It was Miller's job to coordinate the new Homeland Security Awareness system with the network following the revamp of the color-coded advisory system. Taking a cue from the Amber Alert, the missing person's emergency broadcast system, Homeland Security devised a program that would keep the nation in a state of constant awareness regarding the level of national security.

A four-pointed graphic was designed, resembling the four points of a compass, to be broadcast continuously in the lower right-hand corner of all television programming. Proceeding clockwise, the shaded area between points lit up according to the level of risk. Level One indicated a low risk of attack; Level Two, a significant risk; Level Three, a high risk; and Level Four, a severe risk. The graphic flashed when an attack was in progress.

Radios broadcast beeps every hour on the hour, one beep for each current level of risk.

Improving on the previous color-coded system, now each city and region had its own level of awareness that reflected threats to specific targets. For the director of Homeland Security to set the risk at Level Three nationally was an indication the entire country was under high risk of attack.

"Grant, has the government given any indication which terrorist group might be behind this attack?" Helen asked.

"Has any group claimed credit for the deaths?" Sol asked.

Grant shook his head. "At present, the government's reporting zilch. Scuttlebutt is that everyone's stumped. Anyone else hear anything?"

Heads shook all around the table.

Sydney said, "An attack of this magnitude would limit the number of terrorist organizations that could be responsible, wouldn't it? Who has the resources to do something this large?"

"Good point, Sydney," Helen said.

"Any number of organizations, or countries, for that matter, could pull it off," Hunz said, without naming any specifically.

"But considering the deaths are worldwide," Sydney said, "couldn't we just look for a nation that is reporting no death watch–related deaths? I mean, they wouldn't kill their own people just to cover their tracks, would they?"

Sol Rosenthal flipped through the printout pages from the news wires. "Saudi Arabia. Afghanistan. Iraq. Iran. Pakistan. Palestine. All report deaths."

"It's flawed reasoning," Hunz said. "Terrorists have no qualms about killing their own."

"All right, then," Helen said, before Sydney could respond, "bottom line is, we have nothing. We'll keep track of the newswires here at the station. Sydney, you and Mr. Vonner see what you can dig up locally. Begin with the accident victim. See if his family knows anything. Find out how he died. See if the police have any leads on the telegram."

"Helen," Cori Zinn said.

"Yes?"

"In light of recent developments, wouldn't it be better if Sydney covered the governor's news conference? That would free me to—"

"No," Helen said curtly. "Sydney doesn't have your contact with the governor's staff. We're counting on you for an exclusive. However, make sure you get a quote from the governor on these death watch notices."

Cori started to object.

Grant Forsythe cut her off. "So we're officially labeling this story Death Watch?"

"That's what the terrorists are calling it in their notices," Helen said.

Grant shrugged. "Just asking."

An intern placed a pile of pink telephone memo notes in front of Helen. She sifted through them quickly. There were at least a dozen. As the meeting broke up, she handed them to Sydney.

"These are the calls that have come into the station in response to the noon broadcast, people who say they've received a death watch notice," Helen said. "Follow up on them."

Sydney shuffled through the notes. "Have any of them passed the deadline?"

"What do you mean?" Helen frowned.

"Each death watch notice gives its victim forty-eight hours. Have any of them lived past their designated time to die?"

"Good question," Helen said. "Find out." She turned toward her office.

"What if we could find one of them," Sydney called after her. "Someone who has received a death watch notice who is targeted to die before the eleven o'clock broadcast? We could put them in protective custody, so to speak. Have a doctor standing by. Security. The whole nine yards. Do everything we can to keep them living past their designated time to die."

Sol joined them while Sydney was talking.

"A waste of time," Hunz said.

"For what purpose," Helen asked, "other than the obvious one of saving a life?"

"If we can interview someone who has survived a death watch threat," Sydney said, "it'll prove the threats are not always fatal. It'll give people hope."

"We're not here to save the world," Hunz said. "Our job is to report the news."

"I like the idea," Helen said.

"People will see KSMJ as crusaders against the axis of evil," Sol added. "They'll view us as saviors. The station with a heart. It'll make an industry splash. Let's do it! A live feed from the scene."

"Run with it," Helen said. "Only don't take any unnecessary risks. We still don't know who's behind this. This whole thing is scary."

Grant Forsythe walked up, overhearing Helen's comment. "If the deaths continue at this pace, we're going to see panic in the streets. Riots. Global anarchy."

"Do you really think it'll go that far?" Sol said.

Cori Zinn joined them. She handed Sydney another pink memo slip.

"My intern just handed me this," she said. "It's a lead on your story."

Sydney took it reluctantly. She read it.

Billy Peppers. McArthur Park. 4 p.m.

"He wants to meet you. Says he knows who's behind all the mystery deaths."

"Is he a credible source?" Hunz asked.

Cori tried her best to hold back a grin. She couldn't.

"Remember that story I did last year on mental insanity among the homeless?" She had everyone's attention and was milking it. "One of the guys I interviewed called himself The Rev."

"The guy who said he talked to angels," Grant said.

"That's the one." Cori looked disappointed that Grant had stolen her thunder. "Anyway, he called the station. You weren't available so the call was passed to me. I asked him if he wanted to leave a message. He said he wanted to meet you. I asked what it was about. And when he told me, I insisted I needed more information if we were to take him seriously. So he told me who is behind all the deaths. We can stop wondering now."

"Well, who is it?" Helen said.

Cori held out for as long as she could.

"The Devil!"

Everyone laughed.

"He's serious!" she cried.

CHAPTER SEVEN

Jeffrey Conley's house in Covina was shut up tight. Bright yellow police tape across the front and rear doors marked it as a crime scene. There were no cops around now.

Sydney and Hunz interviewed Conley's neighbors. They learned that Jeffrey Conley was a retired accountant. A widower. He and his wife purchased this house in 1958 when they moved to California from Pittsburgh. Conley had two boys, both grown, both living out of state. He'd been in the hospital a year ago for angina when two metal stents were inserted into his heart arteries to hold them open. Other than that, there was nothing unusual about Mr. Conley.

He had the usual credit card debt. Didn't associate with known criminals, and as far as Sydney and Hunz could determine, no one had a motive to kill him and no one profited from his death, other than the payoff from a mediocre life insurance policy and the outrageous price his boys would get from selling his Southern California property.

From Covina, Sydney and Hunz drove to the Hollywood substation on Wilcox Avenue to see if they could get any more information from the officers on the scene of the accident. Everyone was tight-lipped. The area commanding officer referred them to Special Investigations downtown on Spring Street. Sydney hated driving downtown. Nevertheless, she waded into the mire of traffic and managed to find a parking lot two blocks away on Broadway.

The only thing they were able to get out of Special Investigations was that from all the evidence on the scene and the testimony of eyewitnesses, it appeared Jeffrey Conley had a heart attack. He ran a red light at the intersection of Sunset and Vine, smashing into the back of a large black truck, make unknown. The driver of the truck fled the scene. No one got a license plate, but the accident was clearly Jeffrey Conley's fault. The driver of the truck had not been located.

The detective confirmed that Conley had a death watch notice in the car when he died. He refused to give them a list of the other six victims. No amount of prodding and posturing could get him to budge. While Hunz took a call on his cell phone, Sydney remembered Wilt Chamberlain. By the time Hunz was finished with his call, Sydney had the list.

"How did you get it?" Hunz was clearly impressed.

"Just used one of my reporter tools," she said as they looked over the list on the way back to the car. "Look here, it's just like Officer Pollard said. Every death at the exact moment stated in the notice."

"I don't buy it," Hunz said. "Conley had a heart attack. How can somebody know the exact moment when that's going to happen?"

"Maybe the time triggered the heart attack," Sydney said. "Think about it. Your heart's bad. You're given the equivalent of a death sentence. As the time approaches, your anxiety increases to the point you set off a heart that's already primed and ready to explode."

Huntz looked at her. "So you're saying the death watch notices are sent to people with preexisting conditions and that the notice is designed to push them over the edge?"

In the parked car now, Sydney and Hunz flipped through the police printouts. "Your theory doesn't hold," Hunz said. "Here's a twenty-nine-year-old dentist. True, he died from a previous heart defect, but no one knew he had it."

"Someone knew," Sydney said stubbornly.

But the report she was looking at didn't bear out her theory either—an out-of-work actor was hit and killed while crossing the street in a controlled intersection. The car was driven by a schoolteacher with a spotless record. Her transmission jammed in second gear. There were twenty other people in the intersection. Only the actor was hit.

They read the various reports to each other: A city worker was crushed when the tunnel he was digging collapsed on him. An experienced hang glider got caught in a downdraft and plummeted to the beach. A high school student was hit and killed on the freeway while he was fixing a flat tire.

"The only thing they have in common is that they all received a death watch notice," Sydney said, "and they all died precisely when the notice said they would."

It was half past four. The parking lot was already engulfed by the shadow of the bank tower on the far side of the street. Sydney handed the police report to Hunz and turned the ignition switch. Hunz readjusted himself, grabbing for the seat belt and clearing a space for his feet by kicking aside empty coffee cups and PowerBar wrappers with his expensive black European dress shoes.

"Want to get a bite?" Sydney said. "We may not get another chance."

"A bite? Is that dinner?"

"Yeah. We could duck into a restaurant if you'd like. There shouldn't be any lines this early. Anything you were hoping to try while you were in the States?"

"I was told to try your fish tacos. Are they good here?"

Sydney laughed. "Who told you that?"

"A close friend. Was she having fun at my expense?"

Sydney looked at him a moment before answering. This was the first personal comment she'd heard Hunz Vonner make. Until now it was as though he had no life other than news broadcasting. Now it seemed he had a close personal friend, a female.

"No. She wasn't making fun of you. Did she say where to get these fabulous fish tacos?"

Hunz mentioned a fast-food chain.

Starting the car, Sydney said, "Well, the ambiance leaves something to be desired, but you'll like the tacos."

Ten minutes later they were seated at a bright red table next to a window overlooking a busy intersection. Fast-food wrappers served as plates as the German newscaster, still dressed in a black suit, took his first bite of fish taco. Three small plastic containers of hot sauce were lined up in front of him.

Sydney grimaced. "I can't believe Sol took you to Ago's and I take you to Taco Hut."

A few more bites and Hunz fanned his mouth. "This one's too hot," he said. "The green's good, but I like the red better."

"Most people prefer the mild sauce starting out," Sydney said.

On the table beside her taco wrapper were two sheets of paper stapled together. Her cell phone sat on top of them. The papers were a compilation of the people who had called the station during the noon newscast to report that they had received a death watch notice. The list was arranged by time; those who were scheduled to die first were at the top of the list.

Time had already passed on the first two names.

Maxine Hoffa   2:36 p.m.
Charles Bishop   3:55 p.m.

Were they dead?

Sydney took another bite of taco and gazed out the window. A silver Mercedes turning right stopped for a woman pushing a baby stroller in the crosswalk. His turn signal blinked impatiently. The Mercedes inched forward needlessly, dangerously. Californians were always in a hurry.

She felt her anger rising at the needless endangerment of life. Yesterday, she would have watched the same scene and thought little of it, other than the fact the guy behind the wheel of the Mercedes was a jerk. This morning's death watch notice changed all that. Now everyday life seemed more fragile.

She remembered having a similar feeling on September 11, 2001, after watching the two World Trade Center buildings collapse, after watching the burning of the Pentagon and the tragic plane crash in Pennsylvania. The world felt different. It lost its innocence. It was as though the world was told it had cancer, and the prognosis wasn't good. Nothing was the same. Everything was tainted by the news— work, home life, purchases, vacation plans, relationships, even simple things like getting the mail—because even during those everyday moments, in the back of your mind, you knew you had cancer. And the name of the cancer was terrorism.

Death Watch was just another symptom that she was living in a sick world. What kind of person or organization went around killing people indiscriminately? What kind of monsters taunted their victims for forty-eight hours before killing them?

And how could anyone sit at a fast-food restaurant and enjoy a fish taco knowing that people were being handed numbers and told to stand in line for their turn to die?

"These are really good," Hunz said, his mouth full. "I'm going to get another one. Want anything?"

"I'm fine," Sydney said.

Hunz slid out of the booth. "You going to call them?" He pointed to the list.

"Yeah."

While Hunz stood in line for another fish taco, Sydney called the first two names on the list. The news was bad. Both Maxine Hoffa and Charles Bishop were dead.

Sydney couldn't bring herself to ask how they died, or at what time, mainly because she couldn't think of a way to ask, "Did your loved one die according to schedule?" Fact was, they were alive for the noon broadcast, and now they were dead.

She looked at her watch. The third name on the list was Jennifer Magill, thirty-one, a grocery store checker. According to the sheet she had less than three hours to live.

Sydney wrapped up her half-eaten taco with resolve. Somehow, she was going to keep Jennifer Magill alive.

Hunz slid back into the booth. The taco was unwrapped and a bite taken before he sat down. "They dead?"

"Yes."

"Both of them?" He took another bite and chewed thoughtfully. "You know, this idea of trying to keep someone on that list from dying is a waste of time. We need to find out who's behind it and stop them."

"That's a heartless thing to say," she snapped.

Though Sydney had never met Jennifer Magill, the image of a young, vibrant woman came to mind. She found it hard to think of the woman's life as a waste of time.

Hunz appeared taken aback by her anger. "Look, even if you succeed in saving one person's life, what good does it do?"

"It gives everyone hope," Sydney said. "If we can prove that death is not inevitable for those who receive these notices, it will provide immeasurable relief to a lot of people."

"Granted. But my point is, you can't protect them all. From everything we know so far, more people are going to die. Hundreds. Possibly thousands. Wouldn't it be better to use our time tracking down the people behind this assault and stop them? Cut off the head of the snake, and he can no longer bite you."

"So you suggest we just turn our back on Jennifer Magill?"

"Who's Jennifer Magill?"

"The next person on the list."

Hunz chewed. "What's the time on her notice?"

Sydney consulted the sheet. "7:22 p.m."

Hunz checked his watch. He sighed. "All right," he said, "but just this one. Then we do it my way."

CHAPTER EIGHT

As it turned out, Jennifer Magill didn't want to be saved by television station KSMJ. For fifteen minutes Sydney pleaded with her to get her to change her mind. But Jennifer Magill stood firm. "I'm not going to die in front of a bunch of television cameras."

Sydney had no choice but to go to the next person on the list, Lyle Vandeveer of Pasadena. His notice had a time of 10:05 p.m.

Hunz wasn't happy about losing an additional two and a half hours. "I have better things to do than hold an old man's hand."

"Does that mean you're not going with me?"

"I'll go, but I'm not going to waste time sitting around."

"What are you going to do?"

"Something productive."

The KSMJ team descended on Lyle Vandeveer's house in force—a mobile news truck, an ambulance with two paramedics, a car with four armed private security men, and Sydney's beige Volvo. Their arrival drew stares from Vandeveer's neighbors on Fair Oaks Avenue, an older section of town lined with palm trees.

Even in the dark it was clear Vandeveer kept his house nice. The lawn was carpet smooth and trimmed. The house was white with green trim.

It was 7:56 p.m.

When Lyle Vandeveer opened his front door, he seemed staggered by the commotion just outside his house. "Wasn't expecting all this," he said, as the technicians raised the satellite dish on the van.

Sydney introduced herself and Hunz, and Vandeveer invited them in.

Lyle Vandeveer was a sixty-one-year-old machinist who had taken early retirement. The aerospace industry had brought him and his first wife to California from Texas in 1964. Of medium build, Vandeveer had a round face and a belly that stretched his shirt. He was wearing beige shorts, white socks, slippers, and an open flannel shirt over a T-shirt that read: REAL RAILROADERS DO IT WITH STEAM.

"Mind if we go back here?" Without waiting for an answer, he led them to the back of the house. "It helps if I keep my hands busy."

He flipped on lights as they went from room to room, passing through a kitchen that was orderly and clean. A single plate, cup, fork, and knife had been washed and were in the dish drainer. A new liner was in the trash can.

"For a man who lives alone," Sydney said, "you sure keep everything spick-and-span."

Vandeveer stopped and looked at her. He smiled. "Haven't heard that phrase in years. My mother used to use it."

He flipped on a light switch in the next room. A spacious area came alive with scenic color.

"Oh my, this is lovely!" Sydney said.

Two concrete steps led down to a room addition that looked like it had once been a recreation room. Now it was a miniature countryside, complete with mountains, bridges, valleys, and streams.

"This is what keeps me busy," he said.

Model train tracks wove their way through a miniature countryside that was intricately detailed with trees and bushes. Figures created mini scenes: a train station with a man reading a newspaper on a bench; a line of people purchasing tickets, with a woman holding a child's hand; and another scene with people on an embankment, waving to a passing train.

In one corner of the room there was a workbench with a magnifying-glass light on an arm, bottles of model paint, brushes, pictures everywhere, and stacks of magazines—*Great Model Railroads*, *Model Railroader*, and *Trains*.

With shaking hands Vandeveer donned a blue-and-white-striped engineer's cap. He settled down into an overstuffed chair. There was an identical chair beside it, which he offered to Sydney. Hunz started to sit on the wooden stool at the workbench, then hesitated, checking it first. He was obviously worried about getting paint on his suit pants.

The paramedics entered the room, carrying boxes of medicine and equipment.

"We're going to hook you up to an EKG so we can monitor your heart," Sydney said. "The paramedics will also monitor your vital signs. Blood pressure. That sort of thing."

One of the paramedics asked Vandeveer to take his shirt off.

Vandeveer looked at him with wide eyes. "Can I keep this one on?" He tugged at the open flannel shirt.

The paramedics hooked him up, checked his vitals, and took a history. Vandeveer's blood pressure was elevated, but not to the point of concern. His medical record showed him to be in good health. There was no reason for this man to die tonight.

On the wall was a clock, an oversized pocket watch complete with chain, the kind old-time stationmasters used to keep trains on schedule.

It read 8:17 p.m.

According to his death watch notice Lyle Vandeveer had one hour and forty-eight minutes left to live.

"It's not a very good layout." Vandeveer gestured toward the model countryside.

Hunz had left the room, saying he wanted to check on the security guards. Three were posted outside. One was in the kitchen.

Checking on the guards was obviously an excuse. Hunz used his cell phone to contact his people in Germany. A nine-hour span of time separated them, which meant the early-morning news team at EuroNet was already at work. Sydney figured Hunz wanted to find out if the station had developed any new leads on the death watch phenomenon.

"Why would you think this isn't a good layout?" Sydney said. "It looks impressive to me."

Vandeveer shook his head. "To be a top-notch layout, all the elements should have a unifying theme. The time period, the geographical setting, the architecture, the scenery, the people—all of it should be influenced by the type of railroad you're running. This is just a hodgepodge of things I like. Sort of a picture postcard of my ideal world, I guess."

Sydney walked over to get a closer look. Vandeveer's world was orderly, colorful, and serene. All the resin figurines appeared content. Happy.

Vandeveer, standing beside her, pointed out his scale locomotives and cars, the precision of the re-creation, the separately applied handles, the real metal springs on the trucks, the directional lighting, and the five-pole skewed armature motor with dual flywheels for optimum performance at all speeds. "Museum quality," he said with pride. He calmed as he talked about his trains.

He ran the train, making sure she listened to the authentic sound of the locomotive bell and whistle, the squealing brakes, and the Doppler effect.

The film crew captured it on tape.

"Some people go overboard with all this," Vandeveer said, "the historical detail, precision re-creation of a time period. Some guys run their trains precisely on a designated schedule. I know one man who synchronizes his pocket watch with the atomic clock at the Naval Observatory every morning. That kind of detail takes all the fun out of it for me."

Sydney looked at the wall clock.

8:55 p.m.

At 9:05 p.m., precisely one hour from the death watch time, the medical technicians gave Vandeveer another checkup. The results were the same. He was in good health.

"Tell you one thing," Vandeveer said from his chair. "If I'm gonna go, this is where I want to be, with my trains and a pretty young thing at my side."

He reached over and patted Sydney's hand.

She didn't mind. "Tell me about your family," she said.

Vandeveer glanced at the clock, looked at her, and took a deep breath. "Outlived two wives," he said. "The first died early. We hadn't been married two years."

"I'm so sorry," Sydney said. "That must have been difficult for you. Was it sudden?"

"Cancer. She was dead two months after they discovered it."

"What was her name?"

He smiled. "Mildred. Great gal. Guess when we were married."

Sydney leaned forward. "When?"

"November 22, 1963." He laughed.

"The day Kennedy was shot."

Vandeveer raised a lecturing finger. "Learned a lesson that day. Never get married on the day a president is assassinated. Makes for a lousy wedding reception."

"That must have been horrible for Mildred!"

"She was a trooper. Big gal. Strong. She was one of those girls who could handle anything. I always thought she'd outlive me by a couple of decades." He drifted away for a moment, caught up in a private memory of Mildred. "Anyway," he said, "a year and a half later, I married her best friend, Bea."

"You knew Bea when you were married to Mildred?"

Vandeveer grinned. "Mildred's maid of honor. Close as sisters. They used to talk about me. Anyway, we had a daughter, Cindy. That's her." He pointed to a framed picture on his workbench. A happy young woman with bangs and a dazzling smile. It looked like a high school yearbook photo.

"Where is Cindy now?"

A shadow passed over Vandeveer's face.

"With her mother," he said.

"Oh, I'm sorry," Sydney said. "I didn't know."

"Lost both of them on the same day in that airbus crash in Queens, November 12, 2001."

"Oh, my."

"Yeah. Cindy worked at the museum in New York. She restored old paintings. You know, spruced them up, took off layers of dust and grime, that sort of thing. We thought it was funny that she chose that particular profession since we couldn't get her to clean her room."

Sydney's heart went out to this man who was so well acquainted with grief. In his perfect world, the one through which his model trains traveled, there was no hint of his pain. All the figurines were smiling.

"Bea flew out there to visit Cindy. We hadn't seen her in a couple of years, and Cindy kept hounding us to come to New York."

"Why didn't you go?"

"Couldn't get the time off. You see, the trip was supposed to be more than just New York. Bea had always wanted to see the Caribbean. She said, 'You can have Paris and London and Rome. Before I die I want to see the Caribbean.'" Vandeveer's eyes teared.

"Anyway, Cindy had some business down there. Something about scheduling an artist for a show. Not usually her job. She was doing it as a favor to the museum. Bea and me, we'd always talked about going. We'd get the brochures from travel agents and sit at the kitchen table and plan it all out, but then we'd start to worry about who was going to water the yard, and we'd have to stop the mail . . ." His mouth clamped shut; his lower lip trembled.

Sydney reached over and covered Vandeveer's hand with hers.

"Got the call that morning," he said. "The news said the plane went straight down. Almost vertical."

Neither spoke for a time.

The clock on the wall ticked off a minute.

Vandeveer lay back in his chair and stared into space, his shirt open. Wires stretched from a machine to the white circle patches on his chest.

"Do you have any other family?"

"A brother. Both parents are dead. Never knew my dad. I was the product of one last good-bye before he shipped out. He was killed at Guadalcanal. My mother raised us. She died of lung cancer a few years back. Everybody smoked in those days."

Sydney was almost afraid to ask, "And your brother?"

"Canada," Vandeveer said. "He's a minister of a church up there. He was always the good one. Ever since he was little he had a religious streak in him. You know how kids pretend they're a cowboy or Superman? Lawrence would line up chairs, use a table for a pulpit, and pretend he was Billy Graham."

He shook his head. "I never bought into it, myself. Especially after Mildred died. She was a strong Christian woman. Look how much good it did her."

Sydney wanted to disagree with him, but now didn't seem the time. "Have you talked with your brother recently?"

"Ah!" Vandeveer straightened himself up in the chair. "Glad you mentioned that. I've been meaning to tell you something. Lawrence called yesterday. Strange, really. Said he'd received a phone call about me. The caller didn't identify himself. The caller told Lawrence I was marked for death or something like that. He called to see if I was all right."

Sydney leaned forward. "Was it someone who knew about your Death Watch?"

"That's the funny thing. I hadn't told anyone yet. I was about to call Howard Kressler—a guy I know, another model train hobbyist—when the phone rang and it was Lawrence. Why? Is that important?"

Sydney was writing on her notepad. "It's the first time we've heard of someone other than the vict . . . other than the person to whom the death watch notice is addressed, being notified. You're certain he received a notice about you and not him?"

"Who would want to kill Lawrence? He's perfect."

Sydney wrote down Lawrence's phone number.

The sound of hurried footsteps came from the kitchen. Hunz Vonner could be heard saying, "Hold on, I'll ask him." As he stepped through the doorway, he covered the mouthpiece of his cell phone. He didn't ask if he was interrupting. "Vandeveer, have you had any injections recently? Say, within the last four or five months?"

Lyle Vandeveer looked up, searching his memory. "No . . . not that I can recall . . . I've been pretty healthy, haven't seen the doc . . . wait, injection? I had a flu shot last Christmas. Is that what you're looking for?"

Hunz Vonner's eyes widened. He spoke into the cell phone. "That's affirmative. A flu shot. Yeah. It does, doesn't it?" He turned and left the same way he came. Heels clicking, his voice grew softer, then dissipated completely with the closing of the front door.

"What was that all about?" Vandeveer asked Sydney.

"I have no idea."

"Can I ask you a question?" Vandeveer said. "What on God's green earth is going on with these notices? I mean, it's sick, isn't it? Who's behind it?"

Sydney was amazed Vandeveer hadn't already asked this question. She attributed it to the invasion of cameras, equipment, and personnel. All of it at once could be intimidating. Under similar circumstances Sydney had once interviewed a man who couldn't remember his wife's name on camera.

"Mr. Vandeveer, we're as perplexed as you are."

Vandeveer thought about this a moment. "Do you really think you can save me?"

"We have security, medical personnel, and equipment. You're going to beat this thing, Mr. Vandeveer."

"Did I tell you when my wife died, the plane fell vertically?"

"Yeah."

"It landed on some houses. Killed the people inside. Security and medics couldn't have done anything to save those people."

"I don't think a plane's going to fall on your house, Mr. Vandeveer."

"Yeah, you're probably right. Still . . ."

It was 9:41 p.m.

Twenty-four minutes remained.

CHAPTER NINE

Sydney learned that the US Post Office delivered Lyle Vande-veer's death watch notice together with a MasterCard bill, an offer to join the History Book of the Month club, a fund-raising letter from Azusa Pacific University—Cindy had attended there for two years before transferring to USC—and a page of pizza coupons.

The envelope and letterhead matched: cream-colored linen paper. A simple *DW* appeared at the top of the page, centered, TrueType Castellar font, thirty-six point. There was no address, nor was there any return address on the envelope. The message was identical to the one Jeffrey Conley received in telegram form, only the time stamp was different. No fingerprints other than Lyle's and the postman's were on the envelope. It had a Pasadena postmark.

Lyle reported receiving a confirmation phone call, only he wasn't home to take it. It was on his answering machine. The police had both the letter and the answering machine tape.

A broadcast van technician poked his head in the room. "Mr. Vandeveer? There's a crazy broad out here and she says she won't go away until she talks to you. Says she's your neighbor. Opal Whitcomb?"

Vandeveer nodded at Sydney. "He's right, she is a crazy broad. Lives next door. She wanders the neighborhood with a coffee cup, on the prowl for java handouts and gossip. But she's a good neighbor and good company when she wants to be." He looked back to the technician. "Tell her I said I'll call her in the morning and fill her in. Oh, and tell her I bought some of that hazelnut cream blend she likes."

It was 9:55 p.m.

Ten minutes left.

Hunz Vonner strode into the room. There was no sign of a cell phone.

"Has your German station developed any leads?" Sydney asked.

"I'll fill you in later. Mr. Vandeveer, how are you feeling?"

"Like a movie star," he said. "I haven't had this much attention since . . . come to think of it, I've never had this much attention. Can I put my shirt on when the cameras start rolling?"

"Certainly," Sydney said. "We'll be live on the eleven o'clock news."

"Can you show my train layout? Like I said, it's nothing special, but it'll drive Howard Kressler up the wall to see it on TV. He thinks he has the best layout on the West Coast."

9:59 p.m.

The paramedics checked Lyle Vandeveer's heart pressure. They ran another EKG and gave a thumbs-up sign.

"I feel great," Vandeveer said.

His voice was shaky.

10:00 p.m.

Billy Peppers leaned against a palm tree on the other side of Fair Oaks Avenue opposite Lyle Vandeveer's house. He held a Nike shoe box under his arm. With his free hand he scratched his bearded cheek.

He hadn't had a good bath in nearly a month, just a little splashy-splash washup in a fountain now and then. Whenever he went that long without a bath his head and beard got itchy to the point of distraction.

Pockets of people stood around and, like him, watched what was going on. They paid little attention to each other, and no attention to Billy. They were all waiting for something to happen. Apparently this unexpected episode of reality TV on their own block was better than the *West Wing* rerun that was on tonight.

Just then, camera lights switched on and the house across the street lit up like it was some kind of Hollywood premiere. Billy half expected to see Tom Cruise or Nicole Kidman walk in front of the cameras and wave. But all he saw was an old woman carrying a coffee cup, standing cross-armed and looking angry at what was going on.

Then the lights went off.

Just a test, apparently.

Billy had to blink a couple of times to get his night vision back. He looked at his watch, a cheap digital that had a pink strap and Tinkerbell on the face.

10:03 p.m.

There was no descending ball to mark the last minute. No one gathered in Times Square. No one had any idea where Dick Clark was at the moment, nor did they care. All eyes were on Lyle Vandeveer, retired machinist and model railroad hobbyist.

10:04 p.m. and thirty seconds.

Vandeveer was smiling. "Never felt better," he said.

The paramedics nodded. All indicators were good.

Hunz Vonner had pulled a chair from the kitchen. One of the paramedics had set a piece of equipment on the workbench stool he'd sat on earlier. Hunz was leaning forward, arms on his legs, staring intently at Lyle Vandeveer.

Sydney held Lyle's hand.

10:04 p.m. and forty-five seconds.

"You're going to give a lot of people hope tonight, Lyle," Sydney said.

Lyle gave her a sheepish grin. "Seems silly, doesn't it? I haven't done nothing but sit in my chair."

Ten seconds.

A paramedic started counting down. "Ten, nine, eight . . ."

Sydney caught his eye and shook her head.

He stopped.

Everyone watched the clock on the wall, the one that hung over Lyle Vandeveer's peaceful valley like a huge sun—everyone except for the paramedic who had his hand on Lyle's wrist pulse. His eyes were on his watch.

Three seconds.

Two seconds.

One.

10:05 p.m.

For a moment, everyone held their breath.

Lyle grinned. "Made it," he said.

Hunz Vonner clapped a single clap. "Excellent!" he said, jumping out of his seat. "I'll notify the station." He pulled out his cell phone and strode into the kitchen.

Sydney fought tears. All she could think of was the pain Lyle had endured all his life. The guy deserved a break and tonight he got one. She gave him a hug.

Lyle Vandeveer blushed.

"After a hug like that from such a pretty woman," he said, "I could die a happy man."

A machine alarm sounded.

A queer expression came over Lyle Vandeveer's face. He jerked stiff. His back arched.

"I don't believe this!" one of the paramedics cried.

Sydney took a step back. "What's happening?"

Hunz ran in from the kitchen. He caught sight of Lyle Vandeveer—limp now, for a moment his eyes wide with surprise, then expressionless, staring emptily at the ceiling.

"No!" Hunz shouted.

With a sinking feeling, Sydney watched as the paramedics shocked, pounded, and injected Lyle Vandeveer with medicines to keep him alive. Their efforts were useless.

Lyle Vandeveer was dead.

"Ten-oh-five exactly," said the paramedic.

"No," Sydney cried. "We all watched. It was . . ."

"Ten-oh-five exactly," the paramedic repeated. He held up a fist and tapped his wristwatch. "Atomic. Linked to the Naval Observatory in Colorado. Mr. Vandeveer's clock is thirty seconds fast."

CHAPTER TEN

Hunz Vonner thrust his cell phone at Sydney. "Rosenthal," he said.

"Sydney? This is Sol. We're going to lead with your story tonight. Grant will introduce it, then we'll cut live to your location. Look, Sydney, we're going to have Vonner do the report."

Before she had time to object, Sol continued, "I know this is your story, but Vonner is good exposure for the station. What better way to introduce him to our audience than to show him on the front lines fighting this thing? It'll make a splash."

"Sol, it's 10:53! He hasn't prepared. I did the background. I interviewed Mr. Vandeveer. Most of the time Hunz wasn't even in the room." She sounded whiny, even to herself, like a five-year-old begging to stay up past her bedtime.

"Sydney, we don't have time to argue. Give Hunz your notes. He's a professional. And give him any assistance he needs."

The line went dead.

Sydney handed the phone back to Hunz Vonner. "You're doing the live feed."

"I know," Hunz said.

She held out her notepad. "We have a couple of quotes from Lyle," she said. "I thought we could lead with . . ."

Hunz waved off the offer of her notes. "I won't need those," he said, walking away.

The media spotlight made the exterior of Lyle Vandeveer's house glow, set off by solid black shadows. Something newsworthy had occurred here. In this case a mysterious death, which was always good for ratings.

Hunz stood with perfect posture, self-assured, listening to instructions in his earpiece, making a last-minute adjustment to his tie. A microphone with the station's call letters was handed to him. As the station cued him, his eyes crystallized with concentration. He peered calmly into the camera.

"A few minutes ago, in this quiet suburban neighborhood, a man died, another victim of a mysterious and frightening plague of deaths that has been sweeping the globe. What makes these deaths so frightening is their sudden, random nature, and that each of them is preceded by a written notice of death. Who is behind these tragic deaths? That remains unknown. But the scope and alarming accuracy of these notices points to a terrorist organization of immense size and resources."

Sydney stood beside a sound technician as Hunz related the growing number of death watch victims locally, nationally, and internationally. Out of the corner of her eye she could see Opal Whitcomb, Vandeveer's neighbor, the one he'd said he'd call in the morning. She was standing on the edge of the television lights watching the broadcast, arms folded, coffee cup dangling from a finger. She wiped away tears.

Moments after Lyle Vandeveer's death Sydney insulated herself from everything but the task at hand. It was something she'd taught herself to do whenever life's load threatened to bury her. She imagined herself donning a coat made of Teflon. Nothing except the needs of the moment stuck to it. Emotions couldn't penetrate it.

The first time she used the Teflon coat was out of necessity. She'd been dispatched to cover an automobile accident. Three dead. A mother and her two daughters, ages three and eighteen months. They'd been broadsided by a drunk driver running a red light. The drunk walked away with a bump on his head. The car with the family had blood everywhere. Ceiling. Steering wheel. Dashboard. CD player. Then, the unthinkable happened. The volunteer police chaplain arrived to console the family of the victims, only to discover it was his wife, his children, who had been killed in the car.

The only way Sydney could hold it together and report the family tragedy was to don her Teflon coat.

Tonight, the moment she felt the shock of Lyle Vandeveer's death wearing off, she put it on again. She had to shut out all personal thoughts and feelings for Lyle Vandeveer and his family. If she didn't, she wouldn't be able to do her job.

Later, when she was alone, she'd cry for Lyle Vandeveer. She'd cry for Bea and Cindy, who were taken from him so suddenly. She'd think about Lyle's peaceful, happy valley and cry, knowing that it was a far better world than the one in which he lived. She'd cry in frustration over having medical help within arm's reach and still being unable to save him. She'd cry with anger over the sick, twisted mind that was behind this torturing of innocent people. And she'd cry tears of guilt for making promises to Lyle Vandeveer she was powerless to keep. She'd cry because he'd believed in her, trusted her.

"Lyle Vandeveer is the latest death watch victim," Hunz reported to the viewing audience. "Everything humanly possible was done to keep him out of harm's way, yet somehow whoever is behind this cowardly crusade of terror managed to get to him, at the precise moment announced, which makes one wonder: Is there no hope for those who find themselves under the death watch executioner's blade? Is any among us safe?

"This is Hunz Vonner of EuroNet News on special assignment to KSMJ, Los Angeles."

Hunz didn't relax. He listened to his earpiece. "Yes, Cori, it was KSMJ's own Sydney St. James who spearheaded this failed effort, but I don't think transporting Mr. Vandeveer to a hospital facility earlier would have made any difference."

Hunz nodded at the camera, then it was over.

During the broadcast the street was still. No one moved. Everyone focused on the man standing in the spotlight. When the lights were switched off, they blinked, milled about for a few minutes, then walked home in the dark.

Sydney flipped open her cell phone. She punched in the numbers that would connect her with Lawrence, Lyle's brother in Canada. It was late and he was probably asleep, but with the chance the networks might pick up Lyle's story, she didn't want him hearing about his brother's death on a morning news report.

Phone held to her ear, she waited for someone to answer. She caught sight of a black man standing beside a palm tree across the street. With a shoe box tucked securely under one arm, he stared at her intently. Given the setting, a staring man was not unusual. Most people are fascinated by the way television personalities look in real life.

She smiled and waved. The man with the box didn't wave back, neither did he smile. He just stared.

Sydney made a quarter turn away from the staring man to better concentrate on the phone call.

"Hello?" The voice on the other end of the transmission was male and groggy.

"Hello. Is this Lawrence Vandeveer?"

"Yes. Who is this?"

Sydney took a deep breath.

There was a time for everything. That's what the Bible said. After a day like today it was time to crawl under the bedcovers and pull them over her head.

Sydney steered her Volvo onto the Hollywood Freeway heading north with thoughts of bed. She was tired. The lights of monster trucks and SUVs in her rearview mirror hurt her eyes. They were giving her a headache.

"That was a waste of time," Hunz Vonner said. "A total waste of time. We lost an entire evening."

Sydney glanced over at him. His jaw was set. He was angry. Unbelievable. "A man died tonight," she said.

"And a lot more are going to die until we find out who's behind these death watch notices, and we're no closer to finding them than we were six hours ago."

"You're forgetting Lawrence Vandeveer. He was notified of his brother's death watch notice. That's the first we've heard of someone other than the victim receiving a notification."

Hunz shook his head. "An anomaly, if it's true. Nobody else has reported a third-party confirmation."

"What if it's not an anomaly? What if it means something? Why would Lyle Vandeveer's brother in Canada be sent a notification? And if he didn't, why would he and Lyle make up something like that?"

"It could have been a misunderstanding: one brother says something; the other jumps to a conclusion. It happens all the time. Never take something someone says as fact until you check it out yourself."

"I did check it out," Sydney said.

"You talked to Lyle's brother? When?"

"When you were wrapping up the shoot."

Hunz looked at her as though he didn't believe her. "What did he say?"

"I called to inform him of his brother's death. When I told him the details, he told me about the phone call. It was just as Lyle described."

"I still say it's an anomaly. Meanwhile, we have a definite pattern that has proved true in every case: a person receives some form of printed notification which is followed up by a verbal confirmation."

Sydney stared through a dirty windshield at the traffic. The freeway was deserted at this time of night, which meant there were only a couple hundred cars on it rather than a couple thousand.

She said, "Do you have a rental car at the station, or should I drop you at your hotel?"

"What are you talking about? We have work to do."

"It's nearly midnight and I'm exhausted. Besides, shouldn't you be experiencing jet lag or something?"

"I don't require much sleep," Hunz said. "Two, three hours, and I'm good. I want to talk to someone in the FBI. Someone with authority. Do you have any contacts, any home phone numbers?"

"No," Sydney said incredulously.

Hunz muttered something about rookie reporters. "Who's next on the list then?"

"I'm not knocking on people's doors in the middle of the night."

"It's not as though they're going to be asleep," Hunz said. "Put yourself in their place. If you were scheduled to die in a couple of hours, would you be asleep?"

"You do whatever you want to do," Sydney said, "but I'm going home. You may not require sleep, but if I don't get seven hours, all I do the next day is stare at walls. Where should I drop you?"

"Seven hours? Who knows how many people are going to die in the next seven hours if we don't stop whoever's behind this!"

The fact that people were dying had never left Sydney's mind. She didn't need a reminder. Problem was, people died every day. They were assaulted, robbed, raped, shot, stabbed, and murdered. There was always someone who needed help, or who had a story of injustice to tell. At some point, for the sake of her own sanity, Sydney had to shut the world out. It wasn't easy to do, but after a couple of years in the industry, it was getting easier. Was that a good thing? Besides, she still had a couple of hours of crying to do before she could get to sleep.

"Hotel or the station?" Sydney said.

Hunz's cell phone beeped. He answered it.

"Vonner."

Still having received no destination information, Sydney continued heading north on the freeway.

Hunz flipped his phone closed.

"How far away is UCLA?"

"About twenty miles. Why?"

"That was the news desk. There's a boy at Dykstra Hall who claims he just survived Death Watch."

CHAPTER ELEVEN

Dykstra Hall was on the western edge of the UCLA campus. Built forty-five years ago, the ten-story structure was the oldest of four high-rise residence halls. A couple of late-night coeds entered Dykstra a few steps ahead of Sydney and Hunz.

It was quiet outside. Moonlight splashed against the side of the building. All was peaceful. The peace ended the moment they stepped into the hall. Inside it was more like twelve noon than twelve midnight.

Every light was on. Music in a half-dozen or more flavors poured from open doors. There were people everywhere. Reading. Studying. Chatting. Shouting. Eating. Watching television. Throwing things. Chasing each other. Dykstra Hall was a coed anthill.

Sydney was greeted with catcalls the moment she walked through the door. It was readily apparent that both she and Hunz were overdressed in this world of shorts, jeans, and T-shirts—a world where shoes were apparently banned.

They inquired after Jeremy Boles, the name given to them by the news desk.

"Jeremy hangs out on the third-floor lounge, dude," a sandy-haired student told Hunz. "Hey, you're the dudes on TV, aren't you? Were you really with that old man when he croaked?"

After being pointed toward the elevators, Sydney and Hunz made their way to the third floor. Already, they'd gained a substantial following.

The elevator doors opened to a lounge that smelled of popcorn, cigarette smoke, and unwashed socks. Sydney was reminded of her university dorm. Same walls and bulletin boards, same furniture, same students draped over it. From the scene before them it was obvious that the students here took the word *lounge* as a command.

They found Jeremy Boles hunkered over a table in a corner with three other guys. The table was littered with beer cans, several kinds of chips, and candy wrappers. They were playing Texas Hold-'em poker. A quick survey of the stacks of bills indicated Jeremy was losing.

The red-headed boy was short, barely five feet. His grin stretched wide when he was told news reporters wanted to interview him.

"Hey, where are the cameras?" A bare-chested boy, one of the poker players, trotted along on Jeremy's heels.

"On their way," Hunz said, taking charge. "Do you have the death watch notice? We'd like to see it."

Eager to show them, Jeremy pulled a folded piece of paper from his back pocket. Hunz took it.

"It's an email," Jeremy said.

As Hunz scanned it, Sydney read it over his shoulder. The sender was unidentified. The text was identical to all the other notices. Jeremy pointed to the time the email was transmitted.

"See, 10:59 p.m. Two days ago. I was supposed to die at 10:59 tonight and I didn't." He shrugged happily as though to say he couldn't explain it, but wasn't complaining.

"We watched you on the news tonight," the bare-chested boy added. "Too bad about that old guy. That's why we called the station. All the others have died, right? All except Jeremy here. Does he get some kind of prize or something?"

"Yeah, he gets to live," someone said.

"For Boles, that's not a prize, that's a punishment," someone else said.

Hunz handed the paper back to Jeremy. "Tell me exactly what happened when you got the notice."

"When I first saw it?" Jeremy said. "I nearly filled my pants, man."

Everyone around him laughed.

"I mean, this is some serious stuff, isn't it? With all the people dying and everything?"

"Where were you at the time?" Hunz asked.

"Um . . . the computer lab, over at De Neve Plaza." He twisted his torso to point in the direction of the plaza.

"Then what happened?" Hunz asked.

"Well, as soon as I picked myself up off the floor . . ."

Another laugh. He was playing to the crowd now.

". . . I ran back to my room and showed it to Tony here."

He jerked a thumb at the bare-chested boy.

"Him and Fredo." He looked around the room but couldn't find Fredo. "The three of us, we share a room."

"And after that?"

"Well, then I kinda just about fell apart, man. I mean, to be told you're gonna die and all."

"He was crying," the bare-chested boy said. "Then he called his mommy, and she made him feel better."

"Hey!" Jeremy said. "You don't know what it's like. This kinda thing puts a whole different spin on the world, you know what I mean? Until I got this thing, about the worst kind of note I ever got was from the IRS saying I owed them money."

"Death and taxes," someone said.

"IRS? Give me a death notice any day," someone else said.

That got a laugh.

"What did you do when you got the notice?" Hunz said.

Jeremy looked a little sheepish. "Called my mom first," he said, then quickly added, "but then I called the police."

"What did they say?"

"They wouldn't even send a squad car over to take a look at it. The dispatcher said that a whole lot of other people were getting them. Said the police couldn't do nothing. Said I was to call them back if I died."

Another round of laughter.

Hunz's eyes bored in on him. "Do you have a phone in your room?"

"Nah. We all got cells." He pulled his cell phone out of his front jeans pocket. It was a mini model, barely the size of his palm. "So are you gonna interview me on television now?"

"No," Hunz said.

The finality of his response silenced the room. A round of groans came from those looking on. A couple of people walked away.

"Hey, why not, man?" Tony's face fell.

"Simple. Jeremy's notice is a fake. He was never under any real threat of death."

"Fake? It's just like all the others," Tony said.

"Interesting that you would know that," Hunz said. "You're right, the text is identical to all the other death watch notices. It's what happened afterwards that's different. Something that hasn't been publicized. Jeremy, I'm afraid you've fallen victim to a rather cruel practical joke. And if I were to guess I'd say that Tony here had something to do with it."

Jeremy turned on his roommate. "Nah, he wouldn't . . . hey, man, you didn't . . ."

"No, man! I wouldn't do something like that to you!"

"Yeah, you would."

Tony grinned. "Yeah, I would," he said, laughing. Then took off running.

Billy Peppers crawled under a fir tree in the front yard of a quaint two-story house on La Loma Road in Pasadena. Looking under the branches, he had a nice view of Brookside Park across the street—trees, benches, rolling grassy hills highlighted by a silver moon. From behind him the porch light filtered through the tree limbs. He liked that. Sometimes it could be too dark when there was no moon overhead and when businesses didn't replace burned-out lightbulbs over back doors. On those nights Billy didn't sleep much. Rarely did good things happen in the dark. It was a cover for all manner of evil. And on those nights time slowed and the darkness seemed to stretch into forever.

Billy settled beneath the tree. He had never been to Pasadena. Now that he was here, he liked it. It was quiet. There was no banging of dumpster lids. No freeway noise. No squealing tires. No gunshots. The thick layer of needles and soft ground beneath the tree, though damp, would make a nice bed, so much nicer than a concrete alley with its odors of rotten meat or vegetables or urine. It smelled of pine here.

Stretched out, Billy scooted the shoe box in front of him. He removed the lid. Reaching inside, he pulled out a ceramic figurine of an angel. He smiled. This one was his favorite. Illuminated by the yellow porch light, the angel's face appeared radiant. Its white wings were spread gloriously. It was obvious this angel was proud to be a messenger of God.

"Just like in real life," Billy muttered.

He set the figurine down and reached for the other one. There were only two in the box. This one was broken. Its base was a cloud upon which the angel was touching down, or lifting off. Who could tell for sure? Half the cloud and the angel's left foot were missing. This angel's expression was serious, approaching stern. Billy called this one the "bad news angel." When this angel appeared, plagues of locusts or some such disaster most surely followed.

Also in the box were pictures torn from magazines and posters and boxes. All the pictures were of angels. Some were realistic renditions; others were cute cartoon drawings. Billy lifted one and examined it. He'd found this one in a dumpster, torn from a box that had once packaged a Precious Moments Bible. This adorable little angel looked like a happy, plump two-year-old with wings. Billy smiled when he looked at it. He always smiled when he looked at this angel.

He set the little angel on the branches of the tree. One by one, he pulled the pictures from the Nike shoe box and similarly arranged them on the limbs of the tree. Soon he was surrounded by angels overhead. He placed the ceramic angels on two of the sturdier limbs. Then he lay back with his arms behind his head and stared up at them.

"Just like Bethlehem," he said.

He imagined this was what it must have been like for the shepherds all those years ago—the sky filled with angels, their radiance so bright the entire hillside lit up like it was daytime.

At that instant, Billy's world became as bright as day with a light so bright he could barely see his angels in the tree. He could barely see anything at all. Billy raised his hand to shield his face against the brilliant white light.

The light shuddered, then moved off him a moment. In that moment, between blinks, Billy saw a police squad car at the curb in front of the house. Then the light was on him again, and he saw nothing but glaring light.

He heard car doors open.

Billy sat up quickly, his head hitting branches. Grabbing angels as fast as he could, he threw them into the Nike shoe box. First the pictures, then the ceramic figurines. The second figurine into the box made an awful clank, and Billy was afraid he'd broken it, possibly broken both of them.

Throwing the lid on the box, he scooped it under his arm and scrambled from beneath the tree and out of the spotlight. Two lesser lights hit him in the face. Flashlights held by two policemen. The two lights drove Billy from the La Loma Road residence.

He hurried down the street, periodically looking over his shoulder. The Pasadena squad car followed him until he crossed the city limits.

CHAPTER TWELVE

Cheryl McCormick stood on swollen feet in the aisle of Flight 858 from Chicago waiting to deplane. No Santa Anita thoroughbred was ever out of the gate faster than Cheryl was out of her seat at the sound of the seat-belt tone, despite being pregnant and pulling a three-year-old behind her. She managed to get ahead five rows of seats before the aisle clogged with passengers reaching into overhead bins for their carry-on bags. .

It had been a torturous four-hour flight. Cheryl's back and legs ached horribly, confirming what she already knew to be true—that women in their third trimester should not fly on airplanes. When the boarding agents inquired at the boarding gate how far along she was, she lied. Cheryl told them she was twenty-nine weeks along, when she was really thirty-six weeks pregnant. She felt bad about lying. She punished her fourth-grade students for lying. But this was an exception. She had to get on this flight. And now she had to get to the hotel in Century City. Tens, maybe hundreds, of thousands of dollars were at stake.

Cheryl craned her neck to see what was holding up the line. An elderly couple in first class helped each other out of their seats: *What do I do with this blanket? Hand it to the stewardess, dear. Did you get your sweater? My eyeglasses! Where are my eyeglasses? Around your neck, dear. Here, take my arm. I'm not helpless, you know. Did you call Roger? We'll call him in the airport. Did you bring his phone number? I thought you had it. No, I handed it to you when we were walking out the door.*

Finally, the line began to shuffle forward at a pace matching that of the elderly couple. At least they were on the move.

"Mommy?" Little Stacy rubbed her eyes with her free hand. She was asleep on her feet, still wearing her pajamas. Cheryl had yanked her out of her bed at midnight to get her to the airport. As it turned out, they had to wait for hours at O'Hare for a flight.

"What is it, sweetie?"

"Is it morning yet?"

The line started to move. Cheryl adjusted the two straps slung over her shoulder—luggage and her purse—refreshed her grip on her daughter, and maneuvered her swollen belly up the aisle. Once they were in the passageway that connected airport and airplane, she had room to move.

"Excuse me. Excuse me." She pressed past the flow of departing passengers, pulling her daughter behind her.

Stacy began to whimper.

"Stay with Mommy, honey," Cheryl said. "We're almost there now."

Cheryl burst into the waiting area at Gate 27 as though the airplane had spit her out. She'd flown infrequently and had never been to Los Angeles, but she knew what to look for. She hesitated only for a moment before spotting it.

BAGGAGE CLAIM

Taking off as fast as her stomach, a three-year-old, and two heavy bags would allow, she ran in the direction of the arrows. Within moments her breathing was labored, her back was on fire, her calves were cramping, and she was sweating like an El Centro day laborer. Still, she ran.

People were staring at her. She didn't care. Women were telling her to slow down. Not so much with words, but by the stares they gave her. They thought she was a terrible mother. Cheryl told herself it didn't matter what they thought. But it did.

Little Stacy was crying now.

They reached the baggage claim area. A long line of carousels with computerized letters identified airlines and flight numbers.

Cheryl ran past them, even though she'd checked two bags in Chicago. She'd worry about them later. Right now, she was looking for another sign.

She saw it.

GROUND TRANSPORTATION

In a moment, she was out the door, stumbling, waving for a taxi cab. The first in the long line of cabbies saw her and pulled up to the curb.

"Into the back, honey." Cheryl lifted Stacy off her feet and almost tossed her into the cab. Then, grabbing the top of the cab, the door, the seat, she maneuvered her bulk into the cab. The driver had gotten out to assist her. She was in the backseat and had the door closed before he could get around the car.

"I would have helped you, lady," the driver said, climbing back in. He was a short man with a dark complexion and white teeth. His English was broken. Cheryl guessed him to be Filipino.

"Century City," she said. "Excelsior Hotel. And please hurry. In fact, there's a twenty-dollar tip if you get us there fast."

The driver looked over his shoulder. "It's just a short way up the 405. I can have you there in twenty minutes."

"Make it fifteen, and there's forty dollars in it for you."

The cab driver hit the accelerator.

"Mommy?"

"We'll be there in a few minutes, honey."

Cheryl brushed fiery red strands of hair out of her eyes and pulled Stacy next to her. She tried to catch her breath.

Traffic was thick. The cab slowed. Cheryl peered through the windshield pointing out openings when she saw them. Each time, the cab driver was on it even as she was pointing, so she decided to let him drive on his own.

She looked at her watch. The last ten hours had been crazy. Had anyone told her ten hours ago she'd be in Los Angeles the next day, she would have laughed. She had no desire to see Los Angeles.

Which reminded her: *Call Vivian. If she shows up for lunch and you're not there, she'll race to the hospital only to find you're not there either. Then she'll worry.*

Cheryl looked down at Stacy, who had fallen asleep against her. Her firstborn had black hair and alabaster skin like her father, which was a blessing. While people always commented that Cheryl's fair and freckled skin was beautiful, they didn't have to live with it.

Larry had loved it. He couldn't keep his hands off of it. Which is what got her in this condition in the first place. Twice. Cheryl wondered if she'd be doing this if Larry were still alive. Possibly. He'd always been the crazy one. The spontaneous one. The one who would jump up from the couch and say, "Let's go get an ice cream," or "Let's go dancing," or he'd want to canoodle at inappropriate times and places, like in her parents' living room, and in the back of the church, and in her fourth-grade school classroom closet.

Cheryl laid her head back against the seat. Her heart was pounding so hard her chest hurt. Less than twelve hours ago, she'd been looking through *TV Guide* for something to watch. Flipping to channel seven had set in motion a series of events she never would have imagined possible.

The cab driver steered off the freeway.

"Are we almost there?"

"No one gets you there faster than me," the driver said.

The cab swung onto the Avenue of the Stars. When she saw the street sign, Cheryl chuckled to herself. Nobody was as infatuated with Hollywood as Hollywood.

In the distance the twin towers of the Excelsior Hotel rose up against a flat gray overcast sky.

Cheryl pulled herself to the edge of her seat.

Stacy stirred. "Mommy?"

"We need to run again, honey. Last time. Mommy promises." Even as she spoke, she was digging in her purse for the fare, reading the meter, adding forty dollars to the total. She threw the money on the front seat just as the cab was pulling up to the doors of the Excelsior Hotel.

While the cab was still moving the back door flew open. Cheryl was out, Stacy tucked under one arm. The little girl was crying again.

Cheryl could see the front desk through the glass doors of the lobby: her goal line.

A man and woman, middle-aged, nicely dressed, reached the lobby door before her.

Cheryl panicked.

Could that be them?

Taking no chances, she ran for the door, her swollen belly bouncing side to side, her daughter taking giant steps behind her.

His hand on the door, the man saw her coming. His mouth dropped open. Seeing his expression, his wife turned. "Oh my!" she said, jumping out of the way.

The man held the door open and Cheryl bolted through it, Stacy in hand.

Please, not them, not them, please. She'd feel so guilty if it was them.

Two employees in hotel uniform stood behind the front desk. Both young. A male and a female. The woman had been watching Cheryl from the moment she bolted from the cab. The male glanced up from a stack of printouts, started to look down again, then did a comic double take.

What's the matter, haven't you ever seen a pregnant woman sprinting before? Cheryl wanted to ask him. Instead, she said, "I'm Cheryl McCormick. I'm—"

"Ah! Mrs. McCormick." The female receptionist smiled. "We've been expecting you!"

Cheryl glanced back at the couple who held the door for her. They seemed in no hurry. She turned to the receptionist again. "Am I the first one?"

The woman beamed. "You're the first."

Cheryl started to cry.

The receptionist's smile widened as she handed her a tissue. "We get that reaction all the time," she said. She began punching keys on a keyboard.

Cheryl turned to the couple behind her, almost afraid to ask. Little Stacy clung to her leg. "You're not here for . . . *Wonder Wheel*, are you?" The expressions on their faces told her they didn't know what she was talking about. Cheryl felt better. When she turned back to the receptionist, there was a room key on the counter and a map of the lavish Excelsior facilities.

"I'll need to see picture identification and a credit card."

Cheryl dug in her purse.

"We'll have someone help you with your bags," the receptionist said.

"Oh, that's all right. They're still at the airport. I came straight here."

"If you'll give me your baggage claim tickets, we'll have someone pick them up and deliver them to your room."

Cheryl fought back a second wave of tears. This was really happening! "Thank you," she said softly.

"And good luck on *Wonder Wheel*, Mrs. McCormick."

Cheryl gathered the key and map, pried Stacy from her leg, and began to move in the direction of the elevators.

"Oh! One thing more," the receptionist called to her. She disappeared behind a side door, then returned a moment later. "This came for you." She handed Cheryl an envelope.

Cheryl thanked her and stood to one side so the nice couple behind her could register.

The envelope was buff color with a linen texture. It had an expensive feel to it. The only marking on the envelope was her name in Courier font as if it had been typed on an old typewriter. There was no return address and no corporate logo, which was odd since the only people who knew she was in LA were the folks at the television station.

It wasn't sealed. Cheryl looked inside, thinking it might be coupons or vouchers for restaurants, or possibly free passes to Six Flags, Knotts Berry Farm, or Disneyland. But there was nothing colorful inside, only a single sheet of stationery that matched the envelope. Probably a welcome letter and directions to the television station. Cheryl tucked the envelope in her purse. She'd read it later.

The elevator ride was a long one. All the way to the top floor Stacy was hugging her leg again, nodding off on her feet.

"Almost there, honey," Cheryl said.

When the doors opened she located their room and slid the electronic key in the slot. Her plan was to get Stacy down and order room service.

She gasped as the door swung open. This wasn't a hotel room; it was a palace with more floor space than her house in Evanston. A gigantic fruit basket greeted her with a bright red bow. There was coffee in a shiny silver carafe and an assortment of pastries, enough to feed her entire fourth-grade class.

Cheryl began to cry again.

After tucking Stacy between ocean-blue sheets, she slumped into an overstuffed striped chair in front of floor-to-ceiling windows overlooking the Los Angeles basin. It was a hazy day, but still the view was breathtaking. Her thoughts turned to the pastries, but she was too tired to get up. Her feet felt like she'd walked from Chicago to California. She propped them up on an ottoman.

Beside her on an ornate cherrywood end table, which probably cost more than she'd paid for her entire dinette set, was her purse. The envelope with her name was sticking out of it.

Cheryl reached for it.

Her breath caught in her throat as she read:

Cheryl McCormick,
 You have been selected for death. Precisely forty-eight hours from the time of this transmission you will die.
 This is an official death watch notice.

CHAPTER THIRTEEN

Sydney didn't get much sleep, and even that was restless. After depositing Hunz Vonner at his hotel, despite his continued protests in which he called her professionalism into question, she arrived home at 2:30 a.m. after promising to pick him up at 6:00 a.m.

Falling into bed, she wrestled with the bedclothes for an hour and a half, sleeping fitfully with dream vignettes of Lyle Vandeveer looking up at her with startled eyes as he drew his last breath.

Her phone woke her at 4:30 a.m.: Hunz, reminding her to pick him up at six. It rang again at 4:45 a.m.: Sol Rosenthal's assistant telling her to be at the station at 7:00 a.m. and not to forget to pick up Hunz Vonner.

Sydney flung her legs over the side of the bed. The way she felt, it would have been better had she not tried to sleep at all. There were rocks under her eyelids that burned when she blinked. Her head spun and swiveled like a toy gyroscope.

Willing herself into motion, Sydney switched on the thirteen-inch television set she kept in the corner of the bedroom.

Death Watch dominated the news. Overnight, the phenomenon had escalated dramatically. With the rest of the globe already well into the day, a mounting wave of panic was about to hit the West Coast like a tsunami.

Sydney listened to the newscast as she washed her face.

In the lower right corner of the screen, the Homeland Security Awareness Symbol, popularly called the Terror Meter, was set at Level Three.

Deaths are listed in the thousands. Among those dead are Dame Edna Bingham, a member of Great Britain's House of Lords; Joey LaMott, Baltimore Ravens first-round draft pick; and Andrea Scott, femme fatale of the popular daytime series Days of Our Lives.

While there are rumors that among the dead are one state governor, two congressmen, and a member of the president's cabinet, confirmations are being withheld for security reasons.

Beyond the personal tragedies of these deaths are the catastrophic effect they're having on transportation, commerce, and civic functions. It's reported that a pilot for Western Airlines died in flight between San Francisco and Dallas. A death watch notice was found in his pocket. The copilot managed to land the plane safely. Airline officials say they will immediately begin screening their pilots using voice stress analysis machines before allowing any pilot or crew member to board the plane.

Despite the assurances of the airlines, many passengers are canceling their flights. Due to the apparent 100 percent accuracy of death watch notices, some commuters fear that a passenger marked for death could possibly doom the entire plane. Amtrak and bus lines are experiencing similar problems.

Meanwhile, in Boise, Idaho, a third-grade schoolteacher died in front of her class. Officials found a death watch notice in her grade book. And traffic in New York's Holland Tunnel was brought to a standstill when a big-rig truck jackknifed and overturned, spilling hundreds of gallons of milk. The driver was a death watch victim.

Authorities are urging everyone who has received a death watch notice to stay home.

And in Morgantown, West Virginia, the residents of Hillwood Drive are taking matters into their own hands by barricading the entrance to their street. Armed with shotguns, they refuse to let the postman deliver the mail, fearing that he might deliver a death watch notice.

Still others are attempting to avoid death watch notices by refusing to answer their email. According to officials at Microsoft and

Yahoo, cyber mailboxes are bulging with unanswered mail, creating a backlog that is taxing available space on the servers. Ironically, most of the mail is spam.

5:59 a.m.

Hunz Vonner was standing outside the hotel waiting for Sydney as she drove into the circle drive. He was opening the door before the Volvo came to a stop.

"I've been waiting for you," he snapped.

She would have arrived early; however, before leaving home she'd made a phone call. Even so, she wasn't late. "You told me to pick you up at—"

"Take me to the FBI field office."

"We have a meeting—"

"It's on Wilshire Boulevard."

"I know where it is."

"Why aren't we moving?"

Sydney looked over at him, bit back the comment that was on the tip of her tongue, put the car in gear, and pulled into the street. Downtown traffic was already sluggish.

"Just pull in front. I'll only be a minute," Hunz said when they arrived.

"It's a red zone."

He looked at her in exasperation. "Just do it, all right?"

Hunz disappeared into the building. Five minutes later, Sydney was still waiting for him, motor running, sitting in a red zone. Two pedestrians informed her she couldn't park there. She thanked them.

Ten minutes passed. A police cruiser pulled up beside Sydney. A two-man unit. The officer in the passenger seat rolled down his window. He didn't say anything. He just stared at her.

"I'm waiting for someone," she said, motioning to the FBI building.

Apparently, the officer felt his stare communicated well enough. It did. He had those mirror-reflector style of sunglasses. Sydney didn't have to wonder if she looked as ridiculous as she sounded. She could see herself in the reflection. She produced her press pass.

"My partner just ran in to get something." She hoped he wouldn't ask for details, because she'd already told him everything she knew.

"Move it," said the officer.

Sydney looked at the front door of the FBI office, hoping to see Hunz. She didn't.

"Look, lady," said the officer. "We're going to circle the block. If you're still here when we get back, I'm gonna write you up."

He rolled up his window. The squad car continued on its way.

With one last glance at the front door, Sydney had no choice but to click on her turn signal and pull out into traffic.

She circled the block. Once, twice, three times. On her fourth circuit, Hunz was standing curbside. He was shouting into his cell phone.

Sydney pulled into the red zone to pick him up. He was stepping into the street as she did so, and she almost hit him. He yanked the door open.

"I have no idea where she went," Hunz shouted into the phone, "but she's here now." He snapped the phone shut. "I told you to wait for me."

"And I told you this is a red zone." Sydney hit her turn signal. She checked her side mirror just in time to see a police squad car pull up beside her. It angled to block her in.

While Hunz Vonner stewed in the passenger seat, the police officer with the reflector sunglasses took his good sweet time writing Sydney her traffic ticket.

Sydney and Hunz were thirty minutes late for their morning meeting at the station.

CHAPTER FOURTEEN

The news team was assembled and seated at Command Central when Sydney and Hunz arrived. As usual, Sol Rosenthal and Helen Gordon were in the positions of power. Coanchor Grant Forsythe was in his place next to the producer. Beside Grant was Cori Zinn, in a none-too-subtle staging meant to convince people she belonged at his side in a professional capacity off camera as well as on. Josh Leven and Phil Sanders were absent, as were production crew and interns. Sydney remembered Josh had flown to Chicago the night before to cover a Lakers away game.

Hunz was several steps ahead of Sydney. He pulled out a chair next to Helen and opposite Grant, which left Sydney the chair opposite Cori.

However, before she reached the chair Sol Rosenthal zeroed in on her. He shoved back his chair and pulled her aside. "A minute," he said. Whether he was asking Sydney for a minute or telling Helen he needed a minute was unclear. All Sydney knew was he was fired up and ready to unload on her a short distance from the table.

"I told you to assist Hunz Vonner in any capacity needed," he shouted. His voice was easily heard by everyone at Command Central. "Do you have a problem with that?"

"That's what I've been doing," Sydney said.

"Have you? Then why did you refuse to drive him to locations last night? And this morning you drove off and left him standing on the street."

"I was in a red zone," Sydney said.

But Rosenthal wasn't listening. He didn't want a discussion, he wanted contrition and compliance. He also wanted to display his authority, which had been bruised yesterday in front of his European guest. Sydney knew defending herself would be useless. Showing him the parking ticket would be useless. So she said nothing.

"I have to say I'm disappointed in you," Rosenthal said. "I didn't expect this kind of behavior from you."

What kind of behavior? Sydney felt like she was a teenager being chewed out by her parents for something she didn't do. To complete the image, Cori sat a few feet away sniggering like a spoiled sibling.

Sol Rosenthal gave her an unblinking stare, finished for the moment at least. But this wasn't the last Sydney would hear of this. She knew from experience Sol would bring it up again in meetings and conversations and snide comments for the next month or two. He was the kind of guy who never let you forget an error, real or perceived.

Sydney followed him back to the table.

Helen took charge. "Overnight this death watch thing has turned into an international nightmare," she said. "Not since 9/11 have I seen our nation react to something so immediately and universally. People are scared. I'm scared. So what do we have?"

"I have a lead," Hunz said. He was so eager to tell what he had, he trampled all over the end of Helen's question.

A thin leather binder and a manila folder lay in front of him on the table. It was the same folder he'd picked up at the FBI field office. The tab at the top was marked CONFIDENTIAL. Pushing aside the FBI folder, he opened the leather binder and shuffled some loose papers.

"My team in Berlin and I think we may have a promising lead," he said. His papers in place now, he looked up. Confident. Assured. As he spoke, he directed his comments to Sol Rosenthal and Grant Forsythe. "To begin: Whoever is doing this has to have vast resources with operatives in every major city of the world. That eliminates a lot of groups."

"Al Qaeda, for one," Grant said.

"Exactly. Even before the US invaded Afghanistan, I doubt al Qaeda had the resources to execute something of this size and scope. It has to be someone with almost unlimited resources."

"Wait a minute," Sol Rosenthal said. "You're not going where I think you're going with this, are you?"

Hunz didn't respond. He let Sol answer his own question.

"You're not thinking the United States is behind this," he said. "The army? The CIA?"

Hunz Vonner squared his shoulders and looked Sol Rosenthal in the eye. "We haven't ruled that out," he said.

Helen said, "But what possible reason would—"

Hunz cut her off. "There's a more likely candidate," he said, "though you have to admit the United States is one of the few entities in the world that has the resources to do something on the scale of Death Watch."

"As do several other major countries," Helen said.

"So who do you think it is?" Sol frowned.

Hunz Vonner paused like a television detective does just before revealing the identity of the murderer.

"His name is Feliks Baranov," Hunz said.

"That name's familiar," Helen said.

Hunz nodded. "You probably know him from when he was a general in the army of the Soviet Union."

"Part of the attempted coup when Gorbachev was vacationing in the Crimea," Helen said.

Hunz nodded. "A hardliner who violently opposed Gorbachev's *glasnost* and *perestroika* initiatives."

"Openness and reform," Grant said, eager to demonstrate he knew the meaning of the words.

"So you think it's the Russians who are—," Cori said.

"Russians, yes," Hunz said. "But not the government. The Russian mafia."

After a moment of stunned silence several questions were fired at Hunz at once. He waved them off.

"Hear me out," he said. "I know at first it sounds like a 1950s movie plot, but only to people who don't know the facts of the modern Russian mafia. Hear me out before dismissing the idea."

Hunz took their silence for consent.

"After the failed coup against Gorbachev in 1991, General Baranov managed to elude capture. He disappeared, but he didn't go away. We have documents indicating he teamed up with Vassily Sorokin."

"The Russian mafia kingpin," Grant said.

"Over the years they built an organization that literally spans the globe. Believe me when I say they are a viable world power. They own banks. They purchase weapons from the Russian army to supplement what they make in their own weapons factories and then sell them on the black market. They are established in Western and Eastern Europe, Canada, the Middle East—primarily Israel—and nearly every country in Africa. In South America they have established links with the largest drug cartels. Companies who do business in Russia routinely pay them up to 20 percent of their profits. And according to Swiss court documents, they have laundered over sixty billion dollars through Swiss banks. Baranov and Sorokin have more money and more resources than most countries."

He patted the FBI manila folder.

"The Russian mafia has what they call combat brigades in major US cities—New York, Miami, Houston, and here in Los Angeles. Their daily bread and butter includes extortion, counterfeiting, drug trafficking, arms dealing, prostitution, contract killings, and blackmail. Recently the head of the FBI identified the Russian mafia as the greatest threat to American national security. It's a matter of record."

Hunz had their attention.

"This Baranov character," Sol said, "you think he's trying to take over the world?"

"Is that so hard to believe?" Hunz leaned forward, his expression intense. "That was his goal when he was a general of the Soviet Union. And while his country has changed, he hasn't. What better way to announce a new world order than with thousands of precision deaths proving that no one is out of his reach?"

"Are they taking credit for these death watch killings?" Helen asked.

Grant Forsythe scoffed. "Who *isn't* claiming credit for death watch notices now?" He produced a sheet of his own and read. "The Hamas. The Felix Cordova drug cartel. Abu Sayyaf, the Philippine guerilla outfit. The Islamic Liberation Front. The Japanese Red Army. As for pointing the finger at others: Islamic leaders are blaming Christians and Jews; Christian television preachers say it's a fulfillment of prophecy and that the Muslims are behind it all. There's even a group of militant senior citizens in New Jersey who say the killings will continue until their Medicare benefits are increased."

"To answer your question," Hunz said to Helen, "no, the Russian mafia has not claimed credit for the deaths. However, it's early. They specialize in terror. You have to understand the mentality of these people. They'll shoot you just to see if their gun works."

"All right," Sydney said. "Let's assume the Russian mafia is behind this. How are they doing it? Last night Lyle Vandeveer died at precisely the instant they said he would."

Hunz pulled out a photograph from the manila folder and tossed it into the center of the table. "Yuri Kiselev," he said. "Scientist. Disappeared two months ago."

The man in the black-and-white photo was a pale, hollow-cheeked Russian with piercing eyes and a bad comb-over.

"You think Baranov grabbed him," Sol said.

"That, or he went willingly. It's sketchy, but Baranov and Kiselev knew each other during their Soviet days. Kiselev worked with the army to develop experimental weapons. Baranov was the head of that project."

"What kind of weapons?" Helen asked.

"At this point, it's speculation," Hunz said. "The project simply provides a possible tie between the two men. It's what happened after the collapse of the Soviet Union that's important. Yuri Kiselev is Russia's foremost authority in an emerging technology."

"Nanotechnology," Grant Forsythe said, stealing Hunz Vonner's thunder.

"What's that?" Cori asked.

Hunz looked to Grant. The silent exchange had an edge to it. Did Grant want to field the question? The coanchor deferred to Hunz.

"Basically," Hunz said, "nanotechnology is an attempt to manufacture products on the atomic level, arranging atoms as though they were colored Lego bricks. Kiselev is experimenting with molecular robotics. He's building devices that are one one-thousandth the width of a human hair. These machines—called nanobots—are then inserted into the human bloodstream."

"You asked Mr. Vandeveer if he'd had an injection recently," Sydney said.

Hunz nodded. "We believe they may be contaminating batches of popular medicines with nanobots. A person goes in for a flu shot and they get a programmed molecular robotic injected into their bloodstream."

"Is that possible?" Helen asked.

"Scientists the world over are working on nanotechnology. Some of the projects on the drawing board are to use them to clean arteries, repair DNA, repair damaged cells, find and eliminate viruses, and even clean the inside of our lungs."

"Our greatest strides in aviation occurred during time of war," Grant said. "Could it be that our greatest strides in microrobotics will come as a result of terrorism?"

"So Lyle Vandeveer . . . ," Sydney prompted.

"Two possibilities," Hunz said. "One project that's being explored is the use of nanobots as cancer killers. The robot would be programmed to seek out cancer cells and inject them with a poison that would kill them."

"Substitute a cancer-killing poison with a fatal poison," Helen said, "released with computerized precision."

"The other possibility is the use of nanobots to fight thrombosis, or blood clots. Ideally, the nanobot would patrol the bloodstream and search for unwanted developing internal clots. We all know that a stray clot in the bloodstream can cause a heart attack if it clogs an artery or gets into a lung, or it can cause a seizure if it goes to the brain."

Helen tapped her pencil on the pad in front of her. "So, have they determined the cause of Mr. Vandeveer's death?"

Sydney felt the blood drain from her face. Before leaving the house this morning she'd called the medical examiner to get a report on the cause of Lyle Vandeveer's death. "He died of a blood clot," she said.

CHAPTER
FIFTEEN

An uneasy feeling wormed inside Sydney. Could it be that as she sat next to Lyle Vandeveer last night a nanobot was swimming in his bloodstream? A ticking time bomb smaller than a human hair? Could that really be what killed him?

She turned to Hunz, who still had the floor at Command Central. "Can they be detected? These nanobots. Is there a scanner that can detect them?"

"They're microscopic," he said. "I know that those who implant them can give them acoustic signals. Other than that ..." He shrugged.

"Something worth looking into," Helen said.

"What about Baranov and Kiselev?" Grant Forsythe asked. "Do we know their whereabouts?"

"The FBI has men on it."

"Good," Helen said. "What else do we have? Sydney?"

It took Sydney a moment to make the mental transition. She was still thinking about Hunz's nanobots. When she realized Helen was expecting some kind of report from her regarding Death Watch, her heart stalled. Just like in high school. The one time you don't do your homework and the teacher calls on you. Everything she had was reported by Hunz last night on the air.

"We have the follow-up on Lyle Vandeveer's death, that he died of a blood clot," she said lamely. "And there was a hoax last night at UCLA."

"A dormitory hoax?" Cori scoffed. "Hardly breaking news."

"Anything else?" Helen asked.

"Oh! Lyle Vandeveer's brother says he received a confirmation regarding Lyle's death watch notice. We haven't found anyone else who's received a corroborating notification, but it might be something."

"Good," Helen said.

Trying to make up for the lack of substance with quantity, she forged ahead. "And this morning, I plan to go to the Homeland Security Internet page. They've been logging the death watch notices. I thought I'd download the information and see if I could find any patterns."

"Be sure to make a list of any injections they've had," Hunz said. "Location. Date."

"And don't spend too much time playing solitaire," Cori said.

"Is that all?" Helen asked.

Sydney grinned sheepishly and nodded.

"Helen," Cori said, "I think it's pretty obvious Sydney's in over her head. Maybe I should take over for her."

"Why?" Helen said. There was a sharp edge to the question. "Do you have a contact with the Russian mafia's press secretary?"

Cori Zinn's face reddened. Next to her, Grant Forsythe chuckled. From the tone in Helen's voice, Cori was not on her list of favorite people right now.

"In case anyone hasn't heard, seems she lied to get the governor's interview," Grant said. "No exclusive."

"Shut up, Grant," Cori said.

"How about a death watch clock on the news set?" Sol Rosenthal said, changing the subject. "You know, like the ones they have that keep an ongoing tally of American debt. How about a clock that updates the total number of deaths as they're reported? We could have it running behind the anchor desk."

"That's rather ghoulish, if you ask me," Helen said.

"I think it'll make a splash," Sol said.

Which meant it was as good as done.

Sydney sat down at one of the station's computer terminals just after Sol propelled Hunz into his office for coffee and croissants. She rubbed her eyes as she waited for the Department of Homeland Security homepage to load.

She took a sip of orange juice she'd grabbed from the vending machine and stared at the screen. There were actually two Internet sites for Homeland Security. One, a subdirectory of the official White House site, featured current news related to national security. The lead story today was about the death watch killings. An announcement indicated the president would be addressing the nation this evening on the subject of Death Watch. It was rumored in the newsroom he'd raise the Awareness system to Level Four, which meant government and public buildings would be closed; transportation systems would be monitored, redirected, and constrained; and emergency personnel mobilized.

Two raises in two days was unprecedented.

How do you mobilize a nation against nanobots?

She scanned the rest of the site to see if it said anything about the Russian mafia. She found nothing.

Switching over to the Homeland Security site, she found an organizational chart of the Department of Homeland Security; a photo of Wallace Perkins, the department's second director; and instructions to follow in case of emergency or disaster. After Hunz's briefing, Sydney realized how dated the information was. It was based on prior terrorist acts—the role of fire and police departments in an emergency, how to report suspicious activity around bridges and high-profile buildings, and so forth. There was nothing about how to guard against a subatomic nanobot attack.

She found a link to recent news items and clicked on it. A new screen appeared. At the top, a banner headline: Death Watch Notifications.

Bingo. One more click and a list of known death watch victims appeared. It could be sorted by name, state, or chronologically.

Sydney clicked on the date and time column.

Jeffrey Conley appeared twenty-first on the list. The seventh person to die in Los Angeles, the twenty-first in America. He died minutes after a woman in Montana and a West Virginia man.

The length of the list chilled Sydney's flesh. A black dot appeared by the names of those confirmed dead. It reminded her of *Treasure Island*. The cursed black spot.

Halfway down the list the times caught up with the present. There was an hour lag between the placing of black dots and present time, nothing to indicate this was anything but an administrative lag as the deaths were confirmed.

Sydney printed out the list, then clicked on the state column to get a list of California names. Lyle Vandeveer's name stood out. Sydney wondered who would inherit his trains and scenery layout.

Sydney bit her lower lip to fight back her emotions.

She'd promised him he would beat Death Watch.

After printing out the state list, she scanned the lower half for LA residents, those people who were counting the minutes until they died. One name didn't fit. The address was a temporary one, the Excelsior Hotel in Century City. An out-of-town visitor had reported receiving a death watch notice.

"Welcome to California," Sydney muttered.

Before logging off, she checked her email. It was a reflex, something she did several times a day. Today, however, the moment she hit Enter, while the computer accessed her account, her heart caught in her throat at the sudden realization of what she might find in her in-box.

The screen changed, and she wished she hadn't initiated the process. She hadn't really prepared herself for what she might see. She'd forgotten how everything had changed since yesterday.

Checking email. Opening a mailbox. Answering the phone. Answering the front door. Yesterday these were ordinary events. Today, a person's life could change by any one of them.

Her personalized email screen came up.

Thirteen new messages.

Sydney stared at the number for several moments. A mouse click would list the messages by subject. Was she sure she wanted to do this?

Her breathing was shallow. She was spooked, she admitted it. And the longer she sat there staring at the screen, the more spooked she became.

She reached for the mouse and clicked the program closed. She didn't want to know. It was better not to know, wasn't it? It was unnatural for a person to know the precise moment of her death, wasn't it?

Terminally ill patients knew, but they were given a general time frame. You have six months to live. You have a year to live. To know the exact time was to share an experience with death-row prisoners, but they'd done something to deserve their fate. Even then, some people argued that knowing one's time of death was cruel and unusual punishment.

It was better not to know. You could put off thinking about it. You could deny it would ever happen to you. You could believe you were going to be the exception to the history of humankind and live forever, or that like Enoch and Elijah, God would spare you the penalty of death and take you straight to heaven. Jesus could return at any moment, couldn't he?

Sydney stood and backed away from the computer. The screen had returned to the station's homepage.

She stared at it without looking at it.

Wanting to go. Wanting to know.

She sat back down and logged in. She clicked on the button that called up her email. Since it had already been retrieved, it came up faster this time.

Thirteen new messages.

Taking a deep breath, Sydney clicked on her in-box icon. She scanned the list, looking for two words.

She recognized several online store names, merchandisers from whom she'd ordered who now bombarded her daily with ads. There were replies to emails she'd sent; forwarded email, usually junk poems with animated pictures encouraging you to pass the email to ten friends.

Three quarters down the list she saw it.

Two words.

Death Watch.

CHAPTER SIXTEEN

Sydney's mind wasn't on her driving.

She was thinking about the death watch email she'd found in her in-box. It had been sent from the public library by The Rev, the same man who'd tried contacting her yesterday. He claimed he knew who was behind the death watch notices and, this time, wanted her to meet him at the Hollywood Memorial Park Cemetery at noon today. He didn't give a description of himself, said it wasn't necessary. He knew what she looked like.

What had Cori said about this guy? That she'd interviewed him for a mental insanity news feature—that was it, wasn't it? Wasn't he the guy who claimed he could talk to angels?

Sydney had deleted the message, but she couldn't stop thinking about it. Probably because the death watch subject heading had scared ten years off her life, and then when she realized it wasn't what she thought it was, she'd gotten angry at him for scaring her.

But even if she had the time, which she didn't, she wouldn't have followed up on the story. Newscasters get tips for stories every day from people who, nine times out of ten, have an ax to grind or are crackpots.

Pulling to a stop in the middle of a downtown intersection brought Sydney's mind back to the present. Her left signal blinked repeatedly while she waited for a break in the traffic. A steady flow of cars streamed past. The signal light turned yellow. The cars kept coming. Red. Still the cars came, two, three, four, five, before finally someone stopped, but by then, the cross traffic was crowding into the intersection, honking at her because she was in their way.

Driving in LA used to bother her. Not so much anymore. If you wanted to get around in LA, this was the kind of thing you had to deal with.

Moving again, Sydney shifted her thoughts to the Homeland Security Web site and the growing list of death watch victims. The list was limited to deaths in America. Other Web sites attempted to tally worldwide totals. It was these numbers that would power the KSMJ death watch clock to tick with relentless horror.

Sydney found that scanning the worldwide list of names was in some ways like reading headstones in a cemetery. You're aware that they were all dead people, but it didn't impact you emotionally because you didn't know them.

Reading Lyle Vandeveer's name on the list was different. His name got to her. It was personal.

She told herself this next interview would be different. She'd made a mistake with Lyle Vandeveer. She let herself get too close to him. She knew at the time it was a mistake, yet she did it anyway. A reporter is supposed to remain detached. Objective. She wouldn't make that mistake again.

The twin towers of the Excelsior Hotel rose up in front of her. Sydney began preparing herself for the interview, to distance herself mentally and emotionally.

CHAPTER SEVENTEEN

Sydney St. James fell in love with Cheryl McCormick the instant she laid eyes on her. She fell in love with little Stacy a second later. Mother and daughter greeted her with smiles.

"My, they sure grow them pretty out here," Cheryl said, when she first saw Sydney.

"Actually, I'm an Iowa girl," Sydney said.

Cheryl invited her in while Stacy stared at her from behind her mother's legs. For a woman who had just recently learned she was going to die, Cheryl seemed unusually chipper. A show of strength for the little girl's sake?

"Honey, why don't you color in the other room," Cheryl said. "Mommy's going to talk to this nice lady."

Sydney was impressed that Stacy agreed without a fuss. Before going, however, she had to show Sydney some of the pictures she'd already colored.

"Wonder Woman!" Sydney flipped page after page of green scribbled faces. "I love Wonder Woman! I used to pretend I was Wonder Woman when I was a little girl."

Stacy beamed.

While Cheryl deposited her daughter in an adjoining room, Sydney took a quick look around. The suite was immaculate, but cold. Tile floors. Gold inlaid pillars. Cathedral ceiling. Polished ferns strategically placed. Maybe the subject of her visit was influencing her, but it reminded her of a mausoleum.

Cheryl returned and joined Sydney in a little alcove overlooking the city.

"When are you due?" Sydney asked.

"Less than a month," Cheryl said. "Will there be cameras?"

"The cameraman's about thirty minutes behind me. I like to do a precamera interview. That way we both know what to expect."

"How considerate. Thank you. Is what I'm wearing all right?"

Cheryl was dressed in an emerald green maternity top that draped gracefully over her form and set off her red hair.

"You look beautiful," Sydney said.

It was the truth. Cheryl McCormick had an aura of pleasantness about her that had nothing to do with her expectant condition and everything to do with her personality, which troubled Sydney even more. How could this woman be so composed under the circumstances?

"May I see the letter?" Sydney asked. She found it difficult to say *Death Watch*, as though saying it would confirm it. It wasn't needed anyway. Cheryl knew what she was referring to.

Without getting up, she groaned in an effort to reach across her belly for her purse. Sydney jumped up to help.

"Thank you," Cheryl said. "Sometimes I feel like a beached whale at low tide."

With Cheryl directing her, Sydney found the envelope stuffed in the purse. She opened it. The wording was identical to all the other death watch notices. The time of notification was at the top: 7:28 a.m. The exact time she checked in. Cheryl had less than forty-two hours to live.

"Did anything happen after you got this?"

Sydney was hoping Cheryl would say no. That this was someone's idea of a joke, like the one played at Dykstra Hall.

"How did you know?" Cheryl said. "I got a phone call shortly after we settled in. It was the strangest voice." She wrinkled her nose. "I couldn't tell if it was male or female. Weird, huh? Sort of like special effects. And it was as though it knew I was the one going to answer the phone, you know what I mean? No hello. It didn't ask who it was speaking to. It just repeated what was in the letter."

Sydney's heart ached. This was the real thing. "No, it doesn't sound weird at all. And it conforms to prior experiences."

"So what's this all about? Are you at liberty to tell me?"

Sydney glanced out the window. An entire city lay before her. For most people, this was an ordinary workday. For death watch victims like Cheryl, there was no such thing as ordinary anymore.

"We don't know," Sydney said. "At this point, we really don't know."

Cheryl smiled.

Smiled.

Why would Cheryl smile?

"You seem so calm about all this," Sydney said. "If I were in your shoes I'd probably be a blubbering puddle of emotion right about now."

Cheryl glanced down at her hands that were folded serenely across her belly. Her expression was that of a game show contestant who knew the answer to the million-dollar question.

"I have to admit," she said, "I have some experience in this sort of thing."

"You do?"

"A degree in theater. I'm used to being under the lights, to thinking on my feet. We did a lot of improv."

"You're talking about the game show."

Cheryl nodded. "I'm hoping my experience will give me an edge. We can really use the money."

"And the death watch notice?"

"I was surprised at first. Off the record? It shook me. That's why I called the police. Then I remembered where I was. Hollywood, with all those reality shows." She looked around. "It wasn't hard to figure out. They put us up in these rooms outfitted with hidden cameras, introduce an unexpected element when I check in—the letter—designed to throw me off balance, then send someone to interview me. All part of the game." She leaned forward conspiratorially and whispered, "When I answered the door, you confirmed my suspicions. You're far too pretty to be a reporter."

Sydney was stunned. Cheryl McCormick had no idea she was going to die.

"Haven't you watched the news lately?" Sydney asked.

"Will there be a lot of current-event questions? For the last week, I've been so tired, all I've done is take care of Stacy. Last night was the first time I'd turned on the television in a week. Talk about good timing. You know, I called *Wonder Wheel* on a lark, never expecting to get through, and when I did, I certainly didn't expect to win. After that, everything's pretty much a blur."

The poor thing didn't know.

There had been times when Sydney was appalled at how little people were aware of world events, until she realized that this was her chosen field, not theirs. It was sort of like dentists who are appalled at how little thought people give to their teeth, and nutritionists in arms over how little concern people give to their diets.

She fingered Cheryl McCormick's letter and thought of little Stacy in the next room, and of the unborn child Cheryl was carrying. How to break the news to her? All of a sudden Sydney knew how doctors feel when they say, "I'm sorry, it's cancer." Or police knocking on the door in the middle of the night with "I'm afraid I have some bad news."

"Cheryl, there's no easy way to tell you this," she said.

The pregnant woman looked at her with an unassuming grin.

"This notice? It's not part of the *Wonder Wheel* game. It's not Hollywood. It's real."

Sydney spoke in a hushed voice so Stacy wouldn't overhear. She told Cheryl about Jeffrey Conley's car accident, about Lyle Vandeveer, about the escalating terror that was gripping the world, and about the 100 percent fatality rate.

Cheryl listened intently. At times a hint of a smile tugged at the corner of her mouth. She still wanted to believe this was part of the show, that it was Sydney's role to sell the charade. But there was something about Sydney's earnestness that began to sink in. Her cheerful foundation began to weaken until, at last, her footing gave way and she plunged into icy reality—in less than two days she was going to die.

"My baby," Cheryl said. A trembling hand caressed her belly. "If I die, my baby will die."

She broke down and sobbed.

There was a knock at the door.

Torn between comforting Cheryl and answering the door, Sydney answered the door because she thought she knew who it was. She was right.

Fred Zappa, the clothes hamper with legs, lumbered in with his KSMJ camera atop his shoulder. "Here comes bad news," he said cheerfully.

Sydney grabbed him before he got two steps into the room.

"This isn't a good time," she said.

Zappa saw the weeping woman on the far side of the room. "I can't hang around," he said. "I have to be at city hall in forty-five minutes or Cori will have my head."

"What about after that?"

"Sorry."

Sydney looked at Cheryl. It would be cruel to put her in front of a camera now.

"Just tell them we couldn't get the interview. I'll explain when I get back to the station."

"We have a slot for it at six," Zappa said.

"I'll take responsibility for it," Sydney said, turning him toward the door. The cameraman offered no resistance.

"Your funeral," Zappa said, shaking his head. "But, hey, I'm easy. This way I can grab a donut."

He ambled out.

Sydney rejoined Cheryl in the alcove. She was flushed red and wet with tears.

"What am I going do?" she cried.

Sydney put her arms around the woman. So much for remaining detached and objective.

How desperately she wanted to tell Cheryl it would be all right, that she would use the full resources of the station to protect her. Then she thought of Lyle Vandeveer and how much her assurances had helped him.

"I'll contact the station," Sydney said, "and tell them you're not going to be able to go on the game show tonight."

Cheryl nodded, dabbing her nose and eyes with a tissue.

Then, suddenly, she changed her mind.

"No, I have to go on tonight."

"Cheryl, you're in no condition."

"I need the money. Especially now. Who's going to take care of my babies after I'm gone? If I win, at least they'll have money. If I win big, maybe they'll even have enough for college."

"You're putting a lot of pressure on yourself."

But Cheryl had made up her mind. "I have to do it."

"What about relatives? Is there someone you can call?"

"We're alone. Both my parents died when I was young. I was raised in foster homes. Larry's father died a few years ago. His mother is sickly and needs round-the-clock care. And his only brother is younger. He's in the Marines in Afghanistan."

Sydney took her hand. "You're not alone. We'll work something out. I promise you." She meant it, though she had no idea how she could complete the promise. It didn't matter. The way she felt right now, she'd lead a crusade to see that Cheryl's children were taken care of.

"I should make airline reservations for after the show tonight," Cheryl said. "No offense, but I don't want to die in LA."

"Can you fly this late in your term?"

"I lied to get out here. I can do it again."

Sydney said, "Let me take care of getting you back to Chicago."

"Evanston, actually," Cheryl said. "And I should call my obstetrician. If I'm going to die, I'm not taking this baby with me."

CHAPTER EIGHTEEN

Billy Peppers sat beneath a tree with an open Bible on his lap. The sky was clear and blue, the grass was green. A beautiful sight even though Billy was surrounded by death.

His angel shoe box beside him, he read while keeping an eye on the Santa Monica Boulevard entrance to Hollywood Memorial Park Cemetery. In the distance he could see the Hollywood sign in the hills. Behind him was the historic Paramount Studios back lot.

Billy was waiting for a beige Volvo to pass through the gates.

He read:

But mark this: There will be terrible times in the last days. People will be lovers of themselves, lovers of money, boastful, proud, abusive, disobedient to their parents, ungrateful, unholy, without love, unforgiving, slanderous, without self-control, brutal, not lovers of the good, treacherous, rash, conceited, lovers of pleasure rather than lovers of God—having a form of godliness but denying its power.

He heard a car approaching. He looked up. A dark blue Bonneville.

The reporter from KSMJ was late. He'd emailed her to meet him here an hour ago. He'd wait another thirty minutes. She might have been delayed. After all, she was an important person with a lot of responsibilities. But then, so was he. At least it was pretty here.

Billy placed his Bible in the shoe box, careful not to bend or wrinkle any of his angel pictures. He took out his favorite ceramic piece and held it. The angelic figurine didn't seem out of place here, not like it did in the trashy alleys. Maybe it was because this place was frequented so often by angels.

Oh-oh. Trouble.

The driver of the Pontiac Bonneville had gotten out of his car. He was talking to two groundskeepers. The driver was pointing at Billy and talking. The groundskeepers did some head nodding, then came walking toward him.

It always amazed Billy how people could ignore paper and plastic trash in streets and alleys, but couldn't pass by a man in ragged clothes and not try to do something about it.

Billie knew the drill. He gathered up his box. He'd save them the trouble and leave.

Something interrupted him.

"Chicago?" he exclaimed. "How am I supposed to get to Chicago?"

The two groundskeepers slowed, eyeing him like he was crazy.

"I didn't say I wouldn't go," Billy said.

"Then go, already," one of the workers said.

"I wasn't talking to you," Billy said. "Can't you see I'm busy? I'll be with you in a minute."

The groundskeepers exchanged glances.

"Impossible!" Billy said to the air. "It'd take me a couple days at least."

"Listen, buddy," one worker said.

"Fly?" Billy shouted. "In case you haven't noticed, not everyone in this conversation has wings!"

"Hey, buddy!" the worker shouted. "I don't know what you're on, but we don't want any trouble here."

"I said I'd be with you in a minute," Billy replied. Then, picking up his first conversation: "All right, I'll get there. Are you going to tell me why I'm going to Chicago?"

Billy threw up a hand in frustration.

"That's enough, fella!" the worker shouted.

Billy didn't hear him. Pressing past the groundskeepers he said, "Sorry, guys. Can't talk now. I have to get to Chicago."

CHAPTER NINETEEN

The first thing out of the receptionist's mouth when Sydney arrived back at the station was a clipped, "Helen wants to see you." The message wasn't totally unexpected.

She knocked on Helen's door and entered.

"What happened?" Helen said the instant she entered.

Sydney took a deep breath. It would be a mistake to presume Helen's friendship, such as it was. The woman was a professional; Sydney's job was to get the story.

"The poor girl thought the death watch notice was part of the game show experience. When I told her the truth, she took it hard. She was in no condition to give an interview. She's pregnant and frightened."

"No condition to give an interview? Since when is that a requirement for a news story? We cover people immersed in tragedy every day, pregnant and otherwise."

Sydney made no effort to reply.

"And what are we going to fill that fifteen seconds with?"

It was a rhetorical question. At least Sydney hoped it was a rhetorical question.

"Cheryl is still going on the show. Then she plans to return to Evanston, Illinois. She wants to induce labor and have the baby before her time runs out. Let me follow up on it. There's still a story here."

Helen punched a button on her phone. "Get Cori in here," she said to her assistant on the other end.

"There's a problem," Sydney continued. "It's doubtful the airlines will let her fly considering how far along she is."

"Irrelevant. They won't let her on the plane once they find out she's received a death watch notice."

Cori Zinn and Josh Leven entered the office.

"About that," Sydney said. "Cheryl wants to keep her death watch notice quiet. She doesn't want people to know about it until after she's been on the game show. I told her we'd honor her wishes."

Helen slapped her pen down on the desk.

"You're a reporter, not a social worker," she snapped. "Your job is to get the story, not to cater to everyone's wishes!"

Sydney could feel Cori's pleasure over witnessing this scene. Josh looked like he didn't want to be here.

"You've lost your objectivity," Helen said, "and your focus, which is understandable if what I suspect is true."

The conversation had just taken a left turn, which made Cori and Josh's presence all the more mysterious.

"Cori came to me earlier today," Helen said. With a nod she indicated that Cori should take it from here.

"We know about your death watch notice," Cori said.

"What?" Sydney cried.

"This morning I received a confirmation call," Cori said. "Josh was with me at the time. The caller identified you as the recipient of a death watch notice."

Cori Zinn turned to Josh. He backed her up with a slight nod.

"This is ridiculous," Sydney said. "I haven't received a death watch notice."

"I'm afraid I'm going to have to take you off this assignment, Sydney," Helen said.

"Helen, on my honor, I have not received a death watch notice!"

"Have you checked your home mailbox lately?" Cori said. "Maybe it's there. You're familiar with the pattern. A written notice followed by a confirmation."

"Along with a verbal confirmation to the victim," Sydney added. "I haven't received a verbal confirmation either."

She was fighting for her life here. Sydney could guess why Cori Zinn was doing this to her, but Josh?

"Take the rest of the day off, Sydney," Helen said. "Get your affairs in order. Cori, you're now officially on the death watch story."

That was it! That's what Cori wanted! She'd orchestrated this whole thing to wrestle away the death watch story from her. And she'd gotten Josh to go along with it. What had she promised him? It had to be good.

"Josh, help me out here," Sydney pleaded. "Tell the truth. How do you know who Cori was talking to?"

"Sorry, Syd," Josh said apologetically.

"Let's see how the next forty-eight hours goes," Helen said. "If this is all a mistake, we'll know soon enough."

"Helen, don't do this!" Sydney pleaded.

"I won't have an employee of mine running around with a Death Watch hanging over her head. The liability to the station is too great. Go home, Sydney."

This was ridiculous. Cori Zinn was capable of dirty politics, but this was beneath even her.

There was a single rap on Helen's door. Hunz Vonner poked his head in the door.

"There you are," he said, looking at Sydney. "Helen, can I steal her away?"

"Sydney St. James is on a temporary leave of absence," Helen said. "You'll be working with Cori from here on out."

For a moment it appeared Hunz would accept Helen's decision without question. Then he said, "Is it disciplinary?"

"Personal," Helen said.

"They think I've received a death watch notice," Sydney said.

Hunz Vonner studied her with eyes that narrowed to slits. "Have you?"

"No."

"Good enough for me," Hunz said. "Let's go."

Sydney looked to Helen. After a long moment, the assignment editor reluctantly nodded her consent.

Cori Zinn's protests could be heard through the closed door as Sydney and Hunz left.

CHAPTER TWENTY

On the way to the FBI field office on Wilshire Boulevard, Sydney's hands shook, but overall she was feeling good about sticking up for herself in Helen's office. It wasn't like her to do that. Having been taught all her life to respect authority, she usually acquiesced. This time, she fought, and she was glad she did. If she hadn't, she'd be on the Hollywood Freeway right now heading home.

Still, she wished she'd said more. She wished she'd told Cori to her face she was a liar. She wished she could have said something to convince Helen to believe her. She wished she'd expressed her disappointment to Josh, shaming him into telling the truth. That was one conversation she would most definitely revisit.

When she and Hunz reached the field office, this time instead of having her circle the block, he had her accompany him inside. She took this as a positive sign. Maybe he was beginning to think of her as a coreporter instead of a Barbie-doll chauffeur.

They were issued badges at security, then ushered into a ten-by-ten office with barren walls painted sea-foam green. It was a sickening neutral color that had been splashed on the walls of every government building in Southern California. Apparently someone at cost control had made a killing on a shipload of the stuff. No wonder. Anybody with a shred of taste would never pay good money for this color.

Agent Victor Fernandez stood to greet them. "Have a seat."

He offered them two plastic folding chairs, then perched in front of them on the edge of a desk stacked high with paperwork.

Fernandez himself looked as disheveled as his desk—his unimaginative blue-and-red-striped tie was pulled loose, his sleeves were sloppily rolled up to his elbows, and his salt-and-pepper gray hair was mussed.

Hunz introduced Sydney as a reporter at KSMJ. He didn't give her name.

"I'll make it short and sweet," Fernandez said. "We've been following up on your Russian mafia theory and have located General Baranov on Barbados. He owns a villa on the island, which pretty much serves as a transshipping point for narcotics bound for Europe and the US."

"Have you made contact?" Hunz inched forward in his seat.

Fernandez crossed his arms. They were thick and hairy. "It's not exactly the kind of villa Jehovah's Witnesses would call on, if you know what I mean. We're working in cooperation with the Royal Barbados Police through the Barbados consulate here in LA. They'll attempt to make contact soon."

"Soon. You mean in a matter of hours?" Hunz asked.

The agent's eyes squinted with suspicion.

Hunz seemed to read his expression. "Every hour people are dying. The sooner we nab this renegade, the more lives we can save."

Fernandez nodded. "Four to six hours."

"What about Kiselev?" Hunz said. "Any leads on a lab connected to Baranov that is capable of nanotechnology research?"

"Nothing yet."

"You'll call me as soon as you hear anything?"

"I'll call you in the morning."

"Agent Fernandez, the sooner this information gets out to the public, the better. Think internationally. The middle of the night here is daytime in Europe."

Sydney was impressed with Hunz Vonner's style. He had a way of pressing without coming across as annoying.

"I'll call you as soon as I hear something," Fernandez said.

So now we wait," Sydney said, back in the car. The key was in the ignition. She hadn't turned it.

"We press forward," Hunz said. "What else have you got?"

Not much. She'd spent most of the morning at the hotel consoling Cheryl McCormick. After that, Cori Zinn had waylaid her in Helen's office.

She reached into the backseat and grabbed the folded printouts she'd shoved into her purse. "This is a list of death watch victims from the Homeland Security Web site. There are a few personal details, but not much. No record of immunizations or flu shots."

Hunz scanned the names. "They could be using a different delivery method for the nanobots." Apparently he hadn't spent all morning eating croissants with Sol Rosenthal. He'd done some investigating on his own.

He flipped a page. The one with Lyle Vandeveer's name on it. If the reminder of the previous night had any effect on him, he didn't show it.

"Cheryl McCormick," he said, coming to her name. Sydney had highlighted it.

"Visiting LA from Illinois," Sydney said. "She's a contestant on a game show. *Wonder Wheel*. Ever hear of it?"

"No. Illinois. Is it far from here?"

"Halfway across the continent. I've sort of taken her under my wing," Sydney said. "She's asked me to be there with her tonight."

Hunz looked up. That wasn't something he wanted to hear. "Another hand-holding evening?"

Sydney's anger flared. She did her best not to let it show. "Cheryl is recently widowed, has a three-year-old daughter, and is pregnant. She's due in a month."

"A pregnant woman with a death watch notice flew halfway across the continent to go on some kind of game show?"

"She was handed the death watch notice when she checked into the hotel. She's a widow and needs the money."

"The notice was waiting for her when she arrived?"

"That's right."

"How far in advance are these appearances scheduled?"

Sydney brightened. "You see, that's the thing! She was a phone-in contestant the night before and won some money. That qualified her along with other phone-in contestants to appear on the show. The first qualifier to arrive at the designated hotel becomes a contestant. She grabbed up her stuff, didn't tell anyone, and flew to Los Angeles on a red-eye."

"A red-eye?"

"A middle-of-the-night flight."

"The game show people knew she was coming?"

"Not until she arrived."

"Interesting."

"That's what I thought!" Sydney said.

"Still"—Hunz shook his head—"this McCormick girl's a waste of time."

"For Pete's sake!" Sydney shouted. She tried to hold it back. Couldn't. "Just because she doesn't fit your theory, doesn't mean she's a waste of time! You know, for some people these death watch notices are more than just a news story. These are human beings we're talking about. Show a little compassion."

Hunz sat back, obviously surprised by her outburst. But he didn't dwell on it long. "What's this?" he asked. He held up the email printout from Billy Peppers, the one instructing Sydney to meet him at Hollywood Memorial Park Cemetery.

"He claims to know who is behind Death Watch," Sydney said.

"What do you know about him?"

Sydney sighed. She couldn't shift emotional gears as fast as Hunz Vonner. "He lives on the street. Cori Zinn did a spotlight news story on the number of homeless people with mental problems. She interviewed him. He preaches on street corners. Says he talks to angels."

"You've met him?"

"I've never met him."

"So you didn't keep this appointment."

"An appointment is agreed upon between two people. I never agreed to meet him." Sydney was feeling defensive. "I told you, I was with Cheryl McCormick."

"Let's go talk to him."

"Now?"

Hunz was buckling his seat belt.

"He asked me to meet him hours ago."

"You said he lives on the street. He might still be there. It's not as though he has other pressing business."

Sydney started the car. "Cheryl McCormick is a waste of time, but a mentally deranged transient isn't?"

"We won't know that until we talk to him," Hunz said. Then he added, "If there's one thing I've learned over the years, it's that to be successful in this business, you have to be a bloodhound. Relentless. You have to track down every lead. Ninety percent of them waste your time. And sometimes, if you get lucky, your best information comes from the least likely sources. We know Cheryl's story; now let's go get the angel-talker's story."

CHAPTER
TWENTY-ONE

Sydney's beige Volvo trolled the narrow roadways of Hollywood Memorial Park Cemetery at a five-mile-an-hour pace, meandering past mausoleums, old-fashioned headstones, and obelisks that marked the final resting places of Hollywood's greatest legends. Douglas Fairbanks was buried here, so was Rudolph Valentino, Charlie Chaplin, Cecil B. DeMille, Tyrone Power, Victor Fleming, and Darla Hood, everybody's sweetheart of *Little Rascals* fame.

In the passenger seat Hunz Vonner was fidgety. His right leg bounced up and down nervously as he searched among the tombstones for a homeless man. Sydney had never seen Hunz on edge like this. The suave international reporter almost seemed human.

They cruised down Maple Avenue past the elaborate marble tomb of Douglas Fairbanks with its sunken garden. Water lilies shared the pool with sun sparkles. On Sydney's side of the car they rimmed a lake with an island featuring a whitewashed Grecian tomb.

Hunz turned suddenly in his seat, craning his neck.

Sydney slowed the car. "See anything?"

"No," he said, sounding disappointed. He turned back around. His foot kicked empty breakfast drink cans on the floorboard.

"You can just toss those in the back."

He left them there. "Why do Americans insist on living in their automobiles?" Hunz groused. "An automobile is a driving machine, not a living quarters on wheels. Here in the States you eat and drink in your cars; you do business in them, with some people turning them into an office; you take naps in them, watch movies, and now videos; you use them as phone booths for cell phones; you convert them to music halls with elaborate sound systems; and, of course, what takes place in the backseats of American automobiles is legendary."

"What do you drive?" Sydney asked.

"BMW 5er."

"Figures."

"What do you mean by that?"

Sydney shrugged. "You look like a Beamer kind of guy."

"BMW makes a precision machine," Hunz said. "This may come as a revelation to you, but some people purchase automobiles for reasons other than how many cup holders they have."

The road turned gently to the right. Through three towering palm trees, Sydney spotted a couple of men trimming a hedge.

"Let's see if they know anything," she said.

Sydney parked the car and they approached the groundskeepers, who were both wearing safety goggles and manning electric hedge clippers. One of them looked up and saw Sydney. From the expression on his face, you would have thought Jayne Mansfield had climbed out of her grave to stretch her legs. His coworker shared his rapture. Simultaneously they shut off their trimmers and pulled off the safety goggles for a better look.

"Can I help you, darlin'?" one of them said.

If someone had interviewed them later, it's doubtful either of them would have remembered a man accompanying Sydney.

"This may sound a bit strange," she began.

"Darlin', you don't know strange. Herb and I have worked in this here cemetery for nigh onto ten years. We got stories that'll straighten the curls right outta that gorgeous blonde hair of yours."

Sydney ignored the banter. Two or three times a day men made fools of themselves over her. "We're looking for a homeless man," she said. "We don't have much of a description other than that, but he said he'd be here today about noon. Did you happen to see him?"

"Yeah, we did!" the shorter worker, Herb, exclaimed, obviously overjoyed at being able to help out a beautiful woman. "There was this one guy. About noon, too, wouldn't you say, Al? He was a strange one. Real strange. We was gonna run him out 'cause it's not good for business to have bums hangin' around here, you know what I mean? I mean, we get a lot of tourists comin' here to see stars, and the last thing we want them to see is bums layin' all over the place. Gives the place a bad name, if you know what I mean. And, believe me, we get 'em all the time. Two maybe three every—"

His coworker interrupted, "We approached this guy."

"Al! I was telling it. Let me tell it!"

"Then tell it, and quit blabberin' nonsense," Al replied.

"Anyway, like I was saying, he was a strange one. And when we approached him, he was talkin' to someone, but no one was there with him! I mean, he was standin' there all alone, plain as day. And then, when we told him to leave, he seemed real perturbed, you know? Like we was interruptin' a private conversation or somethin'."

"He was talking to someone?" Sydney said. "Maybe he had a cell phone."

"Naw, bums don't got cells," Herb said. "He was talkin' to the air. Usin' both hands, like he was arguing with someone, or somethin'. Only no one was there."

"Hey, Herb. Maybe he was talkin' to Harvey. You know, Harvey? Jimmy Stewart's invisible rabbit?"

Herb guffawed, obviously thinking that was funny.

"Thanks, guys," Sydney said. She'd seen enough of the Herb and Al act.

"Wait! There's more!" Al said. "He kept complaining about having to go to Chicago."

"Chicago?"

"Yeah. Then he said something real strange. He said, 'How do you expect me to get there? I ain't got wings!' That's *exactly* what he said. 'I ain't got wings.' I'm not making this stuff up."

"Al! I was gonna tell her that," Herb complained. "You said I could tell. That's the best part."

"He said he was going to Chicago?" Sydney asked.

"Now I wouldn't say that, darlin'," Al said. "This guy was loonier than Mel Blanc. I've seen his kind before. They talk and talk like that, but it don't mean nothing. After that, he just took off."

"Yeah, we chased him outta here."

"Thank you, guys," Sydney said. "You've been a big help." She and Hunz turned to leave.

"Hey, darlin'," Herb called after her. "If you'd like to stick around, we can give you a personal tour of the place. Show you things tourists don't get to see."

"Thanks, fellas," Sydney said. "I'll take a rain check."

When they were back in the car, Sydney said, "Well, he was here." She looked at her watch. "Where to now? I have about two hours before I pick up Cheryl. I'm taking her to the studio."

Hunz was studying the email printout. "He calls himself The Rev," he said. "Reverend, right?"

"Probably. Though it might be The Revolutionary."

"You think?"

"It's possible. Everybody's political out here. Many of them are still stuck in the sixties. Long hair. Tattered jeans. Tie-dyed shirts. The whole thing. But given the fact that he claims to talk to angels, 'The Reverend' is probably our best bet."

"So, besides alleys and parks, what places would a homeless man with a religious streak frequent?"

"The rescue mission," Sydney said.

"Is it close?"

"Five or six miles."

"Let's go."

CHAPTER
TWENTY-TWO

The Gospel Rescue Mission was located on East Fifth Street in Little Tokyo. Once a thriving Japanese community, the downtown area was in transition. Only a single block of the original Little Tokyo was still intact with oriental markets, clothing shops, and Japanese-language businesses. The surrounding city blocks were a juxtaposition of new development and skid row.

The sleek new Disney Hall was just a few blocks away, while the ten-story Higgens building, built in 1911 and now an eyesore, was an abandoned shell of a bygone era.

Also in the area were the *Los Angeles Times* building, the county courthouse, and city hall with its distinctive sandstone tower, the longtime symbol of Los Angeles, constructed with sand from every county in California and water from the state's twenty-one missions.

Fifth Street had already surrendered to shadows when Sydney turned onto it. Stripped of sunlight the buildings looked even older than they were. Many were boarded up with weathered sheets of plywood and tattered posters several layers deep. The wind toyed with the trash in the gutters, stuffing it in corners. A good number of ragged, colorless, homeless people lined the sidewalks. The luckier ones were camped out in doorways.

"There it is." Hunz pointed to a red brick building.

Protruding at a right angle from the building was a white neon cross with red letters: JESUS SAVES. Beneath it, in block letters: GOSPEL RESCUE MISSION.

Sydney drove half a block farther before locating a parking place. A shadowy chill greeted them as they climbed out of the car.

Hunz Vonner's European-cut suit and Sydney's brilliant blonde hair and clean complexion made them an instant spectacle on the street. Eyes followed them with the detachment of people watching television.

"Have you come to volunteer?" A happy man with short, thinning red hair and wearing a sweater-vest greeted them as they walked into the mission. They stood in a large room filled with wooden chairs lined in rows. A massive wooden pulpit was at the far end of the room facing the chairs. Next to the entrance was a table with stacks of religious tracts. There was an open passageway on the side wall. Kitchen sounds and smells came from it.

"Actually, we're looking for someone," Sydney said.

Happy man's smile turned defensive, but not unfriendly. "Many of our guests prefer not to be found," he said. "May I ask about the nature of your inquiry?"

Sydney handed him her card. "I'm with KSMJ," she said. "This is Hunz Vonner, a visiting newscaster."

The man's eyes lit up in recognition. "I saw you last night on the news," he said to Hunz. "That man in Pasadena who died. The death watch victim."

"It's the death watch notices that bring us here," Sydney said. "Are you familiar with them?"

"I wish to God I wasn't."

Sydney continued: "This morning I received a message from a man who identified himself as The Rev. He said he wanted to meet me, that he had some information on Death Watch."

"Billy?" the man said.

"You know him?"

The man in the sweater-vest nodded and then gestured for them to follow. He led them between a row of empty chairs, through the side door, past a brightly lit kitchen where a dozen workers were stirring steaming pots, lining rolls on baking sheets, and replenishing saltshakers. The end of the hallway opened up to a large dining room set with tables and chairs. They didn't go that far. Halfway down the hallway they entered an office.

"By the way, I'm Ken Overton." His voice was deeper in this room, as though a mantle of authority had been placed over his sweater-vest as he entered the office. He shook Hunz and Sydney's hands crisply, then sat behind a desk that nearly filled the room, not because the desk was that large, but because the room was that small. He offered Sydney and Hunz a pair of old wooden chairs that swayed when they sat down.

Overton interlaced his fingers and placed them gently atop the desk. "Billy Pepper's a good man. Hardworking. Intelligent. Homeless by choice."

"What do you mean by that?" Hunz asked.

"Billy could secure employment. He's been offered jobs. He's chosen to turn them down for religious reasons."

"Working is against his religion?" Hunz asked.

Overton laughed. "No. Billy feels he's been called to minister to the homeless. He's a street preacher. A Samaritan. And a volunteer here at the mission. He does everything we ask of him without complaint. He serves food. Sweeps floors. Makes beds. Preaches. And washes feet."

"Washes feet?"

"Once a month Billy oversees a foot-washing service here at the mission. It's a worship experience. Jesus washed his disciples' feet the last night he was with them. It teaches humility to those who are ministering and reminds all those who participate of the humanity of the homeless, including the homeless themselves. Following each foot-washing service we provide medical checkups by certified podiatrists.

"In fact, when it comes to available services, Billy is something of a roving ambassador for us. You see, we not only hold worship services, serve food, and provide emergency shelter, but we also make available medical and legal services to those who can't afford them. We offer health clinic services through UCLA School of Nursing, dental services through USC School of Dentistry, and legal aid through Pepperdine University. Whenever Billy Peppers comes across someone with a need we can fill, he brings them to the mission."

"The man who contacted me calls himself The Rev," Sydney said. "You're certain he and Billy Peppers are one and the same?"

"I don't recall who first started calling him that, but it's stuck."

"Have you seen Billy lately?" Hunz asked. "Will he show up here tonight?"

"That's hard to say. As a rule, street people don't keep to a routine. I can tell you that he's not scheduled to preach tonight."

"Where else might we find him? Does he have any other places he frequents?" Hunz asked.

Overton rubbed his cheek in thought. "Tell you who might know . . . Here, let me get him."

He disappeared for a few minutes, leaving Hunz and Sydney alone in the cramped office. When he returned, he brought a Hispanic man with him—small, swarthy, muscular arms, mustache. He smelled of dish soap.

"This is Lony Mendez," Overton said, making the introductions. "Lony, these are television reporters. They're looking for Billy."

"Ain't seen Billy for a couple of days," Lony said with a heavy Hispanic accent. "But that's not unusual. Sometimes he's gone for two, three days. A week. No one knows where. He just disappears."

"Do you know him well?" Sydney asked. "It's important that we find him. He contacted me."

"Billy and I go way back," Lony said. "Billy and me were cellies at Calipatria."

"State prison," Overton interpreted.

"Yeah, Billy had two strikes on him for burglary and drugs, same as me, only I stayed away from the nasty stuff. We used to joke about which one of us would be the first to get a third strike and end up at Calipatria forever." He laughed. "But God had other plans."

"God?" Hunz said.

"It was God who dumped a whole bucket of Spirit on Billy's head when he was in prison. Billy ain't never been the same since. At first, it was real hard on me, you know? It ain't easy sharin' a cell with the apostle Paul. But Billy? He was real patient with me. It was him who led me to the Lord. And when I got out a year later, guess who was standin' out there waitin' for me. Billy. He'd hitchhiked all the way from LA just to see me get out."

"Do you know where he is right now?" Hunz asked.

Lony shrugged. "Could be anywhere the Spirit leads him, you know? The guy will do anything to help someone. I seen him give his blanket away on a cold night. And his shoes. That kinda thing just doesn't happen on the street, you know? Did I tell you angels talk to him?"

"So we've heard," Sydney said.

"It's the truth. I ain't seen any of them. They don't just show themselves to anybody. But Billy sees them. They tell him stuff and he does it. Ooooeee, but he pays for it, let me tell you that."

"What do you mean?" Sydney asked.

"Well, Billy sees these angels, but that means he sees demons too, and they don't like being seen. Sometimes they hammer on Billy something awful."

Hunz had obviously heard enough. He stood. "If you see Billy, tell him we're looking for him," he said.

"You gonna interview him? Put Billy on TV?"

"We just want to talk to him," Hunz said.

"When you see him, tell him to call me on my personal cell phone number," Sydney said. She wrote it down for him on her card.

Lony fished in his back pocket and produced a worn and crumpled gospel tract. He handed it to Sydney in exchange for her card. "Are you saved, Miss St. James?" he asked.

Sydney looked at Hunz. Her cheeks warmed. "I'm a Midwestern girl," she said. "I was raised in the church."

"That's not what I asked," Lony said. "I asked if you was saved."

"Let's go." Hunz grabbed Sydney by the arm.

As Sydney and Hunz left the Gospel Rescue Mission, she stuffed the crumpled tract in her pocket.

In the car, Hunz shrugged. "Well, that was a waste of time."

CHAPTER
TWENTY-THREE

Daylight was little more than a thin strip on the western horizon when Billy Peppers reached Los Angeles International Airport. It took three hitched rides, but he managed to get to Century Boulevard exit on Interstate 405. He walked from there, still not knowing how he was going to get a flight to Chicago with no money in his pocket.

The Lord will provide, Billy told himself, toting his Nike shoe box. *Can you fathom the mysteries of God? Not me. No sir, not me.* And so Billy kept his feet moving forward. They were God's feet now. Billy gave them to God, then asked God to use them to get him to Chicago.

Upon reaching the airport boundaries God's feet took Billy in an unexpected direction. Instead of heading toward the passenger terminals, they led him down the road toward the cargo hangars. Names of freight companies were displayed prominently on the sides of hangars and on the tails of airplanes—UPS, FedEx, Transworld Freight, Star Courier, Industrial Express, Global Air Freight.

Billy Peppers smiled.

Global Air Freight.

He knew now how he was getting to Chicago.

One more street, then we have to go," Sydney said.

They'd canvassed the blocks surrounding the Gospel Mission in hopes of finding Billy Peppers. More accurately, in hopes that

Billy Peppers would find them, because they had only a general description at best of what he looked like—black, dreadlocks, jeans, gray jacket, maybe light blue, sometimes with a grocery cart, or as Sydney remembered him, carrying a Nike shoe box. At least she thought that was Billy Peppers she'd seen with the shoe box.

Billy, on the other hand, would notice Sydney on sight, so their slow rolling tour of Little Tokyo was more about being seen than searching. But after a while, the passive approach became too taxing and the need to do something took over.

The direct approach proved equally futile. They found the homeless to be skittish about people approaching them. Some ran away. Others cringed and shut their eyes until Sydney and Hunz left them alone. Still others mumbled incoherently. Among those who would talk to them, who spoke intelligibly, they either didn't know Billy Peppers or hadn't seen him.

"Would you like me to drop you somewhere?" Sydney said.

Hunz didn't answer. He was looking down an alley.

Sydney turned onto San Pedro Avenue. It was getting late. She'd told Cheryl she'd pick her up in thirty minutes.

"Hunz?"

He dialed a number on his cell phone.

"Agent Fernandez," he said into the phone.

On the sidewalk a woman with a brown knit cap pushed a grocery cart overflowing with old rugs. Atop the rug pile, like royalty, sat a Pekingese scratching fleas.

"Fernandez," Hunz said a little louder. "Vonner. Anything?" He frowned as he listened to the FBI agent. "Yeah. Fine. Thanks." Hunz snapped shut his cell phone.

"Anything?" Sydney asked.

"No."

Hunz turned away, presumably to continue looking for Billy Peppers, but before he did, Sydney noticed an odd expression on his face. It was the expression of a man who had just lost a lot of money on the stock market.

"Would you like me to take you back to your hotel?" Sydney said.

"No," Hunz said.

"The station?"

"No. I'm going with you."

"To the game show? I thought you said it was a waste of time."

"It is." Hunz Vonner's jaw was set. The Billy Peppers lead hadn't panned out. All they could do now was wait for the FBI to do their job. And it was obvious that Hunz Vonner was not very good at waiting.

Dwarfed by the size of the cargo planes on the tarmac, Billy Peppers smiled at seeing Buster again. Buster wasn't smiling back.

"Hey, man, I'm glad to see youse and all," Buster said, "but what you're asking me to do is impossible. I could get in a lot of trouble. I could get fired. I know you gots me this job, and I'm grateful for it, believe me I am, but this . . . this is just asking too much."

"I didn't get you this job, Buster. God did," Billy said. "And now it's time to give back to God."

A hulk in a gray Global Air Freight jumpsuit, Buster Kozloski's body resembled an inverted triangle with the sum of his massive shoulders twice that of his hips. Like many cons, he'd spent all his exercise time in the prison weight room. As a result, Buster the parolee was double the size of Buster the defendant.

"I don't know . . ." He looked around for his shift supervisor. "I shouldn't even be talking to you."

Billy had met Buster a little over a year ago. Having reverted to his old ways, Buster was breaking into a Radio Shack store. It was one of those sweltering LA nights, the kind when you couldn't buy a breeze, and Billy was looking for a cool place when he happened upon the break-in. Buster threatened Billy with a tire iron. Billy leveled Buster with the Holy Spirit.

"I have to get back to work," Buster said, apologetically.

"The plane you're loading, it's going to Chicago, right?"

Buster took a step back. "How'd you know that?"

"God wouldn't have led me here if the plane wasn't going to Chicago," Billy said. "I have to get to Chicago, Buster. I'm on a mission."

"What kinda mission?"

"A mission from God."

"That's not good enough. I need to know more if I'm going to get involved."

"You're going to have to take a step of faith, Buster."

Buster was staring at the shoe box. Couldn't take his eyes off of it. Maybe it was the way Billy was carrying it; maybe it was because of all the security measures that had been instituted at airports, all the warnings about packages and bombs.

"What's in the box, Billy?"

"Angels."

Buster's eyebrows rose. "Did your angel visit you again?"

"I'm not going to try to convince you, Buster. This is something you're going to have to do on faith."

"It's about all this death watch stuff, isn't it?"

"Buster, what difference would it make if the whole world needed saving, or just one soul? God's giving you a chance to be part of his mission. You know he won't force you, and neither will I."

Buster looked around again. "Okay," he sighed. "Wait here. Keep an eye on that ramp." He pointed to a ramp leading into the belly of a cargo plane. "When I give you the signal, you skedaddle up the ramp as quick as your old bowlegged legs will carry you, understand?"

"God will bless you for this, Buster," Billy said.

He crouched in the shadows of the hangar for twenty minutes as men and forklifts went in and out of the belly of the cargo plane. The activity became more sporadic; the intervals between forklifts grew longer.

Buster appeared at the top of the ramp. Keeping an eye on the portion of the hangar Billy couldn't see, Buster made a quick waving motion.

Billy scurried out of the shadows and up the ramp into the plane. It was longer and steeper than it looked, and midway up the ramp he was laboring for breath.

"Hurry!" Buster said, frantically checking the hangar.

When Billy managed to make it to the top, bent over and gasping for air, Buster led him to the midsection of the plane, past a section of animal crates—dogs, cats, parrots—where a large wooden crate lay open. Inside, Buster had fashioned a bed of pink packing peanuts. A heavy jacket lay on top.

"It's the best I could do," Buster said, sweating from exertion or nervousness, or both.

Billy ducked inside the crate, pulled on the jacket, and nested in the middle of the packing peanuts.

"You'll need this to get out."

Buster handed him a hammer.

"I'm proud of you, Buster," Billy said.

"Just promise me that someday you'll explain exactly why I risked my job tonight."

Buster lifted the side of the crate to nail it shut.

"Buster?"

"Yeah?"

"Does this flight serve complimentary drinks?"

CHAPTER TWENTY-FOUR

And now, America's favorite game show—*Wonder Wheel!*"

APPLAUSE
APPLAUSE
APPLAUSE

Cued by the flashing sign, the studio audience erupted with noise—clapping, yelling, a couple of wolfish whistles. After all, this wasn't your grandmother's game show; it was a game show for the postmodern generation, one in which the viewing audience participated.

"And the host of *Wonder Wheel*—Skip Hirshberg!"

The smiling, trim master of ceremonies jogged into the bright studio lights, dressed in casual tan slacks and a black polo shirt. He gave the appearance of being an easy-going, fun-loving guy, the kind you'd feel comfortable inviting over to the house for a few laughs. Though in his midfifties, Skip had a perpetual boyish charm about him, largely due to his hair, which was all his, color and all.

"Goooood evening, America!" Skip shouted to the audience. "Are you ready to play *Wonder Wheel?*"

The audience was on its feet, shaking the rafters with their shouts and stomping.

Sydney and Hunz stood in the vomitory, an entrance to the stage cut beneath the stadium seats. Hunz was holding Cheryl's daughter Stacy in his arms, the surprise of the night.

Three-year-old Stacy had taken to Hunz at the hotel the moment she saw him. More surprisingly, Hunz had taken to her. Sydney had never pictured the German newscaster around children. He didn't seem the type.

While Cheryl made one last pass through the motel room, gathering up her things, little Stacy grabbed Hunz by the finger and pulled him into the back room to show him her coloring book pictures and Brenda doll, a knockoff of Barbie with a modest figure. International news broadcaster Hunz Vonner followed enthusiastically.

Actually, there were two surprises at the hotel. Hunz and Stacy were the second surprise. The first was when Cheryl opened the door. She greeted Sydney with an embrace that was surprising for both its enthusiasm and its duration. It was a lingering hug normally reserved for dear friends and long-absent family members.

"I don't know what I'd do without you," Cheryl said, her breath warm on Sydney's ear.

Sydney couldn't remember the last time she'd been hugged by another woman with such genuine affection. The affection soothed an ache in her soul and brought tears to her eyes.

"Tonight will be a lucky night for one of our three studio contestants, or possibly someone at home!" cried master of ceremonies Skip Hirshberg. "It could be you!"

Along with the two other studio contestants, Cheryl McCormick stood behind an electronic podium smiling radiantly, her red hair ablaze under the studio lights.

"Let's meet them, shall we?" Skip said. "Our returning champion and reigning queen of *Wonder Wheel*, Barb Whitlock!"

"Hello, Skip," Barb said with a note of familiarity. A matronly middle-aged woman wearing a conservative print dress, Barb could easily be mistaken for a research librarian with her short brown hair, black-frame glasses, and thickset figure.

"Barb Whitlock is a district manager for Southern California Edison. She lives in Alhambra, California, with her husband, Phil, and pet cockatoo, Sir Talks-a-Lot. To date, Barb has won $123,568!"

Cheryl joined the audience applause, as did the middle contestant, a male in his late twenties, well over six feet tall, with a belly that hung over his belt like a flow of thick ooze, straining his shirt buttons. He weighed three hundred pounds easily.

"Our second contestant is Wendell Wicker Jr., a senior at Cal Poly, Pomona, where he is majoring in computer science. Welcome to *Wonder Wheel*, Wendell."

"C–c–call me Junior, Skip."

As he spoke Junior's eyes bulged, revealing an abnormal amount of white surrounding the pupils. It was as though they were gasping. He repeated this annoying habit two or three times a minute, more when he was nervous.

"Tell me, Junior," Skip said. "When you're not hitting the books at Cal Poly, do you have a hobby? Or a girlfriend?"

The big man tittered. His eyes breathed. "Video games, Skip," he said. "I just changed my major from French poetry to computer science so I can make some really awesome games. You know, Skip, video games are good for society. They keep kids off the streets."

"How often do you play, Junior?"

Junior shrugged. "Five hours a day, minimum."

"Our third contestant tonight is—my, my, my, she certainly is, isn't she?—our third contestant is an expectant mother and last night's winning telephone contestant, an elementary school teacher from Evanston, Illinois. Meet Cheryl McCormick!"

"Clap for Mommy," Hunz said to Stacy, bouncing her up and down.

Stacy clapped happily.

Skip Hirshberg crossed the floor to Cheryl's podium. "May I?" he said, placing a hand on her belly before she could respond.

Cheryl smiled, though Sydney could tell she was uncomfortable with the master of ceremony's presumption.

"You do understand, don't you, that if you deliver the baby during the next hour, the child automatically becomes the official property of *Wonder Wheel!*"

Skip flashed an enormous grin, playing to the cameras.

Cheryl forced a smile. Sydney admired her for it. Had she been in Cheryl's shoes, she probably would have decked him.

"And now, America, let's play *Wonder Wheel!*"

Skip Hirshberg returned to his podium, which was but a few steps away. Sydney remembered her reaction the first time she saw the size of an actual news studio in Iowa City. It was much smaller than it looked on television. This set was just as compact.

The three contestants stood in a row behind a podium bearing his or her name and two electronic displays, one for category and another for winnings to date. The three studio contestants faced the master of ceremonies.

Appearing between the contestants and the master of ceremonies on the back wall, suspended by wires against a black backdrop, was the Wonder Wheel—three stationary concentric circles with flashing lights that moved in alternating directions. Beneath the wheel was a display with ten digits for area code, prefix, and four-digit telephone number.

The Wonder Wheel came alive, the outer and inner circles flashing clockwise, the middle circle flashing counterclockwise. It had a mesmerizing effect.

"Round and round she goes!" Skip cried. "Each contestant will get a chance to answer a question and earn big money depending on the alignment of the Wonder Wheel. The outer wheel determines the question value with a number from zero to ninety-nine. The middle wheel determines the category of the question. And the inner wheel determines the difficulty factor, from zero to nine. The question value and difficulty factor are multiplied together to determine the dollar value of each question. The greater the difficulty, the more money a contestant wins for a correct answer!

"The contestant who spins the highest dollar value goes first. A right answer wins the money. A wrong answer and the dollar amount will be deducted from the contestant's score, and a call-in contestant will be given a chance to win his money, so get ready, America!

"The Wonder Wheel will select tonight's area code and prefix. So television viewers, if you see your area code and prefix displayed, be the first person to call and you can win!

"And remember, contestants. This isn't your grandmother's game show! *Wonder Wheel* rewards only the best! It's winner-take-all. One of you will go home tonight with everything, while two contestants will leave with only the fond memory of having once shared the stage with Skip Hirshberg."

He paused so the audience could laugh.

"Light up the wheel! It's time to play *Wonder Wheel!*"

Applause.

"Contestants! The wheel's in motion. You have five seconds to lock in your selections!"

The *Wonder Wheel* theme music began. The colored lights on the three concentric wheels began to accelerate. The studio audience was deafening.

Junior hit his contestant button quickly, locking in his choices. Barb was next. Cheryl stared at the flashing lights. She looked confused. The music was coming to its conclusion.

"Choose quickly, Cheryl," Skip encouraged her.

Cheryl hit the contestant button on the podium an instant before the computer locked it out.

The results appeared on the contestants' podiums.

BARB
SAY AHH
$30,800

JUNIOR
SINGING FOR YOUR SUPPER
$28,000

CHERYL
ROCKS OF AGES
$6,600

"Barb, you scored the highest dollar value with a question value of eighty-two and a difficulty factor of four for a total of $32,800. The category is *Say Ahh, anatomy for amateurs.* Do you wish to play or pass?"

Barb Whitlock winced. "Ouch," she said, which got a laugh. "I never was good at anatomy, Skip. And though it's hard to pass up that kind of money, I think I'm going to have to pass."

"Junior, you're second highest with a question value of fifty-six and a difficulty factor of five for a total of $28,000. Your category is *Singing for Your Supper, famous actors in musical theater.* Play or pass?"

"Oh, man," Junior groused. "Musical theater? Now if the category was about supper, I'd have a fighting chance. Pass."

"Well, Cheryl, that brings it down to you. You scored the lowest total value with a question value of twenty-two and a difficulty factor of three for $6,600. A rookie mistake. The Wonder Wheel favors the bold, Cheryl, but it looks like things may have worked out for you this time. Your category is *Rocks of Ages, history set in stone.* Will you play, or are we going to give our first caller of the night a chance to win some money?"

Cheryl fidgeted, but only for a moment. "I'm going to play, Skip."

"Your question is: Which of these presidents does *not* have his likeness carved in stone on Mt. Rushmore? (a) Thomas Jefferson, (b) Franklin D. Roosevelt, (c) George Washington, (d) Theodore Roosevelt."

Cheryl didn't hesitate. She smiled and said, "B. Franklin Delano Roosevelt."

"It looks like the schoolkids of Evanston, Illinois, are in good hands," Skip shouted. "Franklin D. Roosevelt is correct, and Cheryl McCormick is our first contestant on the *Wonder Wheel* board tonight with $6,600!"

Amidst the applause, Sydney's cell phone rang. Studio personnel within earshot looked alarmed, then angry, cocking an ear to locate the intrusive chirping.

"Sorry." Sydney pulled her phone from her pocket. "Sorry, sorry." She skulked to the back of the studio, under the unforgiving glare of the floor director, cameramen, and sound technicians. "I'll turn it off," she mouthed to them.

She pressed the answer button to stop the ringing but didn't speak until she was well out of earshot.

Pressing the phone to her ear, she heard, "Syd? Syd? Are you there?"

"Hello?"

"Syd? Josh. We have to talk."

"Yes, we do," she said, instantly angry at hearing his voice. She hadn't forgiven him for selling her out in Helen Gordon's office. Cori may have been the mastermind behind it, but that didn't excuse Josh for being part of it.

"Where are you?" he asked.

She told him.

"I'll be there in fifteen minutes. I have to talk to you."

"What? Now? Josh, we can talk in the morning."

"No. I really need to talk to you now, Syd."

He sounded strange. Upset. *Well, he should be upset*, she thought. *That makes two of us.*

"Promise you won't leave until I get there," he said.

Sydney hit the disconnect button, then programmed the phone to silent mode. She really didn't want to talk to Josh tonight; there was already too much going on with getting Cheryl to the airport, and chauffeuring Hunz.

CHAPTER
TWENTY-FIVE

Grateful for pink packing peanuts, Billy Peppers slouched against the side of his four-by-four-by-four wooden traveling compartment. At times the ride was rough, tossing him around as easily as the peanuts. Three times he slammed his head against the top of the crate. Now, pulling the jacket tight around him, he tried to stop shivering. Frozen fingertips clutched an angel figurine.

He had more pressing problems than staying warm.

He couldn't breathe.

Billy slung his head back, desperately trying to pull air into his lungs. The effort was strenuous, the reward small, like trying to suck liquid through a pinched straw.

Pressing the figurine against his chest, skirting the edge of consciousness, Billy prayed.

CHAPTER TWENTY-SIX

What did I miss?" Sydney asked.

She approached Hunz to thunderous applause. Neither Hunz nor little Stacy were clapping, so the ovation was not for Cheryl. A quick look at the contestants' podiums revealed the damage. Barb Whitlock had taken a commanding lead with $66,500.

"A Bible history question," Hunz shouted over the din. "Burial place of the patriarch Abraham and his wife, Sarah."

Barb Whitlock was pleased with herself. "I knew attending church would pay off someday, Skip," she said.

"What was the answer?" Sydney asked Hunz.

He looked at her strangely. "You don't know?"

"Why would I know?"

Hunz shrugged. "Just thought you'd know, that's all," he said. "Hebron. The city of Hebron."

He handed Stacy to Sydney. "I need to make a phone call," he said.

At first Stacy objected. Hunz assured her he'd be gone for just a moment.

Skip Hirshberg summed up the contestant standings. "Barb Whitlock is our current leader with $66,500, Cheryl McClintock is in second place with $6,600, and Junior has yet to make an appearance on the money board. As for all of you in our television audience, your chance may be coming up right after this commercial break, because anything can happen on America's favorite game show, *Wonder Wheel!* We'll be right back."

A pause, then the set crew and makeup artists streamed onto the set, applying fresh powder to the contestants, and going over notes for the next segment with Skip.

"Mommy!" Stacy reached for her mother.

"Not yet, honey," Sydney said. "Mommy still has more game to play, more money to win, won't that be fun?" She hefted the girl onto her hip. The studio lights and a warm child pressed against her was a hot combination.

Cheryl appeared to be holding her own on the set. In her unguarded moments, she appeared troubled. The gaudy artificial surroundings of the game show were insufficient to mask the death sentence hanging over her. Cheryl scanned the audience for Stacy. From experience Sydney knew she couldn't see anything beyond the studio lights.

"Thirty seconds, people," someone called.

Little Stacy watched the lights of the Wonder Wheel going round and round, oblivious to the fact that in two days she would be an orphan.

The floor director started the countdown. "And we're live in five, four, three, two . . ." His finger signaled one, then pointed at Skip Hirshberg.

"And we're back!" Skip said to the cameras. "Let's put that big money wheel in motion one more time! Contestants, you have five seconds."

This time Cheryl hit her button immediately, as did the other two contestants. The results flashed on the podiums before the theme music finished.

"Cheryl McCormick, you're our high roller!" He leaned toward her confidentially. "It pays to take advice from the ol' Skiperoo, doesn't it?"

Cheryl smiled, happy to have a chance at some serious money. She readied herself for the question.

Hunz returned. Stacy leaned so far out of Sydney's arms to get to him she knocked Sydney off balance. Hunz caught the little girl with an *ooofff*. There was no joy in it.

"What's wrong?" Sydney asked.

"Nothing." But it was a lie. Sydney could tell. "Looks like Cheryl has a chance to pull into the lead," he said, diverting her attention back to the game.

Skip was crossing the stage, something he never did in the middle of a show. "Let me tell you something about this brave little lady," he said, approaching Cheryl. He took her by the hand.

Cheryl looked at him warily.

"I'm sure all of you are aware of the current terrorist threat we face in America known as Death Watch."

"Oh no," Sydney said.

"It's a horrible, horrible scourge, and we can only pray that our leaders will find who's behind it and bring them to justice soon. Despite this little lady's expectant condition, last night she beat two other contestants to the Excelsior Hotel to qualify for tonight's program. Then, within minutes of her arrival, Cheryl McCormick received a death watch notice."

The audience gasped.

"I thought she didn't want anyone to know," Hunz said.

"She doesn't," Sydney said. She had her suspicions who did this.

"In the face of this dastardly threat, we at *Wonder Wheel* would have understood had Cheryl chosen not to appear tonight. However, she insisted. And here she is, Ladies and Gentlemen. Even threat of death cannot keep people from playing America's favorite game show, *Wonder Wheel*! Bless you, my dear. Bless you."

Skip Hirshberg kissed her hand, then returned to the master of ceremonies podium.

Cheryl was shaken. She was trying to see past the studio lights. Looking for Sydney. She was angry.

"I didn't tell them," Sydney said to Hunz. "Honest. I didn't!"

"Scoring the highest dollar value with a question value of ninety-four with a difficulty factor of eight for a total of $75,200 and the lead, the category is *Rocks of Ages*—the second time for you tonight. It was a lucky category for you before, Cheryl, do you want to play or pass?"

"Um . . ." Cheryl looked shell-shocked. "The difficulty factor is eight?"

"Correct. Play or pass? You have three seconds, Cheryl."

"Um . . . um . . . play. Play."

"Here's your question. Possibly the earliest tangible evidence linked to Jesus of Nazareth is a limestone ossuary, or burial box, with the inscription, 'James, son of Joseph, brother of Jesus.' For $75,200, in what language was the inscription written? (a) Hebrew, (b) Latin, (c) Aramaic, (d) Greek.

Cheryl stared at her hands. They were trembling.

"She doesn't know," Hunz said.

"She's a schoolteacher. Schoolteachers know everything," Sydney said.

"Well," Cheryl said, "James and Joseph and Jesus were Hebrew, but the language of commerce in those days was Greek. The New Testament was written in Greek."

She was thinking out loud.

"I'm going to need an answer, Cheryl."

She took a deep breath. "I'm going to say Greek, Skip. D."

A buzzer sounded.

"Ooooooo, I'm sorry, Cheryl. The correct answer is (c) Aramaic. We're going to have to deduct $75,200 from your score, which will put you in the negative column."

Skip Hirshberg's disappointment lasted only a moment.

"But it is *great* news for someone at home! Let's go to the phones!" The display beneath the *Wonder Wheel* began flashing. 727 319-WIN!

"Our computer has randomly selected tonight's at-home contestant location. Here it is! Area code 727. Prefix 319. Seminole, Florida, it's your turn to play *Wonder Wheel*! The first caller from Seminole, Florida, has a chance to win $75,200!"

Cheryl didn't hear any of this. It was obvious she was wrestling with her disappointment, an opponent that was growing stronger by the second. Her expression said it was all she could do to keep from walking off the set. Her situation was hopeless. She was $68,600 in the red. Even assuming Barb Whitlock failed to answer any more questions correctly, Cheryl would have to win $135,100 just to catch up with her. And even if she managed to climb out of this hole and post some positive numbers, it was winner-take-all. All she'd be doing is winning more money for Barb Whitlock and Sir Talks-a-Lot.

Watching from the vomitory, Sydney felt like crying. She knew that for Cheryl this was no longer a game show but a chance to provide for her children after she was gone. With only hours left to live, she'd gambled on staying in LA and lost precious time. She still had to get back to Evanston, convince the doctor to induce labor, and give birth to a child before her time was literally up.

The way Cheryl kept trying to see past the studio lights, Sydney knew Cheryl blamed her for leaking the news of her Death Watch.

CHAPTER TWENTY-SEVEN

Josh Leven arrived at the studio midway through the airing of *Wonder Wheel*.

"Syd," he said, walking up behind her and looking at the contestant totals. "She's not doing too well, is she?"

The podiums told the story. Cheryl had managed to regain a portion of ground—by correctly identifying the meaning of the word *obfuscate*, to darken, to make obscure—which brought her total to minus $22,600, but the gap between her and Barb Whitlock still seemed insurmountable.

Barb was playing it safe. She passed on two difficult questions and correctly answered one low-risk question—in what town was Jesus born?—to pad her lead by $8,100, bringing her total to $74,600.

Junior, meanwhile, had fallen to minus $39,600 and third place with two incorrect answers. He had yet to answer a question correctly.

The contestants had just locked in another round. Barb Whitlock passed on the number of players on an NFL team roster. "My husband will kill me when I get home," she said. And Cheryl passed on the atomic weight of silver.

"Which brings it down to you, Junior," Skip said. "And I have to say, this is a first for *Wonder Wheel*. Never in the history of the show have we had a contestant spin a combination so low. With a question value of one and a factor of difficulty zero, for $100 the category is *Hysterical History*. Pass or play?"

Junior's eyes did his gasping thing. He hesitated. "I'm . . . I'm gonna play, Skip."

"Here's your question: For $100, what color was George Washington's white horse? (a) Dapple gray, (b) Black, (c) Chestnut brown, (d) White."

Junior gripped the side of his podium, his head lowered in thought, his eyes squeezed shut.

"Three seconds."

Junior was in agony.

"I have to have an answer," Skip said.

Junior bit his lower lip. His eyes popped open so wide it looked like they were going to disgorge from their sockets.

"D. White!" he shouted, just as the buzzer sounded.

"Judges, did he get in under the wire?"

A double beep signaled he did.

"White, that's correct!" Skip shouted.

Junior's deficit was erased by $100.

The audience clapped without enthusiasm.

Skip leaned forward. With a smirk, he said, "Tell me, Junior, now that you have answered correctly, it was obvious you struggled with it. Can you tell us how you figured out the answer to the question?"

"Well, Skip," Junior said proudly, "I just thought of the pictures I'd seen of George Washington when I was a kid in school, and in the pictures his horse was white."

Josh whispered to Sydney, "Is this guy for real?"

"You said you wanted to talk," she replied. Sydney really didn't want to get into this now, but there seemed to be no avoiding it. She led him to a quiet corner of the studio.

"Look, Josh," she said, "I'm going to make this easy for you. I know you're infatuated with Cori and that when a guy's in love, his brain freezes up and he does amazingly dumb things. I don't know what Cori promised you to get you to go along with her twisted attempt to steal this assignment from me, and frankly, I don't want to know. We're still friends, okay? Let's just leave it at that. I don't particularly like you right now and it'll take me a few days to get over this, but it's not going to permanently damage our friendship. Just don't do it again, all right?"

"Syd, I got a death watch notice."

"Oh, Josh!" Sydney cried. "Are you sure?"

His eyes were glassy. His chin quivered. Sydney had never seen Josh emotionally distraught before, and it broke her heart. He was the good-natured jock, competitive, occasionally frustrated and angry just like everyone else. But never like this. Never broken. Never scared.

He reached into his back pocket and handed her a folded sheet of paper.

Sydney unfolded it.

An email printout.

It was addressed to Joshua Leven at his KSMJ address. The wording was word-for-word identical to all the other notices.

"Confirmation phone call?" Sydney asked.

Josh nodded.

Behind them, the game show stadium crowd erupted with cheers.

CHAPTER
TWENTY-EIGHT

Under blazing studio lights, Cheryl McCormick blinked back tears. She'd pulled within striking distance of Barb Whitlock, but the pressure, the pregnancy, and the looming death sentence had spun her emotions out of her control.

Since the announcement that she was under Death Watch, she'd become the studio audience favorite. Everyone in the stands was living and dying with each spin of the Wonder Wheel and each breathless second she took to answer a question.

Meanwhile, Barb Whitlock had stumbled; whether out of greed or a moment of confusion, it was hard to say. Instead of passing and protecting her lead, she took a chance on answering a question.

"How many yards is an NFL football team penalized for going offside?"

The risk was relatively low with a dollar value of $13,500. It appeared to be easy money that would put her well beyond Cheryl McCormick's reach.

"I'm a big Raider's fan, Skip," she'd said. "My husband and I haven't missed a game in over ten years. The answer is A. Ten yards."

"I'm sorry," Skip cried. "But the penalty for offsides in the NFL is five yards."

"Wait! No! I was thinking of holding. You said holding, didn't you? The penalty for holding is ten yards!"

But it was too late. Barb Whitlock's total dropped to $61,100.

Cheryl won the next spin and the first chance to answer a question.

"With a question value of ninety-five, and a factor of difficulty of seven, for $66,500 the category is *Rocks of Ages*."

The studio audience groaned. Cheryl had spent most of the show recovering from a wrong answer in this category.

"Pass or play?"

Time was running out. Cheryl might not get another chance to make up this much ground.

"Play, Skip," Cheryl said.

"For $66,500, here's your question: The discovery of the Rosetta stone led to a better understanding of what ancient language?"

Cheryl shook her head. Another language question.

"Is it, (a) Paleo Hebrew, (b) Egyptian hieroglyphics, (c) Attic Greek, or (d) Vedic Sanskrit? You have fifteen seconds."

Each tick of the clock had a dampening effect on the studio audience until it became so quiet Cheryl would have sworn she could hear the heartbeat of her unborn child.

"Eight seconds, Cheryl."

She remembered something about the Rosetta stone being on display at the British Museum in London. A tour brochure, if she remembered correctly. That didn't help.

"I have to have an answer, Cheryl," Skip said.

"B, Skip. Egyptian hieroglyphics."

It was a guess, pure and simple. But she said it with conviction.

"Correct!" Skip shouted.

That's when the studio erupted with noise, the very moment Josh Leven convinced Sydney his death watch notice was real.

Sydney and Josh came running. Hunz filled them in.

"She's within $17,200!" he shouted but could barely be heard. "Not much time left, though. One spin left, maybe two."

"I've never watched this show," Josh said. "What does she need to do?"

"They each stop the wheels," Hunz said. "A combination of factors gives them a dollar number. High number gets first crack."

Josh nodded. As the wheels were once again set into motion, the two men watched with all the intensity of a couple of guys glued to the last seconds of a championship sports event.

Sydney watched, too, but was unable to compartmentalize her feelings like Josh seemed to be doing. Her emotions battled, and she was a casualty. Cheering Cheryl on, she saw a new friend, a dying friend, an unborn life and soon-to-be orphan, while precious Stacy watched her mother with her head on Hunz's shoulder. She saw Josh. Young, energetic, all-around nice guy. Josh, distracted at the moment, but hurting. While all around her, people were cheering for a ridiculous game show. But it was more than a game show for Cheryl; it was the future of her children. A future without their mother or father.

It was just too much. Yesterday morning Sydney's biggest worry was that she was stuck in traffic and couldn't make it to a meeting on time. And now she hurt so badly, she felt as though she was the one dying.

The hands of the three contestants hovered over the buttons that would lock in their choices. The *Wonder Wheel* theme music began to play.

Junior locked in his choice.

Barb Whitlock locked in hers.

As she did on her first spin, Cheryl watched the wheel as the music played and didn't push her button until the last beat of the last measure.

The results appeared on the podiums.

The audience groaned collectively in disappointment.

Barb Whitlock had locked in the highest value, with Junior second, and Cheryl McCormick third.

A total of $17,200 separated Cheryl from first place. She'd spun a question value of twenty-one with a factor of difficulty nine for a total of $18,900. It was enough to win. But she was third in line to get a question. Would she get a chance to play?

CHAPTER
TWENTY-NINE

Barb Whitlock, you have the highest spin. The category is *Royalty Notes, correspondence of literary legends.* Play or pass?"

The leading contestant did not appear as confident as she did when she was sitting on what appeared at the time to be an insurmountable lead. Strands of hair dangled against her perspiring forehead. If she played and won, the game was over. The resulting total would put her out of reach. If she played and lost, it was over for her.

"Play or pass?" Skip repeated.

Barb said nothing.

"I have to have an answer."

More precious seconds ticked.

A buzzer sounded.

"I'm sorry, but that sound means you've forfeited your turn," Skip said.

Barb Whitlock didn't argue.

"She did that on purpose!" Hunz said.

"To run as much time off the clock as possible," Josh said.

"Junior Wicker, you have a grand total of negative $39,500. You just spun a sixty-three and an eight for a total of $50,400 which would put you in the black by $10,900. Not enough to win. Your category is *Noah's Nightmares, annoying animals on the ark.* Now remember, Junior, even if you answer the question correctly, you can't win. You're too far behind. At this point, a gentleman might consider stepping aside for a fellow contestant."

"The network wants Cheryl to win," Sydney said. "Why else would he say something like that?"

"A beautiful pregnant woman who is about to die is good for ratings," Hunz said.

"It'll make a splash," Josh said, tongue in cheek.

"Nah, I'm gonna play, Skip," Junior said.

The audience booed.

Junior took exception to the audience's disfavor. He said something that was deleted from the live broadcast, possible now since all live shows were delayed five seconds as a result of certain indiscretions at a notorious Super Bowl performance.

"Very well," Skip said. His tone was that of a disapproving mother. "For $50,400, here's your question: What is the smelliest member of the weasel family? Is it, (a) Ermine, (b) Skunk, (c) Otter, (d) Mink."

Junior's eyes gasped as he thought out loud. "I don't know what an ermine is, so I don't know if it's smelly or not. And minks, they're not smelly, are they? I mean, women wear them. They wouldn't wear them if they were smelly, would they? Unless it's a trick question."

"Ten seconds."

"Skunks are definitely smelly. Ask me, I know. Whooowee. But a skunk's not a weasel, is it?"

Time was running out, both for Junior and for Cheryl.

"Skunk, Skip."

"Correct!" Skip shouted.

The audience gave a smattering of applause. Junior's tally went from red to black: $10,900. Barb Whitlock clapped the loudest for him. Not only had Junior kept Cheryl from getting another question, but he'd just made Barb Whitlock an extra ten grand.

Skip looked to the director.

"Is there time?"

He was cued to proceed, followed immediately by a wrap-it-up signal. Skip Hirshberg launched into the next question. He spoke so fast each sentence sounded like a single word.

Standing in the vomitory, Sydney and Hunz exchanged glances. Hunz shook his head. He didn't think Cheryl was going to get the question in time. This from a man who was an expert at timing newscasts down to the second.

Josh was riveted on Cheryl. He was smiling at her with a silly half grin.

Skip Hirshberg went supersonic: "Cheryl-McCormick-with-$43,900-you-need-$17,200-to-win-you-spun-a-twenty-one-and-nine-for-a-total-of-$18,900-the-category-is-*Say-Ahh-anatomy-for-amateurs*-for-the-win-pass-or-play?"

"Play," Cheryl said, right on his heels.

She looked remarkable. Her eyes flashed readiness, powered by a quick mind. Sydney teared up just watching her.

Skip gave a quick glance at the floor director.

He was given the signal to proceed.

"Here's-your-question-the-word-*Costa*-refers-to-which-of-the-following:-(a)-Nerve-(b)-Rib-(c)-Gland-(d)-Muscle."

Time had run out. The director was rising to his feet, his hands signaling the cut to commercial. It was one of those moments in life where momentous events occur between heartbeats and decisions are made between ticks of the clock.

In that instant, that fraction of a second, no breath was taken, no pulse had time to beat, no one lived, no one died. Universal time-space hiccuped.

And in that hiccup, Cheryl McCormick said, "B. Rib."

"Correct!" Skip shouted.

The television audience heard only, "Cor—"; the second half of the master of ceremony's word was cut off by a toilet tissue commercial.

In the studio, the audience was popping and splattering with shouts and applause like water on a hot skillet. Barb Whitlock left her podium to complain to Skip that time had run out. Her protests were drowned out by the celebration of not only the people in the stands but the network executives. In the vomitory, Hunz was jostling Stacy for joy. Josh turned and hugged Sydney, who was crying. On stage Cheryl was smiling. Her podium flashed her total winnings: $134,800. She looked tired.

CHAPTER
THIRTY

Twenty minutes after the Wonder Wheel went dark, the hub of activity shifted to the greenroom, a holding area where the contestants could relax before their appearance on the show. Behind the closed door, Cheryl was conferring with studio executives and Skip Hirshberg.

Sydney and Hunz waited for her in the hallway. Hunz had enticed Stacy into going on a treasure hunt for a vending machine. He wanted to put distance between her and the shouting that could be heard coming from the greenroom.

The door opened. An exasperated executive, a short man with glasses that were too large for his face, emerged. Sydney could see Cheryl inside seated on a couch, flanked by another executive and Skip Hirshberg.

"You work for the station, right?" the exec with glasses asked Sydney.

"Both of us do," Sydney said, including Josh.

"See what you can do with her," said the frazzled exec. "She insists on going back to Illinois. Talk her into staying for one more show. Earn your paychecks."

Wiping his brow, he hustled down the narrow corridor to regions unknown. Sydney glanced at Josh. They stepped inside the room.

The three people on the couch glanced up simultaneously. Cheryl was red-eyed with exhaustion.

"Let me talk to her," Sydney said.

The remaining exec, a portly man with balls for cheeks, got up, straightening the wrinkles in his pants. Sydney took his place. Skip gave her one of those "reason with her, will you?" looks.

"Alone," Sydney said. "Josh and I would like to speak to her alone."

The station exec bit his lower lip in thought, then said, "We'll be right outside." Leaning close to Sydney's ear, he whispered, "Don't let her leave this room until she agrees to appear on tomorrow night's show."

Skip stood and lingered a moment. "The station is being more than generous," he said to no one in general. "They've offered her a $50,000 appearance fee. They didn't have to, you know. She signed a contract. Winners return the next day. Those are the rules of the game."

He left, closing the door behind him.

For a long while, no one spoke. Josh shuffled uneasily, then moseyed over to the couch and sat next to Cheryl, trying to appear nonchalant. He reminded Sydney of a junior high boy trying to summon up the courage to ask a girl to dance.

They were surrounded by dozens of photographs on the walls of past *Wonder Wheel* contestants, all smiling. Some held fistfuls of money. Master of ceremonies Skip Hirshberg was in every picture. It was a mosaic of the American dream—go to Hollywood, hit it big, be the envy of everyone in the country. The message to the contestants who waited in this room was clear: *This could be you!*

Tonight Cheryl McCormick qualified to have her picture on the wall along with all the other winners. Unlike them, Cheryl wasn't smiling.

The strong odor of day-old coffee came from a pot at the far end of the room. Next to it was a tower of white cups, a bowl of pink sugar packets, and a cup filled with red stir sticks.

"That coffee's turning my stomach," Cheryl said. She pushed herself up from the couch with effort. She wobbled.

Josh jumped to steady her.

Cheryl didn't seem to notice. "I'm going home," she said.

"I'll bring the car around," Sydney said.

"Don't do me any favors. I'll call a cab." Cheryl's eyes were cold, her words clipped.

"Cheryl—"

"I can manage on my own, thank you very much."

Pressing a hand against her back, the pregnant woman made for the door. Sydney stood and caught her by the arm.

"Cheryl, let us help you."

The response was quick and heated. "I don't want your help," Cheryl spat. "I thought we were friends. Chalk it up to Midwestern naiveté. I should have known reporters don't have friends, only news sources."

The on-the-air death notice announcement. In all the excitement, Sydney had forgotten about it.

"My purse," Cheryl said, scanning the room.

Josh lunged for it and handed it to her.

"Can someone tell me where I can find my daughter?"

"Cheryl, listen to me," Sydney said. "I don't know how Skip Hirshberg found out, but I didn't tell him. You have to believe me."

Cheryl wasn't listening.

Sydney's hands fell helplessly to her sides. What could she say to convince her? "If you don't believe me, ask Skip," she blurted.

Cheryl's hand was on the door.

"Syd's telling the truth," Josh said.

Maybe it was the quiet way he said it, or maybe it was the fact that he hadn't said anything up to now, but whatever the reason, Cheryl listened.

"I was at the station this afternoon," he said. "Syd took a lot of heat for not interviewing you. And I heard her tell our assignment editor you wanted to keep the death watch thing quiet. She took heat for that, too. Any other reporter would have screwed you over."

Josh looked at Sydney. "I can't believe Helen would disregard your promise and give out the information," he said.

"It was Cori," Sydney said.

"Makes sense."

This was the first time Sydney had ever heard Josh acknowledge Cori Zinn's devious side.

"Why would this woman do this to me?" Cheryl asked. "She doesn't even know me."

"It's not you," Sydney said. "Cori is an ambitious, unscrupulous woman. She did it to hurt me."

Josh turned to Cheryl. "You have every right to be angry. It was a cheap shot to boost ratings. But let me tell you something about Syd. She's not like other reporters. She doesn't play those games. If Sydney St. James said she didn't tell the *Wonder Wheel* people about your death watch notice, she didn't."

"One reporter vouching for another?" Cheryl said. "Sort of like one con vouching for another con, wouldn't you say?"

Josh looked down and blinked a couple of times before responding. "Point taken. I'm a sportscaster. But think about it. What possible reason does a sportscaster have for being here tonight? You think reporters have some kind of secret signal they flash whenever they need someone to cover their backside? I'm here because an hour and a half ago I opened my email and found a death watch notice."

That got Cheryl's attention.

"I haven't told anybody yet, not even my parents. I came here tonight because I needed a friend, someone I could talk to, someone I could trust."

Cheryl touched Josh Leven's hand. "Thank you," she said. Josh stepped aside, and she turned to Sydney. "Sydney. I . . ."

"Forget it." Sydney gave her a soft smile.

In a room that smelled of scorched coffee, the two women embraced, as best they could bending over the large bulge between them.

To everyone's surprise they found the hallway outside the green-room empty. Neither the ball-cheeked exec nor Skip Hirshberg was on guard as expected.

"Where's Stacy?" Cheryl asked.

"With Hunz," Sydney said.

"I'll go find them," Josh said.

"They offered me open-ended use of the suite at the Excelsior Hotel if I stayed," Cheryl said, after Josh had gone.

"That doesn't surprise me," Sydney said.

"When I reminded them that I wouldn't be alive to take advantage of it, they offered to arrange for my burial at Forest Lawn cemetery. Said they could get me a grave a stone's throw from Walt Disney, that some network bigwig would give it up for me. They also threw in an amusement park package for little Stacy after I was gone. They said it would cheer Stacy up."

"Oh, Cheryl, I'm so sorry. That's how things work here."

"They didn't offer me the one thing I wanted."

"To go home."

Cheryl smiled. "You do understand, don't you?"

Men's voices came down the hallway. Happy sounds, obviously not the studio executives returning.

As Cheryl gathered herself to leave, she said, "Not being in the hallway just now is the first thing they've done right all night."

Hunz and Josh appeared at the end of the hallway with Hunz carrying Stacy. Sydney couldn't remember the girl's feet touching the ground all night. Stacy was licking a half-eaten fudgesicle. She wore much of the other half on her face. Hunz Vonner's suit was stained where she'd laid her head against him. He didn't seem to mind.

"Oh, honey!" Cheryl cried. "You got Mr. Vonner all dirty!"

A moment later the girl was in Cheryl's arms being cleaned with a tissue.

"I sent Skip Hirshberg and his fellow barracuda on an errand," Hunz said. "I hinted Stacy was partial to pistachio ice cream. I think they went to find her some. Then we found the cafeteria . . ."

While Cheryl was occupied cleaning her daughter, with an amused Josh looking on, Sydney pulled Hunz aside. "I don't have time to take you back to the hotel," she said. "I have to get Cheryl to the airport. You can call a cab, or perhaps Josh can drop you off."

Hunz turned serious. "What are your plans?"

Sydney shrugged. "Get them on a plane to Chicago any way I can. Medical emergency. Hardship case. I'll use my press credentials. Beg. Plead. Bribe. Whatever it takes."

"Use your feminine wiles," Josh said, grinning. Apparently he could watch Cheryl and listen at the same time.

"Private joke," Sydney said to Hunz.

Hunz wasn't laughing. He turned and walked away. Just before he disappeared around a corner, he pulled out his cell phone. Sydney caught a few words.

"Sol. This is Vonner . . ."

She winced. She could expect another angry lecture from Sol in the morning. It angered her that Hunz was acting like a child. *Tattletale! Tattletale!* But she'd didn't have time to worry about that right now. She had to get Cheryl and Stacy to the airport.

Cheryl was looking for a trash can to stow a couple wads of chocolate-stained tissues. Stacy's face was presentable, though there were still a few stubborn smudges on her chin.

Josh offered to take the tissues. Cheryl thanked him and grabbed Stacy's hand. "We're ready now," she said.

Sydney led them toward an exit. "I'll bring the car around," she said. "Wait for me at the top of the steps."

"Can I go with you?" Josh asked. Then, his gaze resting on Cheryl, he added, "That is, if you don't mind."

Cheryl smiled shyly. "I'd like that."

Their gaze lingered noticeably. Under different circumstances, Sydney would have interpreted the exchange as romantic. Reality bludgeoned that thought. Neither Cheryl nor Josh had a future beyond two days. Whatever passed between them was more likely that of two victims sharing a common fate.

All because some egomaniacal Russian general had planted microscopic killing machines in their bloodstreams. To make a statement? To flex his political muscles?

Sydney felt a rage such as she'd never felt before. It was as though she was standing at ground zero of the World Trade Center on 9/11. She could see the planes approaching. She knew what was going to happen, but she was powerless to do anything to stop it. No amount of screaming, no amount of shouting, no amount of anger or rage or tears could prevent the tragedy from happening. And Cheryl and Josh were on the ninety-first floor.

They reached the exit. Sydney shoved the crash bar harder than what was necessary to open it.

In the next instant, a multitude of lights flashed in her face. Camera lights blinded her. A crush of reporters pressed, thrusting microphones in her face. Everyone shouted at once, demanding information about Cheryl, who hadn't stepped from the building yet, who wouldn't step from the building if Sydney could help it.

She backpedaled, nearly bowling over Josh and Cheryl, pulling shut the door with all her might. Several hands tried to stop her and got their fingers smashed.

"What do they want from me?" Cheryl cried.

"You're a hot news story." Hunz walked up behind them. "Popular game show winner and expectant mother who is also a death watch victim. Sells papers. Raises ratings."

Cheryl turned to Sydney. "Is there another way out of here?"

"All the exits are covered," Hunz said.

Josh frowned. "We need a plan."

"Already taken care of," Hunz said.

CHAPTER
THIRTY-ONE

The studio door flew open.

As before, a staccato burst of lights hit with force. His arm around a red-haired pregnant woman, Hunz lowered his head and plunged into the sea of reporters.

"This isn't going to deceive anyone," Sydney said.

"Keep your head down and keep moving," Hunz shouted over the din.

She did. She was hunched over a well-placed pillow and outfitted with dark glasses and a green scarf, compliments of the studio prop department. A red wig flared with every camera flash.

Hunz straight-armed everyone in his way like a running back headed for the end zone with a faux Cheryl tucked securely under his arm as the ball.

A black limousine split the crowd, its horn blaring, warning foolhardy reporters that they'd better think twice about challenging a couple of tons of metal to a head-on competition. The back door opened just as Hunz and Sydney reached it.

Hunz assisted his charge into the limo, but instead of following her, he turned to face the stormy tide. Looking like Moses parting the Red Sea, Hunz raised both hands over his head. He identified himself.

With someone to record and shoot, the rabble quieted.

"My name is Hunz Vonner, newscaster with EuroNet operating out of Berlin, Germany. Some of you undoubtedly recognize me."

He couldn't help himself. Good newscasters have healthy egos, and Hunz Vonner's was making a public appearance.

"As a guest in your country," he shouted, "it has been my privilege to observe your media at work, and compare it to the way we do things in Europe. Where I come from, there is an unwritten code of professional courtesy. Accordingly, as a professional courtesy, I request that you honor the exclusive agreement station KSMJ has made with Ms. Cheryl McCormick. I appeal to your sense of honor and dignity as journalists and trust that your example tonight will forge a new era of cooperation between our respective countries. Thank you."

His speech was a drop of sanity in an ocean of chaos. Hunz ducked into the limo, and it sped off to a chorus of shouts and catcalls.

Beside him, Sydney took off her glasses.

"What was that all about?" she said.

"You didn't like my speech?"

"Professional courtesy in the media? Really?"

Hunz howled. "Are you kidding? They're jackals!"

"You lied."

"And I suppose you never lied to get a story," Hunz said.

Sydney stared at him.

"No, I guess you never have, have you?" he said. "Doesn't matter. But I didn't lie tonight. I said there is such a thing as professional courtesy where I come from, and there is. Just not among journalists."

"What did you hope to accomplish?" Sydney asked.

"Look out the back window."

She turned. A serpentine line of vehicles sped after them from the studio parking lot.

"You taunted them into following us," she said.

Hunz laughed. "Asking for professional courtesy from a pack of reporters is like throwing meat into a shark tank. But that's not why I did it."

"Why then?"

Hunz stomped both feet on the floor gleefully, pleased with himself.

Sydney laughed at his exuberance. This was the second time today Sydney saw a hidden side of Hunz Vonner, the first being when he hit it off with Stacy at the hotel.

"There was always the chance some of them would not take the bait," he said, "that they would suspect some kind of sleight of hand. I know I would. That's why I instructed Josh and Cheryl to slip out right behind us, during the moment of deception, and not wait for the coast to clear."

"And your little speech . . . ," Sydney said, catching on.

"Extended the moment of deception. It also put me in position to watch them make their getaway. I had to make sure they got away safely."

"And did they?"

Hunz sat back with a grin. "As they say in the movies, worked like a charm."

CHAPTER
THIRTY-TWO

When Sydney and Hunz arrived at Los Angeles International Airport, Josh and Cheryl and Stacy were waiting for them.

Having followed Hunz's instructions, Josh had steered the Volvo down a side road to hangars that serviced private corporate jets. The guard at the parking lot security booth told Josh he was expecting them. After a cursory check of the Volvo, he directed them to the appropriate hangar and waved them through.

"You should have seen their faces." Hunz was still laughing as he climbed out of the back of the limo. "Priceless!"

Sydney emerged right behind him. What followed was a breathless duet reenacting the last twenty minutes.

"They followed us all the way to the Excelsior Hotel," she said.

"Some of them were there waiting for us," Hunz said.

"After all, it's no secret *Wonder Wheel* uses the Excelsior Hotel."

"She was marvelous," Hunz said of Sydney. "Inspired."

"It seemed the natural thing to do," Sydney said.

Josh grinned widely. "What? What did you do?"

"Well, when we got to the hotel," Sydney said, "we drove into the drop-off area in front of the lobby doors. Hunz opened the moonroof on the limo."

"And Sydney stood up so everyone could see her. Naturally, they thought she was Cheryl. They piled out of their vehicles and surrounded the limo, shouting questions, thrusting microphones at her, cameras rolling, strobes flashing."

Standing next to Josh and holding Stacy, Cheryl listened intently and smiled as the story unfolded.

"It was fun," Sydney said, glad to see Cheryl smiling again. "I felt like a celebrity wearing those dark glasses."

"Sydney waved to them, one of those regal, Princess Diana waves," Hunz said. "Strobe lights were flashing everywhere. Then she removed her glasses and there were fewer flashes. With a flourish, she pulled off the wig, and the flashes stopped altogether."

"They were stunned," Sydney said.

"But then," Hunz cried, "the pièce de résistance. A stroke of genius!"

"I pulled the pillow from beneath my blouse . . ."

". . . and she tossed it to them . . ."

". . . like a bridal bouquet."

"Then we drove off, leaving them standing there. Stunned. Stunned! Hands down, best time I've had in America," Hunz cried.

I can't believe you arranged all of this," Sydney said, "and in such a short time."

The Dassault Falcon cruised at thirty-six-thousand feet. A Plexiglas panel doorway separated the section of the plane in which Sydney sat from the boardroom where Cheryl had put Stacy down. The little girl was sleeping on a small sofa, her head beneath a large fern. Cheryl sat on the floor next to her, stroking her bangs. Josh reclined in a conference chair nearby, his feet propped up on the table. His eyes were closed, but it was doubtful he was sleeping.

Hunz closed the Plexiglas door behind him and joined Sydney. Four wide soft leather chairs were arranged in pairs, facing each other. Hunz sat next to Sydney, who was watching Cheryl love her daughter.

"And it was nice of you to invite Josh and me along, though I still don't understand why you did." Sydney paused for an explanation. When Hunz didn't offer one, she said, "I've never flown on a private jet before. I've never even flown first class, only cattle car coach."

Hunz slumped back in his chair. He let out a sigh of accomplishment.

"At the studio, you called Sol and arranged things then, didn't you?" Sydney said. "The limo, the jet, all of it."

She just couldn't let it go. The details of the trip. Hunz's reasoning. They were little niggling worms under her skin.

Hunz closed his eyes. "Being an international celebrity has its perks."

"You did it for Stacy, didn't you? You and she have formed quite an attachment."

Hunz smiled, his eyes still closed.

"What did you promise him?" Sydney asked.

"Who?"

"Sol. He's not the kind of guy who gives something unless he gets something in return. You promised him something. What?"

Hunz sighed again, obviously a bit agitated at the question. "Does it matter?"

"It depends on what you promised him."

Hunz turned his head without lifting it to look at her. "An exclusive," he said. "I offered Sol an exclusive."

It took a moment for what he said to register. When it did, Sydney bolted upright. She looked at Cheryl, then back at Hunz.

"You scum!" she shouted. "All this time I thought you were rescuing Cheryl from those game show piranha, and you were just saving her for yourself! You're no better than they are! I take that back. You're worse!"

"Scum," Hunz said calmly. "I don't know that word."

"Dirtbag. Sleaze. Wretch."

"Ah, wretch. Now that's a word I know."

He didn't seem the slightest bit concerned by Sydney's outrage.

Sydney was beside herself. "How could you do such a thing? How could you be so low? Here I thought you were trying to help Cheryl, while all the time you're setting her up to exploit her!"

"Everything has a price," Hunz said. "Cheryl wanted to get back to Chicago to deliver her baby. The price of the airfare was an exclusive interview with a death watch victim at the moment of death—in perfect health one minute, dead the next. Sol liked the idea. Said it would make a splash."

"I might expect this kind of despicable behavior from Sol, but you? I thought you were better than that."

Hunz's face reddened. "Maybe you've forgotten who we are. We're reporters, not a rescue aid society. Reporters report— automobile crashes, burning buildings, natural disasters, murders. Every day people die and we're there live, broadcasting it to our viewing audience. It's the nature of our business. And if you don't know that by now, you're in the wrong business. If you want to save people, join the Red Cross!"

Sydney sat facing him on the edge of her seat, her hands balled in fists.

"But this is Cheryl!"

Hunz was unmoved. "First rule of journalism: Never compromise your objectivity."

Sydney glared at him. "Why now? Why Cheryl? We could have done this story with Lyle Vandeveer."

"Things were different back then."

The way he said it, *back then* sounded like it was several decades ago instead of just last night.

"Back then," Sydney said, "you thought interviewing Mr. Vandeveer was a waste of time."

"Like I said, things change."

Sydney studied him. What had changed? It had to be more than just a matter of passing time. Was it the fact that Cheryl was now a game show celebrity? Or was it something else? What else had changed since last night?

"You heard from the FBI," she said.

Hunz looked away. He said nothing. But he heard her, because his jaw muscles tensed, just like it had in the vomitory when he returned after making a phone call.

After a few moments, he said, "A few hours ago, General Baranov surrendered to FBI agents outside his villa on Barbados."

"That's good news, isn't it? Has he talked? Has he told the FBI where to find Yuri Kiselev?"

Hunz nodded. "Baranov talked."

"And?"

"He's not behind Death Watch."

Sydney was crestfallen. "Oh, Hunz! Is that what Baranov said? He'd deny it, of course. Is the FBI certain?"

"Baranov told them where they could find Yuri Kiselev. He's buried in a basement just outside of Minsk. He's been dead for two months. Apparently, he made the mistake of falling in love with Baranov's mistress."

"And the nanotechnology?"

Hunz shook his head. "There is no production lab. No master plan."

"What about someone else? If the technology is possible, maybe someone else—"

"The theory was based on Baranov's money and Kiselev's brains. And from what the FBI told me, Baranov is as anxious as we are to find out who's behind Death Watch. His mother died this morning. A death watch victim."

Sydney touched his arm with sympathy. "That was our best lead. It all made sense, in a warped, villainous way. So what are we left with? Does the FBI or your EuroNet team have any other suspects? "

"A hundred leads. All long shots."

Sydney looked toward the back of the plane. "That means that Cheryl and Josh will most likely . . ."

"Yeah."

"At least you'll get your exclusive," Sydney said, her tone turning hard. Just because she was disappointed his theory hadn't worked out didn't mean she'd forgiven him for exploiting Cheryl.

"Yeah. Looks like I will," Hunz said sadly. "But that's not why I arranged to get Cheryl back to Chicago."

"But you just said . . ."

"I said there is always a price to pay."

"An exclusive."

Hunz nodded. "An exclusive."

"You have something up your sleeve," Sydney said.

Hunz laughed. "I wish I did." He sighed heavily. It was the third sigh since he sat down. "Actually, this whole enterprise is because of you."

"Me?"

"Last night. The look in Lyle Vandeveer's eyes. It meant everything to him that you were there. I'd be willing to bet he hadn't smiled that much in years. Then tonight, after hearing from the FBI . . . well, I wanted to do something similar for Cheryl, something that would make her smile, make her happy, before . . ."

"Before she dies." Sydney finished his sentence for him.

"No," Hunz said. "Before I die."

CHAPTER
THIRTY-THREE

Of the 51,327 tons of cargo that passed through Chicago's O'Hare airport that month, 167 pounds of it was Billy Peppers.

His feet and hands were frozen, his joints stiff, and his rear end numb from four hours of nonstop vibration. Shut up in the packing crate, in pitch-black darkness, he listened for activity, sounds similar to those he'd heard in LA when they were loading the plane—forklift engines; heavy boots; male voices shouting orders, cursing, talking sports, telling off-color stories. For the last ten minutes or so—who could tell for sure? It was too dark to see his pink Tinkerbell watch—he'd heard nothing except the sound of his teeth chattering.

The vertebrae-wrenching landing would have sent him to the chiropractor tomorrow if he had money for that sort of thing. That was followed by the monotonous rumble of taxiing. With no windows to gauge the distance, it seemed as though they taxied to Cleveland before the engines finally wound down, sounding very much like a huge vacuum cleaner that just had its plug pulled. Soon afterward, Billy felt the fuselage shake as a door was opened. There was activity for a while, then silence.

Buster told him to wait until the workers moved him into the hangar. It was safest that way.

"They'll offload you," Buster had said, "stick you off to the side, and pretty much leave you alone. You're not a priority package, so no one will get to you until morning. That should give you plenty of time to hammer your way out."

Billy didn't take the "you're not a priority package" comment personally.

He strained to hear something beyond the plywood walls. He heard nothing. Buster told him to wait, and Buster knew what he was talking about. But Buster was talking about the way things were supposed to work. Things don't always work the way they're supposed to work.

In the dark this needling doubt pricked Billy repeatedly. What if someone had made a mistake? The guys who load and unload cargo weren't exactly Rhodes scholars. *No offense, Buster.* It was possible they overlooked him, or were intentionally blinded to the markings on the crate. That wasn't out of the realm of possibility, knowing what he knew.

Billy leaned forward at the thought. There were two sides to this spiritual war in which he was involved, with angels on both sides. It stood to reason that if a good angel told him to go to Chicago, there was a bad angel who didn't want him here, and it was certainly within a bad angel's ability to blind the eyes of a cargo handler! If that was the case . . .

He listened for a new sound—the closing of a cargo hatch. What if they were done unloading? What if Chicago was not the plane's final destination? He could end up in Boston, or New Orleans, or Winnemucca.

Setting the Nike shoe box to one side—with the lid unsecured, he'd held it the entire trip to keep the angels from spilling out—Billy felt for the hammer Buster had given him. Grabbing it, he let loose with two good whacks across the upper edge of the crate, then listened, which was harder now because of the ringing in his ears from hammering in such close quarters.

The noise didn't seem to attract attention, but neither did it make much of an impression on the crate. He had little room in which to swing the hammer, and Buster had nailed him in good.

A couple more whacks, harder and louder this time, and he failed to see even a suggestion of an opening along the top edge of the crate. Each blow sounded like firecrackers going off.

It was time for a different approach. Dropping the hammer, Billy pressed his back against the crate and gave the opposite side a couple of kicks with the heel of his shoe.

He saw a strip of light.

A couple more kicks and one entire edge was loose. A couple more and the opening was large enough for him to crawl out.

Tucking his shoe box under his arm, Billy Peppers crouched like a running back prepared to take on a pair of three-hundred-and-fifty-pound tackles. Who knew what he would encounter? But the only thing that hit him when he emerged was the cool Chicago night air.

A quick glance up and down the fuselage revealed he was alone. A huge portal opened up to the airport runway. In the distance, an Aer Lingus Airbus with a green shamrock spotlighted on its tail was landing.

Billy approached the edge of the hatch. He saw no ramp, no ladder. He'd have to jump. It was about an eight-foot drop, maybe ten. Most days this would be a challenge. Tonight, with his feet frozen and his knees feeling like rusted hinges, the jump had *pain* written all over it.

He heard voices, though he couldn't see the men they were attached to. They were getting louder. Billy looked at the tarmac. Jump or hide? Did he have a choice? The crate was yawning open. He supposed he could nail it shut again, but what then? Hide among the cargo? He could possibly get lucky and someone would pull a ramp up to the side of the plane and then leave again so he could walk out. Or they could shut him up in the belly of this silver whale, and the next thing you know he'd be disgorged onto the sands of Winnemucca.

It was time to take a leap of faith.

Billy crouched down, prayed a simple *help-me-Jesus* prayer, and jumped.

There was a moment when he seemed to hang suspended in the air, an exhilarating feeling of flight that ended suddenly and most painfully. The tarmac struck the bottom of his feet with what felt like lightning; his knees cracked and buckled; the Nike shoe box went flying, spilling angels everywhere; and when the rest of him crashed against the cement, he tried to stop himself from falling with outstretched hands and managed to scrape both palms, embedding pebbles in his flesh that looked like little comets with long red tails.

With his cheek pressed against the cement, while various body parts issued emergency signals to his brain, Billy remembered how parachute jumpers dipped their shoulders and rolled upon impact. Sure, now he remembered.

Gingerly, because he had to use his hands to push himself up and they were presently screaming at him, Billy managed to get to his knees. There was a stiff breeze and some of his angels were trying to fly away. They looked like they'd forgotten how, tumbling this way and that.

"Hey! You!"

One of the voices he'd heard earlier took human form. It became a body dressed in gray coveralls with a face that didn't look pleased to see him. In fact, there were three men just inside the hangar. Two were smoking. One was sitting on top of a crate, his feet dangling.

"Get away from that plane!"

All three men were looking at him now. The one shouting had taken a last draw from his cigarette and tossed it aside. He picked up a crowbar and came toward Billy. The crowbar fit his hand with familiarity, much the same way a nine iron would fit in the hand of a golfer, or a bat in the hand of a baseball player.

Billy scrambled to capture the last of the runaway angels and shoved them into the box. The two ceramic angels were scuffed but not broken. His Bible lay open, the wind's fingers flipping its pages.

He grabbed them all and tossed them into the box, then wrestled with the lid. His knees complaining loudly, he managed to get on his feet and—hobbling—put some distance between him and the crowbar.

"That's right, get outta here! Go on. Git! Git!"

Maybe it was a universal thing; Chicago was no different than LA. In both places they used the same language to chase away dogs and bums. Billy hobbled out of the hangar lights and into the darkness.

To one side, in the distance, like a finger pointing heavenward, stood the O'Hare airport control tower. Splayed beneath it were lights, both stationary and moving, a city of people in transit from all quarters of the world.

"Well, we're here," Billy said to the air. "Now what?"

CHAPTER THIRTY-FOUR

Sydney couldn't believe what she was hearing.

"You? A death watch notice?"

"On the flight from Atlanta," Hunz said.

"All this time?"

She still couldn't believe it. From the time she'd met Hunz, he'd been living under the threat of death. At Lyle Vandeveer's house. At Dykstra Hall. At FBI headquarters. Now it all made sense. He hadn't wanted to sleep.

"Who knows?" she asked.

"Sol. Now you."

"You told Sol . . ."

"When I arranged for this flight."

"Why not earlier?"

"You saw the way Helen reacted when she thought you had the Death Watch. I couldn't risk it."

He was right, of course. Helen was ready to bench her, which explained why Hunz acted so cavalierly when he interceded for her in Helen's office.

"On the flight in . . . ," Sydney said, counting back the hours. "That means . . ."

"8:47 a.m."

Sydney looked at her watch. It was after midnight. 12:26 a.m., to be exact. "That means you have . . ."

"Eight hours, twenty-one minutes to live."

"And the live interview you promised Sol. It's not Cheryl."

"Never said it was."

"Oh, Hunz."

"Works out well for you, though," he said breezily. "That's why I brought you along, to wrap up the story once I'm gone. You'll get international exposure."

"Don't joke about that. It's not funny."

"Who's joking? Besides, I know exactly how Lyle Vandeveer felt. Just having you near makes things easier."

"Don't you have someone in Germany?"

Hunz looked at his empty hands. "I've pretty much sacrificed everything to get where I am. Married the job, no time for a social life. You know the drill."

"Family?"

"My mother's gone. Haven't spoken to my father in a couple of years."

"You should call him."

Hunz Vonner's face turned to granite. The friendliness that had been there a moment before was gone. "Don't offer advice about things you know nothing about."

He was out of his chair and walking to the back of the plane before Sydney knew what was happening. She called to him.

He stepped into the lavatory and closed the door.

Sydney looked at her watch, refusing to believe Hunz Vonner had no more than the time of a normal working day to live.

Sydney sat alone, staring out the window of the plush corporate jet, her reflection staring back at her. She looked past it to the lights below. For most of the journey only an occasional light dotted the black prairie beneath them. Now lights were appearing with greater frequency. They came in clumps and strings.

The sound of the engines changed as the plane began its descent. Sydney buckled in, her thoughts and emotions as black as the night outside her window.

She found it hard to give up on the nanotechnology theory. She had no reason to hang onto it; she just wanted to. Not only did it make sense, it was something they could understand, something they could fight. Scientists could come up with something to neutralize the little buggers, couldn't they? The theory had given her hope. Now that it was gone, hope was gone and they were right back where they started, asking the same disturbing questions. Who was behind this? How were they doing it? What could be done to stop them?

On the other side of the Plexiglas partition, Josh stirred. Taking his feet from the table, he stood and stretched. He said something to Cheryl. She smiled and said something back.

Maybe Sydney was mistaken, but she thought she saw a fledgling love sparkle in their eyes, the kind that gives couples a giddy feeling and makes them smile and laugh a lot. No, they hadn't known each other long enough. Besides, there was Cori. And what did Josh and Cheryl have in common besides a very short future?

Little Stacy was still asleep. Josh and Cheryl talked.

Sydney sighed. Five passengers on board, not counting the one in Cheryl's belly. Three marked for death. Later today, after Cheryl was settled, Sydney would fly back to Los Angeles. Possibly alone, possibly with Josh, but he'd be going back to LA to die. For all its leather and polished wood, the Dessault Falcon was a coffin with wings.

Hunz stepped out of the restroom. He joined the others in the conference room. The three adults chatted casually, then both men assisted Cheryl to her feet. It took both of them. Hunz buckled himself into a chair with them, leaving Sydney alone and frightened.

She couldn't help but feel that an invisible terrorist rode in the plane with them. He sat with the others in the conference room, having claimed them as his own. Somehow, Sydney had to find a way to stop him. But she didn't know where to begin, and she was running out of time, and soon she would begin losing people she cared for.

CHAPTER THIRTY-FIVE

The lights of Chicago slid beneath the Dassault Falcon as it made its approach to Midway Airport. Smaller than O'Hare, Midway serviced connector flights for the major airlines and corporate aircraft.

The plane slowed to a stop a short distance from the terminal. Sydney unbuckled and joined the others. Josh was holding a sleeping Stacy upright while Cheryl dressed her in a light jacket. Josh was obviously inexperienced at this sort of thing. The little girl's head and arms flopped this way and that like a rag doll.

"Do we need to arrange for transportation?" Sydney asked.

"Already taken care of," Hunz said.

The man was efficient, you had to give him that.

"Evanston?" Sydney asked Cheryl.

The pregnant woman zipped up Stacy's jacket, then put a hand against her own back to straighten up again.

"I've got Stacy," Josh said to her, picking up the girl.

The girl laid her head on Josh's shoulder. Hunz looked on attentively, several times making motions to help get Stacy situated. He obviously wanted to carry her.

Cheryl answered Sydney's question. "I'm meeting my OB/GYN at Prentice Women's Hospital. It's part of Northwestern Memorial Hospital on Superior Avenue."

"You're not going home first?" Sydney asked.

Cheryl shrugged. "I want to get checked in as soon as possible. My doctor's reluctant to take the baby early. He says all this death watch stuff is nonsense, that once I'm in the hospital I'll be safe, what with all their medical resources and stuff."

That's what Sydney had told Lyle Vandeveer.

"Don't let him talk you into waiting too long," Sydney said.

"I won't."

Sydney knew she wouldn't. Cheryl was quiet, but she was strong and determined. Sydney admired her like no other woman she knew, and felt an incredible urge to hug her. Having had so few close women friends, it pained Sydney to think that now she'd found one, she would soon lose her.

The hatch opened. Single file, they stepped into the brisk September night. A ground crewman pointed them toward the glass terminal door. Josh and Cheryl went ahead. Sydney and Hunz waited for Cheryl's luggage.

The terminal was surprisingly populated for one o'clock in the morning. The interior was brightly lit with a white, open-beamed metal ceiling.

They made their way down Concourse A, following the ground transportation signs where, according to Hunz, a limo was waiting for them. Josh, Cheryl, and Stacy looked like a family returning from vacation. Hunz stepped briskly behind them.

Sydney had to hurry to catch up. "Are we going with her to the hospital?"

"To complete your story," Hunz replied. "You can report how the station helped her back to Chicago, then provided for her safety. It'll make a splash."

Sydney looked at him. Was he mocking her? Or was he mocking Sol? Or was this simply an attempt at humor? She found it hard to read Hunz at times. Of course, his reason for going with Cheryl to the hospital was 100 percent malarkey. That was the kind of thing that could be confirmed with a phone call. Hunz didn't fool her. He was concerned that Stacy would be cared for after her mother died, even though he could do little to help given the fact that his time would run out before Cheryl's less than eight hours from now.

They reached the junction of three concourses. Not surprisingly, it was a food court. In the center of the triangle stood a magazine kiosk. Every newspaper, every magazine had *Special Edition* slashed across the front. Death Watch was the feature story. *Time* magazine featured a large black question mark on the cover, set against a bloody red background, with the words, "Who's Next?" printed beneath it in bold block letters.

The competing odors of deep fried foods—french fries, donuts, fried chicken, fish—commingled at the concourse intersection. Backlit franchise signs vied for patrons with bright colors and pictures of burgers, tacos, pizza, gyros, and hoagie sandwiches.

Even though it was the middle of the night and Sydney's stomach knew better, it was aroused by the odors. They did a job on Stacy, too. She stirred and looked up with half-open eyes.

"Mama?"

"Go back to sleep, honey," Cheryl said. "We're not there yet."

Just then Sydney realized Hunz was missing. She looked around for him and found him standing at an unoccupied American Airlines gate watching a television mounted high on a white pillar. Even from a distance, Sydney recognized the CNN logo in the corner. Nothing unusual. CNN produced a special airport edition of their show. However, this wasn't it. On the bottom of the screen were the words SPECIAL REPORT—DEATH WATCH UPDATE.

Sydney joined Hunz. Intent on the news report, he gave no indication he knew she was there.

The CNN correspondent, an attractive black female, held a microphone and addressed the camera. She stood in front of a Hilton Hotel sign.

Two more bizarre death watch stories came to light today. At the South Pole, photographer Robert Helwys, a member of the National Geographic scientific expedition at the Atmospheric Research Observatory, is reported to have received a death watch notice on his digital pager, even though that device is well beyond normal transmission range. Authorities are unable to explain it.

And in an equally bizarre event, the Russian Space Agency has just confirmed that Cosmonaut Alexei Kovalenko has received a death watch notice while aboard the International Space Station. The trans-mission arrived via highly secure communication channels.

Which begs the question: Who is behind this far-reaching terror-ism? Theories abound, and there is no shortage of terrorist groups claiming responsibility. However, authorities are quick to point out that none of these terrorist groups have the means or resources to pull off a strike of this magnitude. So who is behind Death Watch? One man says he knows.

The camera panned up the side of a glass building to the roof of a hotel where a man stood precariously close to the edge. Tucked beneath his right arm was a Nike shoe box.

"Good Lord!" Sydney cried. "That's him!"

"Who?"

Sydney looked harder. "I'm almost certain it's him. Yes. In Pasadena. He was holding a Nike box!"

"Who?" Hunz cried.

Cheryl and Josh, having doubled back, joined them looking up at the television.

"Billy Peppers!" Sydney said.

"It can't be," Hunz said.

"Peppers," Josh said. "Isn't he the crackpot who keeps con-tacting Cori with end-of-the-world messages?"

High atop the Hilton Hotel at O'Hare International Airport, here in Chicago, a man stands on a ledge. He says he alone has the answer. Police have identified him as William Peppers, a resident of Los Angeles and self-proclaimed gospel minister.

"He must have followed us here," Sydney said.

"How?" Hunz countered. "We just got here. He had to have arrived before us."

"Oh, no," Sydney said.

"What?" Hunz demanded.

"The groundskeepers."

"What are you talking about?"

"The groundskeepers at the cemetery. They said they heard Billy Peppers talking about going to Chicago."

"A coincidence," Hunz said.

"Is it?"

"What are those white patches all over him?" Josh asked, pointing at the screen.

"They look like torn pieces of paper," Hunz said.

On screen, emergency and camera lights reflected off the patches, making it difficult to see what they were. The camera zoomed in for a tighter shot.

"Angels," Sydney said. "They're pictures of angels."

"Why would he paste pictures of angels to his clothes?" Hunz asked.

"That's right!" Josh exclaimed. "He's the crackpot who says angels talk to him."

However, Mr. Peppers refuses to talk to authorities. He says he will speak to only one person—

Premonition. Intuition. Call it what you will, but a sense of anticipatory dread chilled Sydney.

—Sydney St. James, a Los Angeles news reporter. Police are attempting to contact Miss St. James now.

Everyone looked at Sydney.

"How did he know you'd be here?" Hunz said.

Sydney was shaking her head. "He couldn't have known. I didn't even know until we got to the airport."

Hunz's cell phone rang. He answered it. "Yeah, she's right here. We just landed. I don't know. She doesn't know. All right. No idea. All right. Yeah."

He closed the phone.

"That was Sol Rosenthal. The Chicago police are looking for you."

"Did he tell them we were here?" Sydney asked.

"No. He told them he'd attempt to locate you. He wants you to get over there."

"And do what?" Sydney cried.

"Get the story. It's national." Hunz turned to Josh. "Oh . . . and he's looking for you, too. He sounded peeved. Grant Forsythe did the sports tonight."

"You didn't tell anyone you were leaving?" Sydney said.

"I had more important things on my mind than reporting a bunch of scores," Josh said.

Meanwhile, police are trying to talk Mr. Peppers down from the ledge.

The camera cut back to the reporter in front of the Hilton Hotel sign.

When asked if they thought Mr. Peppers could solve the mysterious death watch puzzle, authorities declined comment. But in a world gone mad, where messages transcend normal transmission limits and breach ultrasecure channels in space, who's to say? And if, as it has been said, fortune favors fools and small children, perhaps we should listen to a homeless man who says he converses with angels. This is Chandra Smyth reporting live from Chicago. Back to you, Bill.

CHAPTER THIRTY-SIX

Between the food court and ground transportation curbside the foursome made the decision to split up.

"How far is it to O'Hare?" Hunz asked.

"I'm not very good at distances," Cheryl replied. "You go straight up Cicero to I-90 west. Fifteen, maybe twenty miles, I think."

"We'll meet up with you at the hospital as soon as we can." Hunz held Stacy while Josh climbed into the back of the limo behind Cheryl.

Cheryl reached a hand across Josh. "Thank you for everything," she said to Hunz. She squeezed his hand warmly, then looked up at Sydney. "Sydney, you too, dear friend. Come as quickly as you can."

"We will," Sydney said.

Hunz closed the limo door and it pulled away from the curb.

"You didn't tell them?" Sydney asked.

"And add one more worry to her burden?"

He hailed a cab. Sydney checked her watch. Hunz had barely seven hours to live.

Hunz hadn't spoken a word since they left Midway. He stared out the taxi window at the lights—convenience stores, gas stations, donut shops, strip malls, grocery stores, auto shops, and tire centers.

A man who had less than the length of a workday to live should have something more poetic to look at, Sydney thought, like mountain streams, blue skies, and flowers. Acres and acres of flowers.

She wondered what he was thinking, but didn't ask. Not that she was afraid. They'd been through enough together—walking through the valley of death is the phrase that came to mind—that she felt comfortable asking him personal questions. He just seemed to need some alone time.

What does a perfectly healthy man who knows he's dying think about? The details of his impending death? Will it be an accident? A fall, or possibly a runaway vehicle? Does he have an undiagnosed malady? A heart imperfection, like the actor John Ritter, or a blood clot, like Lyle Vandeveer? The body is such a complex and delicate vessel with a thousand ways to break it.

Whether the stone hits the pitcher, or the pitcher hits the stone, it's going to be bad for the pitcher. Words of wisdom from that immortal philosopher, Sancho Panza.

And then there was the biggest unknown—who was throwing the rocks? Who was smashing vessels of flesh the world over?

Aliens? Had anyone considered aliens? Was this some sort of extraterrestrial prelude to invasion? Some sort of otherworldly war? Of course, it would have to be a technologically advanced race. That went without saying, didn't it? If they had the ability to travel the gazillion light-years scientists said they'd have to travel just to get here, they'd have to be advanced, right? But given the bizarre facts of Death Watch, were aliens out of the realm of possibility?

The cab accelerated onto I-90, leaving the colored store signs behind. It wasn't long before they could see commercial airplanes low in the sky, approaching O'Hare International Airport runway. Huge green overhead freeway signs provided arrival and departure information.

As they neared the airport terminal, red taillights like fireflies began popping up in front of them. The cab slowed. The driver cursed. It seemed odd to encounter traffic this time of night.

With a pudgy, freckled hand the driver gestured at a large white "Pardon Our Face-lift" sign.

"Can you get us directly to the hotel?" Sydney asked.

"Looks like the police got the hotel blocked off. Wonder what's up with that?" the cab driver said.

To their left, barricades blocked the road leading to the Hilton. Hunz opened his door. He threw money at the driver.

"Let's go," he said to Sydney.

The next thing Sydney knew, the two of them were running between rows of cars toward the white lights of the terminal. Because of open ditches and construction scaffolding the length of the loading zone, they had to stay in the roadway until they were parallel to the doors.

To their left was the Hilton Hotel, attached to the terminal, its features bleached in the glare of police spotlights. The overhang on the terminal prevented them from seeing the hotel's roof; neither could they see the street in front of the hotel.

"We have to go down one floor," Sydney said.

Searching for a down escalator, they raced into the terminal, stepping over piles of luggage, brushing past people, sidestepping long lines in front of the ticket counters.

Hunz spotted it first. Sydney had to quicken her pace to keep up to him.

They raced down the escalator, across the terrazzo floor, past baggage carousels, and out the door, once again in the Chicago night.

Playing cop, Hunz stiff-armed traffic to a halt as they crossed lines of traffic. They dashed under the elevated airport transit tracks just as a train whooshed over them.

A policewoman met them. She was short and freckled, with orange-red hair tucked beneath her hat. "Sorry, folks. Hotel's temporarily unavailable," she said. "We got a situation here."

Sydney looked up at the situation. Billy Peppers was seated atop a ten-story building of glass with a convex facade. At the far right, it met the airport control tower. Billy was in the center, his legs dangling over the edge.

"This is Sydney St. James," Hunz said to the policewoman.

"I'm Sydney St. James," Sydney said, a half syllable behind him. She flashed her press pass.

The name didn't register with the policewoman. "Glad to meet you. Like I said, folks, I'm sorry but . . ."

A short distance away, a man coiling cable overheard the exchange. He grabbed the arm of a woman nearby and said something. She swung Sydney's direction. Barking orders, she quickly navigated an intercept course. Sydney recognized her. It was Chandra Smyth.

By the time she reached Sydney, she had a microphone in hand, the area was awash in camera light, and she was asking her first question.

"Miss St. James, what is your connection to William Peppers, the man on the ledge?"

The swift approach of the camera crew took the policewoman by surprise. She obviously didn't like the intrusion but didn't know what to do about it. The lights and sudden movement caught the attention of another officer, a sergeant fifty feet away. He hurried toward them, scowling.

The suddenness of the ambush caught Sydney off guard. She reacted like the proverbial deer in the headlights.

Hunz stepped forward, putting his hand over the camera lens, a move that angered the cameraman. "Miss St. James has no comment at this time," Hunz said, positioning himself between Sydney and Chandra Smyth.

"What's going on here?" said the approaching police sergeant.

Sydney identified herself again.

"Miss St. James, how did you get here so quickly?" Chandra Smyth shouted.

The sergeant recognized Sydney's name.

"Come with me," he said. With a forearm, he shoved Ms. Chandra and her microphone aside, earning for his efforts angry words of protest which he shrugged off as he led Sydney away. Hunz attempted to follow. The policewoman stopped him.

"He's with me," Sydney said.

The sergeant looked Hunz over. "Sorry," he said.

Sydney pulled up short. "I'm not going anywhere without him," she said.

"He your lawyer?" the sergeant asked.

Sydney said nothing. Neither did she move.

The sergeant took another look at Hunz. "All right," he said, and motioned him through the police cordon.

The sergeant led Sydney to a man in a gray suit. Short and stocky, he wore a no-nonsense facial expression as he stared up at the roof and Billy Peppers. Just as they reached him, he lifted a walkie-talkie and demanded an update.

While they waited for Gray Suit to conclude his transmission, Sydney looked up at the roof. Billy sat on the ledge, his feet dangling, surveying the scene below. The CNN camera lights must have attracted his attention, because he was staring straight at Sydney.

She imagined it wasn't hard for him to spot her. After all, it was dark, there was no moon, and all the emergency workers were dressed in dark colors. Her blonde hair must have stood out like a struck match in a pitch-black forest.

When he saw her, he smiled. A mouthful of white teeth were framed by black lips stretched wide. He stood up, a move that agitated the crowd below. Then he spread his arms wide, as though to greet Sydney with a hug, or invite her to join him on his precarious perch.

A shiver shook Sydney, chilling her insides and draining her extremities of blood until they were ice cold. At that moment, a gust of wind arrived from Lake Michigan. It whipped the flags on two impressive poles in front of the hotel. Billy's open shirt, the one on top of several layers of shirts, flapped happily with the flags.

"What is it, Sergeant?" Finished with his conversation on the walkie-talkie, the man in the gray suit turned his attention to them.

"This is Sydney St. James," said the sergeant.

Gray Suit looked her over with a critical eye. Purely professional. He was registering details, forming opinions, and filing away information in some file cabinet in his head. "Why you?" Gray Suit asked Sydney.

"What do you mean, why me?"

"What does he want from you?"

Sydney said, "All I know is—"

Hunz cut her off. "Exactly who is it we're talking to?" he said. "Who are you and what is your position here?"

Gray Suit scowled as though asking questions was his private domain and Hunz was trespassing. "You her lawyer?"

"A friend," Hunz said.

Gray Suit's jaw ground back and forth. Sydney had heard of men who chewed people up and spat them out, and she'd always thought it was a figure of speech. To look at Gray Suit, she wasn't so sure anymore.

The sergeant jumped in. "This is Assistant Chief of Police Leonard Caplan," he said. "He's in charge of this whole shebang."

"Well?" Caplan barked. "Can we get on with it now?"

"I don't know why he chose me," Sydney said.

"You know him?"

"I recognize him."

"From where?"

"He watched us do a live broadcast in Pasadena."

"He watched you. You're certain it's the same man?"

"Fairly certain. He was carrying a Nike shoe box that night too."

Caplan nodded as he chewed on this. "So after seeing you do a live broadcast, he thought it would be nice to invite you to a tea party on the roof of the Hotel Hilton in Chicago?"

"He emailed me yesterday," Sydney said. "He claimed he had information on Death Watch. We"—she gestured toward Hunz—"failed to connect with him. Then, when we did a little investigating, we discovered he lives on the street and volunteers at a rescue mission."

"In Chicago?"

"In LA."

"What's he doing in Chicago?"

"You'll have to ask him that."

"I don't buy it. He asked for an LA reporter thirty minutes ago and now here you are?"

"Coincidence. We're here on a totally unrelated matter."

"You mean news story, don't you?" Caplan ground his jaw. He spat on the ground. "I don't like it. Not one bit."

He squared himself and stood inches away from Sydney.

"This is some kind of media stunt, isn't it? A rivalry between two television stations. Or maybe the payoff on a lost wager."

Sydney didn't answer immediately. Guilty people tended to answer too quickly. She looked him dead in the eye. "We just brought a pregnant woman, a friend, from LA to Chicago so that she could deliver her child at home before she dies. Believe me, Assistant Chief Caplan, if I had any choice in this matter, I would be at her side right now, not here."

They locked eyes.

Caplan grunted. He turned his back, walked a distance, and spoke into the walkie-talkie. A minute later, he returned.

"You'll talk to this guy?" he asked.

Sydney looked up at Billy. His hands were by his sides. He was looking down at her from a distance of ten stories. The reality of what she was being asked to do hit her. She was a reporter, not a counselor. What did she know about negotiating with a suicide jumper? What if he jumped while she was talking to him? What did he want with her anyway?

She was certain of one thing: She didn't want to do this.

"I can ask him what he wants," she said.

In less than a heartbeat—a very short time considering Sydney's heart was hammering furiously against her chest—Caplan moved into action.

To Hunz: "You, stay where you're at."

To the sergeant: "Take the lady up to the roof."

To Sydney: "And you—no stunts. Promise him anything. Get him to back away from the ledge. We'll take it from there."

Caplan walked away, speaking rapidly into the walkie-talkie.

Sydney looked to Hunz.

For what? Assurance? A word of encouragement? A last piece of professional advice? All she knew was that at that moment she craved a positive word from a familiar face.

Hunz flipped open his cell phone. "I'll get everything set up for the live feed later tonight," he said, walking away.

"Yeah," Sydney said to his back.

Get everything set up for his last on-the-air report, the one that would culminate in his death.

Sydney felt the burn of shame. Hunz was the one who was dying, and here she was wanting to be reassured.

She watched him go. Business as usual from the looks of him. She should have said something supportive. But what? Tell him it would be all right? Cream-puff words, all sugar and no substance. Besides, he'd already moved on, and she needed to do the same.

"This way, ma'am," said the sergeant.

With a heavyhearted sigh Sydney followed the sergeant toward a glass façade that rose up before her like an enormous glacier.

CHAPTER
THIRTY-SEVEN

At each level between street and rooftop Sydney's doubts compounded. In the lobby she was struck by a niggling uncertainty as she was escorted to the elevators. Upon reaching the tenth floor the niggle grew to mature apprehension as the elevator doors opened to police with rifles and face shields, while curious hotel guests stood in their doorways in their robes. By the time Sydney climbed the final flight of stairs and emerged on the roof, her doubt had mutated to full-fledged fear.

An expansive canopy of stars opened overhead. This high up there were no buildings to restrict the view, or the wind. It whipped her clothing with authority, reminding her that this was its territory.

It was dark where she entered. Shadowy military figures crouched in every corner. The only one in the light was Billy Peppers. Spotlights from the street and portable lights on the roof crisscrossed on him.

The crunch of gravel announced the approach of two men, one dressed for action, the other in a suit of undetermined color.

The sergeant said, "This is Sydney St. James."

They were expecting her. The armed man held a walkie-talkie, no doubt linked to Caplan.

The man in the suit leaned close and advised her regarding the man on the ledge. "Don't anger him. Try to get him talking. And make sure you stay out of arm's reach."

The armed man added, "See if you can get him to step down off the ledge. We have men in position behind the lights to grab him."

Neither asked Sydney if she was having any second thoughts. They each grabbed an arm and led her toward the light.

The man in the suit lifted a bullhorn. "Peppers, we have Miss St. James, just as you requested."

Billy turned toward the voice. He squinted against the lights. There was no way he could see any of them.

Sydney was pushed forward. Two crunchy steps and she crossed from darkness into light. It was bright. She stopped, holding up a hand, giving her eyes time to adjust, sensing she was close to the edge and that if she took one more step she'd hit the ledge and topple over it.

While it was still too bright for her to see anything, she heard Billy say, "Wow. You look like an angel."

Sydney's defenses rose instantly. She was standing on the roof of a hotel in the middle of the night and this guy was hitting on her? She didn't have time for this nonsense. Cheryl was on her way to the hospital, Hunz had less than—what?—six hours left to live? If this guy had gone to all this trouble to try to pick her up, she was going to push him off the ledge herself.

Her conclusion wasn't without precedence. In Iowa City, working for the PBS station, she would get calls to interview university professors with significant scientific discoveries, or to interview a classical music celebrity, only to arrive and find there was no discovery, there was no celebrity, only some wise guy who saw her on television and wanted to meet her.

The pattern was always the same. First the compliment, then the pickup line. So she looked like an angel, huh? Not very original.

"When you were a kid," Billy said, "did you go to Sunday school?"

If that was this guy's best pickup line, he needed professional help.

"Yeah," she said. "Is that a requirement?"

Billy smiled. "Just wondered why they chose you."

"They?"

"I contacted you in LA," he said. "You didn't meet me at Hollywood Memorial. I waited."

Sydney searched for signs of mental instability or drugs. Nervous gestures. Inability to look her in the eyes. Dilated pupils. She noted none of these things. Billy was casual—if such a thing was possible standing on the ledge of a tall building in a windy city—and his speech was clear. So were his eyes.

"I was detained," she said. "You must have left by the time we got there." She thought a moment. "We went looking for you at the mission."

Stalkers never liked it when someone turned the tables on them by showing up unexpectedly at their home or work. Sydney wanted to gauge his reaction to this bit of news. If anything, Billy appeared flattered.

"Then you met Ken Overton!" He spoke as if they were at some kind of reunion.

"And Lony Mendez," Sydney said. "He told us about your prison background."

Billy Peppers beamed. He folded his arms contentedly, momentarily covering the wooden cross he wore around his neck. He was every inch what you'd expect to see in a homeless man: layers of clothing; old, worn shoes; hair and face that needed washing. One thing was different, though. A quick mind backlit friendly eyes and powered an intelligent tongue.

A gust of wind hit them suddenly, staggering Sydney and knocking Billy off balance. His eyes grew wide with fright, his arms did the windmill thing as he fought to keep from going over the side. Sydney reached for him instinctively. A chorus of male voices from the dark warned her not to do it.

Billy caught his balance. He pressed a hand to his chest as though to calm a heart gone wild. "I hate heights," he said.

"Then let's go someplace safe," Sydney said, her own heart doing triple backflips. "They have conference rooms here. I'm sure they'll let us use one. We can talk there."

Billy fixed his gaze behind her, past the lights, as if trying to discern what was behind them. "My instructions were to deliver the message to you here."

"Instructions from whom?"

"We'll get there soon enough." He paused and stared at his feet for a moment. Then he looked up. "You're looking for the terrorist who is behind the death watch tragedy."

"We have several leads."

"You're looking in the wrong places."

"How can you say that? You don't know where we're looking."

Billy smiled knowingly. "I know where you're *not* looking," he said.

"Mr. Peppers, let's get to the point. Do you know who is behind Death Watch?"

Billy caught her gaze and held it. "Yes."

"Are you going to tell me who it is?"

"He's a terrorist," Billy said. "A terrorist with an organization so strong, so widespread, it makes all other terrorist organizations look like two-bit street punks."

Something caught his eye behind her. He stared hard at it. Sydney turned to see what he was looking at.

The airport control tower. Two men were watching them with binoculars. Police? Bored air traffic controllers? It was impossible to tell from this distance. Sydney wondered how he would react if he knew that a couple dozen feet behind the lights there were men who had guns, not binoculars, trained on him.

Billy pointed at the Nike shoe box near his feet. "Look inside," he said.

The box looked innocent enough. It was an ordinary shoe box. No swastikas drawn on it. No skull and crossbones. No protruding wires. Just a regular Nike shoe box. Size ten.

She reached for it.

All manner of shouting erupted behind her from the dark, warning her not to touch the box.

She recoiled.

"It's just a shoe box," Billy said. "I keep my stuff in there. If you'd like, I'll open it."

He started to reach for the box. Sydney stopped him. There could be a gun in the box. The police would think so too. And though she couldn't be certain, she had the distinct impression that if he touched the box, he'd be shot, and she'd never know what he wanted from her.

"I'll do it." Sydney inched toward the box to a renewed doomsday chorus sung by the choir behind the lights. She touched the lid and hesitated.

He insisted it was personal items. The police suspected a bomb, or something equally dangerous. A chemical weapon? If she lifted the lid of the box and something chemical was released, this wind would spread it quickly and efficiently and there would be no way anyone could stop it.

Which was it? The safest thing to do would be to snatch the box, hold the lid down, and give it to authorities for them to examine. But if she did that, Billy probably wouldn't talk to her anymore.

He'd had it under his arm in Pasadena. Carried it like it was something personal, like he said. Or something dangerous he didn't want anyone to touch until the right moment. Which was it? But then what were the chances of a homeless man carrying around a pocket-size nuclear device or a vial of sarin gas in a Nike shoe box?

Cautiously, Sydney lifted the lid.

She let out a small yelp. Two faces stared up at her.

"My angels," Billy said.

"Yeah," Sydney said, her hand shaking. "You could have given a girl a warning."

"The book underneath," Billy said. "Get it."

Moving the figurines aside, Sydney removed the book. "It's a Bible."

"You said you went to Sunday school. Can you find the book of Job?"

"Yes."

"Find it. Chapter one. Verse six."

Sydney opened the Bible to the middle and found Psalms. From there, she tracked backward to Job.

"All right," she said. "Is this some sort of code?"

"Begin reading with verse six," Billy said.

Sydney looked around, knowing that all eyes were on her even though she couldn't see them. Because of the floodlights, everything on the page was bathed in white light, or blotted out by shadow. She adjusted her stance so the light caught the page. She began to read.

"Aloud," Billy said. "I want to hear it again."

Sydney looked up at him. She cleared her throat and began again, this time reading aloud. At first, the open space and wind swallowed her words whole. She spoke louder.

"'One day the angels came to present themselves before the LORD, and Satan also came with them. The LORD said to Satan, "Where have you come from?"

"'Satan answered the LORD, "From roaming through the earth and going back and forth in it."

"'Then the LORD said to Satan, "Have you considered my servant Job? There is no one on earth like him; he is blameless and upright, a man who fears God and shuns evil."

"'"Does Job fear God for nothing?" Satan replied. "Have you not put a hedge around him and his household and everything he has? You have blessed the work of his hands, so that his flocks and herds are spread throughout the land. But stretch out your hand and strike everything he has, and he will surely curse you to your face."

"'The LORD said to Satan, "Very well, then, everything he has is in your hands, but on the man himself do not lay a finger."

"'Then Satan went out from the presence of the LORD.

"'One day—'"

"You can stop there," Billy interrupted. He was grinning. "What do you think?"

Sydney closed the book and offered it back to him. He didn't take it, so she held it. "I think I remember reading this story in Sunday school," she said. "But what does it have to do with reality?"

"Interesting story, wouldn't you say? Satan roaming through the earth, going back and forth between earth and heaven. One minute among men, the next face-to-face with God."

Someone in the darkness coughed.

Sydney was getting impatient. She shifted her weight, jutting out a hip.

"What of it?" she said.

"The way I understand it," Billy said, "it's happened again. Another convocation. Another challenge. Another agreement."

"You're telling me Satan and God have made an agreement and the result are these death watch notices?"

"Pretty much, yeah."

Sydney was nonplussed. "Is that the best you've got? Because I'm ready to turn around and let the men with the nets and straitjackets have at you."

"Is it so hard to believe? You said you went to Sunday school."

"I did. What of it?"

"You're a Christian?"

"Yeah . . . but . . ."

"Then why are you finding it difficult to believe what I just told you? I can understand them . . ." He waved an expansive hand. "They've bought into a closed system based solely on measurable phenomenon. They've elevated mankind to the status of God. If we can't see it, or measure it, or understand it, it doesn't exist. But not you. Not Christians. The very nature of Christianity is based on the supernatural."

"So you're saying the notices, the deaths, the intricate timing, all of it is supernaturally related?"

"Natural and supernatural. The two realms coexist in time and space." He thought for a second. "Remember Elisha and his servant? They were surrounded by an army of men. The servant was afraid for his life. Elisha told him he needn't be, because those who were with them were more than those who were against them. That poor servant counted only two, himself and Elisha. So Elisha prayed, 'Lord, open his eyes,' and the next thing the servant saw was a whole host of heaven, outnumbering the army of men! Sydney, they're still here. They haven't left!"

Sydney was shaking her head. She'd heard the story before. That was something that happened a long time ago. Things were different then.

"Another one!" Billy looked down, trying to remember. He snapped his fingers a couple of times. "In Genesis. Chapter thirty-four . . . thirty-two . . . somewhere in that area, Jacob was on a journey. He stumbled into an encampment of angels. Can you imagine that? Walking into an angelic camp? That's what happened. He named the place Mahanaim. It means 'two encampments.' His and theirs."

"This is nuts!" she said.

"I'll tell you what's nuts," Billy said. "Believing in a supernatural God and not believing in the supernatural. That's nuts."

Sydney thought about that.

"I mean, Christians involve themselves in the supernatural everyday, Sydney. When we pray, aren't we praying to a Being we can't see? A Being who has revealed himself as Spirit, who inhabits a spiritual realm?"

"Now that's something I can agree to," Sydney said.

"Then you're almost there. The next step is becoming aware that the spiritual realm is nearer than you think. It's right here, Sydney. Natural and supernatural. Side by side. Sometimes touching. Sometimes overlapping. Men and angels in the same universe, sharing time and space. This is the universe God created!"

CHAPTER THIRTY-EIGHT

Surely, this couldn't be the answer. A Sunday school story? Sydney held the Bible to her chest, hugging herself, bracing against the cold Chicago wind, but more than that, against the chill of reality she felt creeping into her life.

Billy Peppers, The Rev, was trying to recruit her as an evangelist. Sydney had been in church often enough to recognize the elements of a call to service. Billy would next zap her with guilt with a long, bony finger, then they'd sing *Just as I Am*, and he'd give an invitation—a call to commitment, pressing her to make his message her message. Only, she wasn't ready to walk the aisle. While this was the most fantastic death watch story she'd heard, it was just that, a story told by an unwashed, homeless man from the streets of Los Angeles, a preacher with prison credentials.

She could just imagine Helen's reaction if she phoned in this story. Or Hunz's reaction. Or Cori's. They'd think she was nuts.

It was obvious Billy Peppers was good at his profession. He had a preacher's arsenal and knew how to use it. Knew where to aim and when to fire. But a reporter was not your typical church congregant. A good reporter should be able to sidestep the emotional arrows to get to the truth.

"Why now?" she asked him.

Billy was feeling the drop in temperature, too. He pulled close his jacket and folded his arms. "We're approaching the end of history. It'll be different than what has gone on before. History has always focused on political, economic, and social events. It's time for the spiritual to come to the forefront. Soon spiritual events will overshadow everything else. This is but the first step."

"Massive, worldwide deaths just to get people thinking about spiritual matters?"

"What's more spiritual than life and death? At birth, the spark of the spirit animates us; at death, it leaves the body."

Sydney shifted uneasily, crunching rocks beneath her feet. "Let me try it out on you," she said. "This is what you're asking me to do. You want me to go on the air and report that Satan and God had a discussion, the result of which, Satan has been granted the power of life and death, and as a consequence we have Death Watch. My source? A homeless suicidal man with pictures of angels plastered all over him."

"Oh, no!" Billy cried. "God didn't hand Satan the power of life and death. God is and always will be the giver of life."

"But people are dying!"

Her emotions rose to the surface as she said this. She couldn't help it. Cheryl and Hunz and Josh were dying!

"All men die, Sydney," Billy said. "The only thing that has changed is the timing."

"So you're telling me there's no hope."

Billy's face became radiant. "With God there's always hope, Sydney! That's the whole point. This time Satan didn't accuse one good man; he accused God of delaying the end of days needlessly, that Christians no longer believe in the power of salvation, that God's grand plan had proven itself a failure, that even if a Christian knew his neighbor was dying, he'd do nothing to save him, I mean truly save him, for all eternity. And so God said to Satan, 'All right, do your worst. Only for every death watch notice you give, you must inform two Christians.'"

Sydney's reporter senses quickened. "Two notices? Anything else?"

"The death watch notice has to be delivered in some form of printed content with an accompanying verbal contact."

Billy knew about the confirmation!

"You're saying there's no way to break the death watch cycle?"

"Of course there is. God is the source of life. Not just for eternity, but for the present."

This was unreal. Sydney stared at him. He'd tossed a lifeline in her direction and she wanted to grab it, no matter how improbable, even though her mind, her reporter's instinct, told her it was an illusion.

She remembered the colored picture of Joseph and his multicolored coat her Sunday school teacher would hold up while telling a Bible story about him and his brothers. She remembered the flannelgraph figures of Jesus and a boy and his lunch of loaves and fish which they fed to five thousand people on a hillside. What was she supposed to do? Use flannel-graph figures on the evening news?

But then, put a scientist on the ledge and have him tell her how he developed a microscopic search-and-destroy submarine that was smaller than a human hair and that could hunt down and neutralize nanobots that had been injected into a person's bloodstream, and she'd rush to the cameras, wouldn't she?

You've bought into a closed system based solely on measurable phenomenon. If you can't see it, or measure it, or understand it, it doesn't exist.

Was it so inconceivable that the realm of the spirit could affect life and death? Was human existence solely physical, affected only by the realm of science?

"So if someone who has received a death watch notice," Sydney said, "if that person is led to God . . ."

"The death watch contract would be broken," Billy said.

"As easy as that?"

"You should know there's nothing easy about salvation. If you've forgotten that, you need to read the gospel tract you were given at the mission."

He knew about that too? Sydney felt her pocket. The tract was still there.

"An angel told you?"

Billy laughed. "No. I know Lony. He doesn't let anyone leave the mission without giving them a gospel tract."

Sydney wanted to believe. More than anything she wanted to believe. It made sense, didn't it? Or had this street preacher just tapped into her Midwestern culture and sold her a bottle of snake oil?

"Can you really talk to angels?"

Billy looked at the pictures on his clothes. "I chose pictures that look like them, because after a while the image fades in my mind."

He bent down and reached inside the shoe box.

"This one's my favorite."

He pulled out a ceramic angel, its white wings flashing in the bright lights.

Billy started to straighten up. His foot slipped. His arms waved. To keep from falling, he had to grab the ledge, releasing the angel. It flew over the side of the building.

Below, there were screams.

Billy caught himself, but the angel tumbled for ten stories, smashing to smithereens on the sidewalk. Billy looked down at the white remains of his favorite angel. He was shaking.

"Oh, this is crazy. This is crazy," he said. "I put the pictures on me to remind myself that I have angels watching over me. I'm scared to death of heights. Oh, this is crazy."

Sydney held out her hand. "Then come down," she said. "Why did you climb up there in the first place?"

"We had to get your attention."

We. Again with the *we*. Despite his obvious sincerity, and his story—well, the jury was still out on that one—it was the speaking in plural that made him sound like an insane man.

"Well, you got it. I'm here. Committing suicide doesn't do much for your credibility."

"I'm not a suicide." He said it most emphatically.

"Then prove it. You've delivered your message. Your work is done. Now you can come down."

Billy thought about that. "Yeah. I like that. I've done what they asked me to do, haven't I?"

He started to get down.

Behind her, in the darkness, Sydney could hear the shuffling of feet in gravel. The instant Billy's foot stepped down off the ledge, they'd grab him.

But Billy didn't step down. He cocked his head. Listened. Then he straightened himself and turned, facing the deadly side of the ledge. He looked straight ahead, toward the runway.

As he stood there, his face changed. His cheeks, which had been quick to ball up into a laugh, fell; as did his jaw. He blinked several times. His eyes glassed over with tears. He nodded, almost imperceptibly, but Sydney saw it.

He hung his head.

"Billy?"

For several moments he stood there, wind whipping, cold. He shivered. Shuffling his feet, he turned his head to Sydney.

"You go," he said.

"Billy, take my hand. I'll help you down."

"I don't think so. I need to hang around here a little while longer."

He spoke with somber resolve like someone who had just received disturbing news.

"It's the angels, isn't it? Billy, did an angel just speak to you?"

Sydney scanned the air in front of him and saw nothing.

"Billy?"

"Take the shoe box," he said. "There's another angel in it. It's broken, but I want you to have it. The Bible too. The front pages, the blank ones. I wrote everything down I just told you on them. Maybe it'll help."

"Billy, step down from the ledge. I have someone I want you to meet. Someone with a death watch notice. You can tell him what you told me. He'll listen to you. In fact, let me put you on the air. Let me interview you. You can tell everyone. The networks will pick it up. We even have connections with EuroNet. Let me help you get your message out."

But Billy was no longer listening to her. He stood straight, his face into the night, his toes over the edge.

"Billy!"

A pair of hands grabbed Sydney's shoulders from behind, pulling her away. She wrenched free, grabbing the Nike shoe box.

Then there were more hands with stronger grips and Sydney St. James was escorted off the roof of the Hilton Hotel.

CHAPTER THIRTY-NINE

Sydney St. James stepped from the hotel lobby. As she did, she turned and looked up. They hadn't grabbed Billy yet. He was still on the ledge, staring off into the distance.

A mob of reporters on the opposite side, cordoned off by the police, shouted questions at her.

"What did he say to you?"

"Did he tell you why he was going to jump?"

"Did you try to talk him out of jumping?"

Sydney wanted to shout back at them that Billy wasn't a suicide jumper, but now she wasn't so sure. Something changed up there. One minute it was happy Billy, positive-preacher Billy, God-has-everything-under-control Billy. The next thing she knew, Billy was wearing the expression of a condemned man and his toes were curled over the ledge.

Hunz came running up to her.

"What did he say? Anything useful?"

"He knew about the confirmation call."

Hunz thought about this a moment. "He could have heard about it from someone. That was a good litmus test earlier, but now . . . I don't know, too much time has passed."

"He says everyone who's been given a death watch notice has had confirming notices sent to two different acquaintances."

"Two? That doesn't ring true. No one has been informed of my death watch notice."

"That we know of," Sydney said.

"True. That we know of. But if they'd heard something, why hadn't they contacted me?"

It was a good question. Why hadn't they at least called to see how he was doing?

"Who does he say is behind it? How are the deaths being carried out?"

Sydney glanced down. She knew the question was coming. All the way down the steps, into the elevator, through the lobby, she knew the question was coming. But she had yet to reach a conclusion as to what to tell him. While she didn't know Hunz well, she knew he didn't have Midwestern go-to-church roots. Even with her background, she found Billy's story hard to believe. What would it sound like to a man with no church background?

"Let's go somewhere we can talk," she said.

Sydney looked around. The police were done with her. No one was paying attention to her. Her debriefing had lasted the amount of time it took to walk down ten flights of stairs. They tried to take Billy's shoe box from her. After showing them what was inside, they let her keep it. In all likelihood, the man on the other end of Caplan's walkie-talkie had already filled him in.

Hunz looked around. "Yeah, let's get out of here," he said.

Leaving wasn't going to be easy. To get back to the terminal and transportation they were going to have to go through a sea of media for the second time tonight, only this time Sydney had no disguise.

Hunz offered her the crook of his arm. "Just hang onto me," he said. "I'll plow the way."

Sydney hooked her arm in his.

They ducked under the yellow police tape and hit the first row of screaming reporters. Immediately Sydney was buffeted by the strength of the human current, and she was nearly knocked off balance. She clung to Hunz with all her strength, clutching the Nike shoe box, which was tucked under one arm.

Cameras and microphones were shoved in her face. High-powered lights blinded her. It was all she could do to put one foot in front of the other and keep from stumbling.

A second later, they were completely engulfed.

"He's gonna jump!" someone cried.

The next instant, the current that threatened to engulf them changed course, the way a school of fish suddenly changes direction as though controlled by a single mind.

Hunz and Sydney turned back.

The area went dark as cameras and lights swung away from them and toward the building.

Ten stories up, Billy Peppers stood tall, feet together, arms extended outward. Military-garbed figures could be seen creeping toward him from both sides. One of them had his hand stretched out. He was talking, though no one could hear what he was saying.

Billy appeared composed. His face showed no emotion. His eyes were fixed forward on the distant horizon.

He stood like that for what seemed an eternity. His shirt and pants legs flapped in the wind, as did the angel pictures, their corners flapping furiously, as though the angels were trying to take flight.

"Billy, no . . . ," Sydney muttered.

Billy looked down at her as though he'd heard her speak. He couldn't have; she barely heard herself.

They locked eyes.

It was one of those moments where distance is irrelevant. Two people making contact with nothing but a gaze; two minds, two hearts, joined by such a powerful link that everyone else, everything else, becomes muted colors without sound or substance, and the universe is reduced to that moment.

Sydney knew she had him at that moment. She knew he wouldn't jump. The fear of heights she'd seen in his eyes before was gone. The anxiety, the urgency, gone. All that was left was serenity. Peace. She took comfort in that. He exuded the confidence of a man who had successfully completed a difficult task, who deserved a rest.

Her heart caught in her throat.

Rest. Billy had resigned himself to rest.

Eternal rest.

Billy, no!

With her eyes she willed him to live.

Billy smiled at her.

With the ease of stepping across a threshold, as casually as a person steps from one room to the next, Billy Peppers stepped off the ledge.

The crowd screamed with a single voice.

Every chin was lifted. Every eye riveted on the man who had just done the unthinkable.

With outstretched arms, Billy did a swan dive, no, an angel dive from the roof of the Hilton Hotel. The rush of wind ripped at his clothes, leaving a trail of angel pictures to flutter to the ground behind him.

He plummeted, looking more like a rag doll than a man.

Sydney couldn't bear to watch, but neither could she turn away. Then she noticed the strangest thing.

The rippling of Billy's clothing changed color from the dark green and blue of the fabric, to pale imitations of the original, then to white, finally to yellow and orange and red. The flapping fabric resembled a thousand tongues of fire.

They spread across him, curling up along the edge of his arms and torso and legs, so that after a moment or two, he looked like a NASA shuttle reentering the earth's atmosphere in a fiery blaze.

Two orbs appeared on either side of him. Brilliant white, luminescent. They took shape. Human form, arms outstretched, but also wings.

Billy's angels!

They flanked him. His descent began to slow, though the flames showed no sign of dissipating, until Billy hung midair, suspended between earth and the sky, ablaze with fire, held in the arms of angels.

So engulfed was he in flame that his body had nearly lost its shape now, but his face and eyes were still recognizable, and functioning, for they looked for Sydney and found her; and, as before, silent communication passed between them, accompanied by a huge, toothy grin.

Billy was happy. Young and vital. Boyish. Like a kid on an amusement park ride.

Then, in a sudden burst, he was gone, as were the angels. For a moment, residue, like a million fireflies, lingered, then it too was gone, and all that was left was the night, and the wind, and the glare of camera lights reflected in the glass building.

"Ooohhhhh!"

The assembled crowd let out a groan.

It wasn't a sound that accompanied fireworks. But a punch-in-the-gut groan.

People turned their heads, sickened.

It didn't make sense. What had just happened was the most amazing thing Sydney had ever seen in her life. Her skin was still tingling. What was wrong with these people?

Ten floors above, men in military garb leaned over the ledge with face-twisting grimaces. They turned away, shaking their heads.

There was similar head shaking among the people on the ground. Camera lights flicked off. A suffocating pall hung heavy in the air. People looked as though they were sick to their stomachs. They avoided eye contact with each other and walked away.

All except Hunz. He fought his way through the retreating crowd. Sydney lost him for a moment when he bent over as though he'd dropped something. He resurfaced and rushed past her.

"Where are you going?" she cried.

His eyes set on something, and determined strides carried him forward. Sydney hurried after him.

The Chicago news station had a van parked a short distance away—white, with a satellite dish on top. The station's call letters were printed in red slanted block letters on the side panel, along with smiling male and female images of their prime-time newscasters and the slogan "Bringing the Windy City News It

Can Use." The back of the van was open. Hunz charged into it like he owned it. Sydney ran as far as the steps, but couldn't seem to bring herself to go any farther. She stood outside, looking in.

There were three workers inside the van. None of them had paid any attention to Hunz, their eyes glued to a monitor that was rewinding the videotape of Billy's plunge. Between the workers' bodies, Sydney glimpsed the video image of Billy Peppers midair, parallel to the ground, arms outstretched, but he was falling upward. His feet touched the ledge and he stood upright atop the building.

Rewind completed, the man controlling the playback punched a button. The tape began to play forward.

Everyone's attention was on the monitor. One of the men shifted positions, blocking Sydney's view, making it impossible for her to see from outside the van.

She glanced around. No one seemed to be paying any attention to her. She had to see the playback—the flames, the angels, every-thing—but to barge uninvited into another station's van?

The first step was hard. After that, she didn't remember any of the other steps. The next thing she knew, she was standing behind Hunz watching the playback monitor.

On the screen, Billy leaned forward and fell. Everything hap-pened much more quickly than she remembered it. And to her astonishment, much differently!

Billy plummeted, his shirt and dreadlocks whipping, his deadly course straight and true and unhindered. The playback recorded no flames. No glow. No angels. No slowing. Nothing but air separated Billy from the ground, and not for long.

"Ooohhhhh!" The men in the truck echoed the earlier cry in the street.

"That's gotta hurt," one of them said.

They grinned at each another. That's when they realized they had company.

"Hey, who are you? You guys cops or something?"

"That's the chick on the roof!"

"Are you spying, man? That's really low!"

"Get outta here!"

Without a word, hunched over, Hunz turned to follow Sydney. With curses hitting them in the back, they climbed out of the van. The door slammed shut behind them.

Sydney was stunned. Not by the crew's outburst, but by what she'd seen on the replay. In a way it made sense, but then it didn't. At least now she understood the crowd's reaction. They saw Billy fall to his death. But she saw fire, angels, and what looked like pixie dust. They watched him die. She watched him . . . what? What did she see? Or had she really seen what she thought she saw? Had she imagined it?

"Something troubling you?" Hunz said.

The understatement of the millennia, she thought. Was she the only person who had seen angels rescuing Billy?

"Yes . . . yes, something's troubling me!" Without explaining, she ran back to the sidewalk entrance to the Hotel Hilton, ten stories directly beneath Billy's position on the ledge.

"There! That's my problem!" she shouted. "There's no body. If Billy Peppers hit the ground, where's the body?"

A uniformed police officer overheard her.

"They just carted it off," he said.

"That quickly? Not likely," Sydney said.

"How long do you think it takes to load a stiff into a truck?" the policeman said.

"But this is a crime scene!"

"A suicide. Happens all the time. That yo-yo tied up the hotel's clientele way too long. You think we're gonna leave him lyin' around the rest of the night? We'd get calls up the wazoo from every guest on this side of the hotel. Not good for the city. Best for all concerned that he disappear quickly."

Feeling desperate, Sydney scanned the area. The place where Billy's favorite ceramic angel had met its doom had been swept clean. "I don't believe you," she said. "You're covering up."

The officer laughed at her. "You reporters are all alike. A guy jaywalks and you see a conspiracy. Sheesh." He continued on his way, shaking his head.

Sydney turned to Hunz. "What did you see?"

"What do you mean?"

"Simple question. What did you see?"

She was in his face. She had to know. Never in her life had she doubted herself like this or felt this edgy. At the moment reality was a greased pig and she couldn't get a grip on it.

Hunz wasn't helping. He looked at her as though the cheese had slipped off her cracker.

"The video playback in the van?" he said. "That's what I saw. Why? What did you see?"

CHAPTER FORTY

Sydney sat at a polished wooden table in front of a large window overlooking O'Hare International Airport, her head in her hands. She moaned. Hunz had charged a suite at the Hilton to the station. He said he needed a quiet place to prepare for the upcoming broadcast, the one that would air his death scene live. With time running out, Sydney couldn't help but think he wanted the suite so he didn't have to die in a studio or on the street.

She glanced at a clock radio on the end table beside the sofa.

5:05 a.m.

Her heart lurched. It couldn't be . . . what happened to the time? She checked her watch.

3:05 a.m.

It took a moment for her tired mind to sort it out. There was two hours' difference between Los Angeles and Chicago.

Well, that little scare got the ol' heart pumping.

She considered changing her watch to local time, then decided against it. If she changed her watch, she'd also have to remember to adjust Hunz's deadline—a word that had taken on a whole new meaning since Death Watch—from 8:47 a.m. to 10:47 a.m. Best to keep things simple.

8:47 a.m. The number to remember.

She urged her tired gray cells to do the math.

Hunz had five hours and forty-two minutes left to live.

Sydney let out a sigh. It was quiet, and she was drowsy. Not many flights landing or taking off at the airport.

Did Billy Peppers have control tower clearance when he took off on angels' wings?

Aahhhh! Where had that come from?

A tired mind, that's where. What do you expect? You're half dead, dead on your feet, dead tired, dead asleep, dead to the world . . .

"Stop it," she growled to herself and stood to wake up. She rubbed tired eyes with the palms of her hands. Maybe she was going loony tunes. When she opened her eyes, would she find herself standing outside on the sidewalk? Had checking into the hotel been a dream?

Tentatively, she lowered her hands. To her relief she found herself standing beside a table on the eighth floor of the Hilton Hotel overlooking the airport runway. She was alone. None of Mel Blanc's loony friends were in the room with her.

With a sigh, she risked sitting down.

Hunz had gone to get coffee. None of that foil-packet hotel brew for him. He wanted the real stuff. He'd seen a coffee shop in the lobby, an all-nighter for true addicts, and went to check it out. He asked her if she wanted anything—a scone, cookie, brownie. What she wanted was forty winks, but she was pretty sure they didn't sell winks by the cup.

Sydney tried calling the hospital to get an update on Cheryl. The only information the hospital would confirm to someone who wasn't a relative was that Cheryl had checked in and that she didn't have a phone in her room. Sydney tried Josh's cell phone and got the standard automated voice message informing her that the phone was either out of range or turned off.

She slumped back in her chair and stared at the Chicago skyline on the horizon. She hated it when life was reduced to being alone and waiting. It wasn't good to give an active and frightened mind that much freedom.

Billy Peppers's shoe box lay on the table in front of her. The white Nike wing dominated a side that was slightly caved in. All four corners of the top were worn and cardboard gray. The box had obviously seen some mileage.

Sydney lifted the lid. Looking up at her was a ceramic angel on his back. Or was it a her? In all the stories she'd heard in Sunday school, angels acted and sounded male. Yet she seemed to remember hearing something about angels having no gender. This angel wore a pale blue unisex robe and he looked perturbed, if not angry. Maybe he was angry because half of his right foot was gone.

The face of the ceramic angel looked nothing like Billy's angels. Billy's angels appeared to be having fun, swooping out of nowhere . . .

"Expressions!" Sydney shouted. "I remember their expressions! If they weren't real, how come I remember their expressions so vividly?"

It wasn't profound, but it was something.

There was a bump at the door. Not a knock. It was too much of a thud to be a knock.

Sydney rose and peered through the security peephole. A distorted Hunz stood on the other side holding a cup of coffee in each hand and clenching a white bag with his teeth.

She opened the door.

"Faannx," Hunz said.

Crossing the room, he set the coffee cups on the table, double jumbo size from the looks of them, and took the bag from his mouth.

"Got myself a cinnamon roll," he said. "Figure, why not? It's not like I have to watch my waistline anymore."

Death-row humor. Sydney smiled halfheartedly.

Hunz fell into the chair opposite her seat and leaned his head back. His eyes closed, but not for long. Pulling himself forward, he checked his watch, then pried the lid off one coffee. Two days ago, glancing at one's watch was a casual act; now, it was no different than a demolitions expert checking the clock of a ticking time bomb.

"If you want," Hunz said, "you can lie down for a while in the bedroom. You look like you're asleep on your feet."

. . . *dead tired, dead asleep, dead to the world* . . .

"No, I'm all right," Sydney said.

She sat down. He shoved her coffee closer to her. On the side of the container there was a checkmark in the box next to the word *latte*. Sydney lifted the lid and was greeted by the warm odor of milky coffee.

"Don't know why you'd want to ruin a perfectly good cup of coffee by dumping all that froth in it," Hunz said.

He drank his black.

Sydney pulled the cup closer. She didn't drink any. The coffee stores always made it too hot. She was used to waiting for it to cool. She stared at the creamy brown swirls and wondered how to begin telling Hunz Vonner what she needed to tell him.

"You're not going to make it as a reporter," Hunz said.

She looked up. He was staring at her.

"That's a cruel thing to say," she said. "Something I'd expect to hear from Cori Zinn."

"Wasn't meant to be unkind, just stating a fact."

"You haven't even seen me in front of a camera. You haven't read any of my copy, or seen any of my video clips. All you've seen me do these last two days is drive you all over Los Angeles, and from that you pass judgment on my professional skills?"

"I've seen enough." Hunz sat back in his chair and sipped his coffee. His cinnamon roll lay atop the white bag on the table, largely uneaten.

Sydney wondered how many condemned men when served their last meal clean their plates.

"All right," Sydney said, returning to the topic. "Tell me. Upon what exactly are you basing your opinion?"

"You're angry," Hunz said. "I didn't mean to make you angry. Let's just forget I said anything."

"Oh, no! You said it, now defend it. What makes you think I don't have what it takes to be a reporter?"

Hunz took another sip. "Let's get to work. Tell me what Billy Peppers said to you on the roof."

"No. You're going to tell me why you think I won't make a good reporter."

Hunz stared at her, exasperated.

Fine. Let him be exasperated. They weren't moving on to the next topic until he gave her an answer. She had more time to kill than he did.

Sydney cringed inwardly. She couldn't believe she'd just thought that. Yes, she was tired, but that was just cruel.

"Fine, I'll tell you," Hunz said. "You're too kind."

Now she cringed visibly.

"Don't pretend you're not," Hunz insisted. "Naturally, no reporter wants to hear that they're kind, but you are. You can't help it. It's part of who you are."

"Hunz . . ."

"Step back and look at yourself objectively. Look at what you did for Lyle Vandeveer, what you're doing for Cheryl. With both of them, there came a point when they were no longer a story to report. There came a point when you were more concerned for them as persons than you were about doing your job as a reporter.

"And again, with Billy Peppers. A good reporter couldn't have gotten down from that roof fast enough to get the story on the air. A good reporter would have been secretly—some outwardly— thrilled that he jumped, because it makes a better story.

"And now, here. Look at us. Sitting, drinking, chatting. If you were a good reporter, you'd be pumping me with questions: What was I thinking about just hours from death? If I could say something to the terrorists behind Death Watch, what would I say to them? How does it feel to come to America only to be handed a death sentence? Why did you choose a cinnamon roll for your last meal? But you haven't asked any of those questions. Why? Because you're more concerned about me than you are about getting the story."

An uneasy silence settled between them.

"I have a question for you," Sydney said. "Reporter to condemned man."

"Too late. If I hadn't goaded you into it, you wouldn't be asking questions."

"Not true. I was thinking about this question before you started evaluating my performance."

Hunz was skeptical, but he said, "Go ahead. Ask your question."

"Are you going to finish that cinnamon roll?"

It was probably the combination of being tired and being a few hours from death, but the question struck them both as hilarious. They laughed until tears came.

CHAPTER
FORTY-ONE

3:36 a.m. (PST)

Hunz Vonner had five hours, eleven minutes left to live.

"Billy wrote everything down in the front of his Bible." Sydney pulled the black leather-bound book from beneath the angel in the shoe box. She laid it open between them.

"He wrote it down?" Hunz said. "He could have saved us all a lot of time by faxing the information to you."

Sydney took a deep breath. There was no turning back now. Billy's supernatural explanation to Death Watch would soon be on the table.

She anticipated a negative reaction. The stuff of fairy tales. A story worthy of the brothers Grimm. And as persuasive as Billy Peppers had been on the roof, a few hours ago, she might have agreed with him. But that was before Billy's plunge.

How could she tell Hunz what she saw?

"The way Billy described it to me on the roof," she began, "the human race is on the cusp of a new spiritual age, where matters of the spirit will soon take center stage."

"Matters of the spirit . . . what does he mean by that? Ghosts and demons?"

"Here, let me show you."

Reaching for the Bible, she read the Job passage to him, where Satan makes an appearance in God's court. Then, though it took her awhile to find this one, she read to him the passage in Genesis where Jacob stumbled upon the encampment of angels.

"Peppers was definitely fixated on angels." Hunz studied the surviving ceramic angel. "Look at the way he covered himself with pictures of them."

Sydney closed the Bible. Hunz picked it up, turning to Billy's notes.

"Doesn't it strike you as simplistic to blame Satan, the original bad guy, for all this?" he said flatly. "People have been blaming him for every evil event since the dawn of history."

Sydney gave no reply; Hunz appeared to have his mind made up.

"The question is why," he said. "Why would Satan do this? Just because he's evil, or does he have something to gain from the slaughter of a massive number of innocent people?"

"That part's fuzzy for me," Sydney said. "Something about proving that God's plan for humankind had gone south, that God had overestimated the goodness of man, that if a man knew his neighbor was dying, he wouldn't do anything to help him. That's why the confirmation notices to two acquaintances. Two Christians."

Hunz listened as he read. "So, according to Billy Peppers, two Christians have been notified that I've received the Death Watch?"

"Yeah. But so far, you've not heard from anyone, have you?"

"Proving the Devil's point, so it would seem."

"That's not fair," Sydney said. "You've been out of the country. Who's to say they haven't tried to contact you?"

Hunz gave her an amused smile before returning to Billy's notes.

"How do we break the Death Watch, did he say, or is this all gloom and doom? How does one battle the Devil? Make a donation to a rescue mission? Enlist a priest to do an exorcism? My head's not going to spin around, is it?"

Now Sydney knew he wasn't taking this seriously.

"You've been watching too many movies," she said. "And I doubt Billy Peppers came all the way to Chicago just to take an offering."

Sydney reached into her pocket. She tossed the crumpled salvation tract onto the table.

"You have to get right with God," she said.

Hunz picked up the tract and examined it. The name and address of the mission was stamped on the back.

"You mean, I have to find Jesus. Get saved. Hallelujah, glory to God, and all that stuff."

"Pretty much."

He tossed the tract back at her.

"I don't buy it."

"Why?"

"Because that would mean the crazy evangelicals were right all along, and that's unacceptable to me."

CHAPTER FORTY-TWO

Cheryl McCormick watched from her hospital bed as Dr. Lewis Boscacci wrote on her chart.

"Your blood pressure is elevated, not to the point of concern, and certainly not unusual considering the circumstances. Your blood work came back negative and the baby's heartbeat is strong."

Dr. Boscacci had been Cheryl's OB/GYN doctor for a little more than six months. He came with the insurance package. With black hair and a substantial nose befitting his ancestry, Boscacci was one of those doctors who was pretty much all business. Prenatal checkups had been brief. He spoke to her through the clipboard. In, out, on to the next patient.

Cheryl lay beneath the covers in a hospital gown, her bed cranked up to a sitting position. Her clothes hung in a plastic bag on the handle of the closet door along with her purse.

Josh sat in a chair against the wall. Next to him, on a makeshift bed of pillows and blankets on the floor, Stacy slept.

The clock on the wall read 5:38 a.m.

The room was bright, as was the hallway. It was still dark outside the window. At the moment, all was quiet at Prentice Women's Hospital, though ten minutes ago a wailing woman had passed by the open door, wheeled into delivery with nurses, doctors, and a man in street clothes—presumably the father—running beside her, all of them talking at once.

"Everything looks good," Dr. Boscacci said to the chart.

"When will you induce labor?" Cheryl asked.

Boscacci didn't answer immediately. He continued writing. Then, clipping the pen in his pocket, he hugged the chart.

Talking to the foot of the bed, he said, "We're not."

"Cesarean?" Cheryl asked. "Why? Is something . . ."

"I anticipate a normal delivery in about a month."

Josh sat up.

"Dr. Boscacci," Cheryl said, "I thought I made myself clear—"

"There is no medical reason to take the baby now," the doctor said. "It would be irresponsible to do so."

"Doctor, I have one day left to live. I don't want my baby extracted from my dead body. The risk is too great. Surely you realize that."

"Mrs. McCormick," the doctor said with forced patience, "you're not dying." He looked at the chart again, lifting several pages. "I have examined your records. You're a healthy woman."

"Josh. In my purse. There's an envelope with my name on it. Would you get it for me, please?"

Josh jumped up and dug into Cheryl's purse. It was odd to watch a man she'd known for only a few hours rummage through her purse.

He handed the envelope to Cheryl, who gave it to the doctor.

Boscacci read the death watch notice. He shook his head. "I wouldn't worry about this, if I were you."

Cheryl stared in disbelief, with color rising in her neck and cheeks. "Not worry about it?" she said, a little too loudly. A scowling nurse appeared at the door and closed it.

"You are a healthy woman," Boscacci repeated.

"Are you aware of what that is?" Josh said, coming to Cheryl's aid. "Or have you had your head stuck in the sand for the last two days?"

"I've seen the news reports," Boscacci said. "Mass hysteria, that's all it is. I assure you, Mrs. McCormick, you will not die."

"Well, I'm going to need more than your assurances," Cheryl shouted. "I want this baby out of me."

The doctor placed the death watch letter on the bed. "I will not authorize it," he said. "But, if you insist, I will admit you for twenty-four hours. Should anything happen, you will be surrounded by medical personnel who are trained to handle every emergency. But I'm only doing this because of your near-hysterical state." He wrote on the chart. "I will also insist you have a psych consult."

"I want another doctor," Cheryl said.

Boscacci's eyes hardened. One more time he wrote on the chart. "Very well. I will ask Dr. Isaacs to look in on you in the morning for a second opinion."

The door swung closed behind him as the last syllable of his last word sounded.

Josh stood beside the bed helplessly. "I can't believe that guy."

"Thanks for being here," Cheryl said.

She held out her hand. Josh seemed eager to take it. He gave her hand a reassuring squeeze, then let go. But she didn't let go of him. His hand was warm. Comforting. It surprised her how much she needed the touch of another human being right now.

"I can't believe how kind you've been," she said. "We haven't known each other for a day and yet you flew halfway across the country with me, and now you're here in the hospital with me."

Josh shrugged. "If we're going to lick this thing, we've got to stick together."

He looked at her with understanding, as only another person living in death's shadow could do.

"Stay with me?" Cheryl said. "I'm scared."

"Shaquille O'Neal couldn't muscle me out of here," he said.

CHAPTER
FORTY-THREE

I take offense to your remark about crazy evangelicals," Sydney said to Hunz. "I am one."

"Really?" Hunz said, surprised. "I never would have guessed."

Sydney didn't know how to take his comment. Was it a compliment or an indictment? She raised her chin a notch. "I was raised in an evangelical church."

"Huh. I just can't see you standing at airports handing out gospel tracts."

"I've never done that."

"Isn't that what evangelicals do?"

Memories of witness-training sessions came flooding back to Sydney. She had attended her fair share of personal evangelism classes, each with a different approach. One had taught her to create opportunities by asking a provocative question: "If you were to die right now and God were to ask you, 'Why should I let you into my heaven?' what would you tell him?" Another class advocated the use of a tract similar to the one Lony had given her. She was taught to read the tract aloud. Four steps led to a prayer of decision. Then there was the approach that tied witnessing to other activities, like visiting first-time guests, holding neighborhood block parties, doing door-to-door canvassing, or inviting people to Bible study.

As with most people who attended these training sessions, Sydney liked the thought of being able to represent her faith if called upon. However, when it came time to actually go visiting or knock on doors, inevitably she came down with an acute case of timidity.

She compared her training to CPR lessons. It was something that was good to know, but something you hoped you never had to use.

Like now. World-renown newscaster Hunz Vonner was sitting across the table from her asking about her personal faith. Why was she so nervous about telling him?

"Actually," Sydney said, taking up the gospel tract, "if Billy Peppers is right—just assuming for the moment that he is—and the Death Watch is a spiritual assault, then this tract pretty much outlines what a person would have do in order to . . . well, the term is to be saved, that's pretty much the evangelical . . . well, actually the Bible, lingo. In this case, though, it would be the way to . . . well, to break the power of the Death Watch."

She never once looked at Hunz as she spoke, focusing instead on the tract in her hands.

"Sydney St. James, are you trying to proselytize me?" Hunz asked.

Sydney sat up, her eyes wide. His was no small accusation. She could get fired for doing what she'd just done. The network had strict rules against proselytizing.

"We . . . we were talking about Billy Peppers," she stammered. "You asked what he said about the Death Watch and . . . well, naturally, in such a discussion . . ."

Hunz laughed at her.

"Relax," he said. "I'm not going to turn you in. I just wanted to see you squirm."

"I . . . well, I . . . you can do what you want," she said. "You asked me. I told you. Simple as that."

Hunz was still smiling at her even as he sipped his coffee. Merry eyes peered at her over the rim of his cup.

"We didn't go to church when I was growing up," he said. "I was thirteen when the Wall came down. I was raised on the Communist side. The State, the Party, was everything. I grew up in the youth organizations. We saluted, marched, sang songs that glorified

Communism. Our god was the land and the Communist philoso-phy. We had churches. Only a handful of people attended them. They were viewed as weak-minded and superstitious, people to be pitied. The first time I stepped into a church, I was twenty-two years old. A wedding. An old friend."

He smiled warmly at the remembrance.

"An old girlfriend, actually," he said, laughing. "She said I was too intense for her. Too work-oriented. Can you imagine that?"

."If I try real hard," Sydney said.

"Had I done it any differently, I wouldn't be where I am today."

"Do you regret losing her?"

Hunz grinned at his coffee cup, which he twirled in his hands.

"I never knew how much I missed her until I met you," he said. "You remind me of her."

That was certainly unexpected. Sydney didn't know what to do with it. All she knew was that it brought warmth to her cheeks.

"To some degree your appearance," Hunz said, "but mostly your outlook on life. Strong, yet always feminine. Compassionate. Caring."

"You said she got married in a church."

Hunz nodded. "That was the other reason I lost her. She met a man who spoke to her of spiritual things. She converted, and that made the gap between us even wider."

."She became a Christian?"

"It lit her up, is that an expression?"

"It's an expression."   .

"It made me angry to think that a mythical philosophy could steal her away from me. Angrier still to think that it could make her happier than I could make her, that she would choose it over me."

Sydney listened. Sometimes you interact, and sometimes you just listen. The tone of Hunz's voice indicated this was a soliloquy, not a dialogue.

What struck Sydney was how much the man delivering the soliloquy had changed in just the last few moments. Hunz Vonner, media celebrity, had left the room; in his place was Hunz, the man. It was as though he'd shed a suit of armor to reveal flesh and blood beneath all the polish and shine.

"To tell you the truth, I haven't given God much thought since then," Hunz said, "which makes these last few hours that much more puzzling." He grew animated. "Think about it. Just for the sake of argument, let's say Billy Peppers is on to something. What I want to know is, what is Satan's strategy? He has the whole populated world to choose from. Why Cheryl McCormick? Why Lyle Vandeveer? Why Josh Leven?"

"Why you?"

"It doesn't make sense that, given the scenario that's been described to us, Satan would respond with a lethal lottery. If indeed there is a battle between him and God, he'd eliminate people in order to gain a strategic advantage, wouldn't he? So the question is: What threat am I to him? What threat is Cheryl?"

"I'm afraid I don't have—"

"And then there's the other side of this celestial drama," Hunz said. "Why Billy Peppers? Who's going to believe a street preacher convict who carries around a shoe box full of angels? And why was Billy Peppers so insistent on delivering his message to you?"

"He said the angels told him—"

"There you are," Hunz said. "Back to all this angel nonsense again."

He was breathing heavily now. Worked up. He dug into his pocket.

"And how do you explain this?" he said, tossing Billy Peppers's cross onto the table, the one he wore around his neck.

"Where did you get that?" Sydney cried.

"It fell to the ground when he jumped."

Sydney examined it. There was no doubt it was Billy's cross.

Hunz leaned forward, both arms on the table. "And when he fell, why was it that you and I were the only ones who saw him—"

"You saw it!" Sydney shouted.

"I don't know what I saw," Hunz said. "Flames. Two men, one on each side . . ."

"Billy's angels," Sydney said with tears.

"Why didn't anyone else see that? Why didn't the cameras record it?"

"You lied to me! You said you saw him fall."

"Of course I lied to you!" Hunz shouted. "Because what we saw is crazy!"

CHAPTER
FORTY-FOUR

7:00 a.m. (CST)

Cheryl was still holding Josh Leven's hand when Dr. Amos Isaacs shoved the door open, talking, walking, and reading Cheryl's chart as he entered the room.

Josh had pulled a chair beside the bed. When the doctor entered, he released his grip and stood up to step aside. Cheryl tightened her grip. She felt stronger holding it.

"Mrs. McCormick," said Dr. Isaacs, looking up. "I understand you want a consult."

Isaacs was of average height, portly, with reddish-blonde hair so thin, you had to look twice to see how neatly he'd combed it over. Fatherly eyes peered over a pair of reading glasses, and he wore a genial expression that had undoubtedly served him well over the years.

He seemed surprised to see Josh.

"Mr. McCormick. I didn't expect you to be here at this hour of morning." He noticed Stacy asleep on the floor. "I see the whole family's here."

Cheryl spoke up before Josh could correct him.

"Doctor, you're mistaken if you think I want a consult," she said. "What I want is to deliver my baby while I'm still alive."

Her directness caused Isaacs to blink. He checked the chart again, flipping pages. "I don't understand. I see nothing on your chart to cause alarm, Mrs. McCormick. Why do you think you're dying?"

She told him about the death watch notice.

"Ah!" He smiled and nodded in a fatherly though condescending way. He furrowed his brow as if pondering a deep thought. "What can I do to convince you that you're not going to die?" he said.

"You can tell me you've solved the mystery of Death Watch," she said.

"I've solved the mystery of Death Watch," he said.

Stunned. At first, Cheryl didn't know what to say. Finally, she managed, "You have?"

"You have?" Josh echoed.

It was too much to hope for. Cheryl's heart beat freely, as though the cords that had bound it for the last twenty-four hours had suddenly been cut.

"Really?" she said.

"Really," Dr. Isaacs assured her.

Cheryl stared up at Josh; he stared down at her. They must have looked like a couple of grinning monkeys, but Cheryl didn't care. For the first time since Los Angeles, she felt hope, and it felt good. It felt so good, it surprised her.

Until yesterday she hadn't realized the effect hope had on a life. She had to lose it to appreciated it, much the same way a person takes her internal organs for granted; but let one of them stop working . . .

And now Isaacs—bless his heart—had revived the invisible organ that dispensed hope, and she was whole again.

She could see beyond tomorrow, a week, a year, decades into the future. She could see Stacy growing up, going to school, falling in love, having children. She would get to know Stacy's little sister or brother. She could look forward to getting to know Josh better, to . . . well, it was too soon to go down that road, but that was the point, wasn't it? She would be going down that road. She would see where it led.

Cheryl had her life back. And Josh, too.

"Oh, Dr. Isaacs, you don't know what this means to me!" she cried. "This is wonderful news! What needs to be done? Is it a painful procedure?"

Dr. Isaacs smiled. He wrote on her chart. "In your case, nothing. It's already been done. Have a good day, Mrs. McCormick."

He turned to leave.

"Wait!" Josh cried.

A single word, and just like that Cheryl found herself back on the edge of the precipice. She felt his alarm. He'd communicated it through their linked hands. She shared it.

Isaacs turned back.

"You said nothing needs to be done," Josh said.

"That's correct."

"How about for me? I have the Death Watch too."

Isaacs smiled. "I suggest you consult your physician."

"Dr. Isaacs," Cheryl said. "Let me put it to you another way. How many death watch patients have you saved?"

Isaacs fidgeted. And with that fidget, Cheryl's fledgling hope died a stillborn death.

The fatherly tone returned. "Mrs. McCormick . . ."

"Just answer her question," Josh said. "How many death watch patients have you treated that have lived past the appointed time of death?"

"Mr. McCormick, there is no need to—"

"The name is Josh. Josh Leven."

Isaacs raised an eyebrow. "You're no relation to this woman? Mr. Leven, is it? I must insist you leave. You are in violation of hospital policy. Visiting hours—"

"They've all died, haven't they?" Cheryl said.

Isaacs made a show of dipping into his reserve of patience.

"They died because they all had preexisting conditions," he said. "Wolff-Parkinson-White syndrome, hypertension, arteriosclerosis, adrenocortical carcinoma. You, on the other hand, are a healthy young woman. To put your baby at needless risk at this stage of pregnancy would be foolhardy and criminal."

Cheryl was squeezing Josh's hand so hard, he squirmed. "Doctor Isaacs," she said, "one way or another, this baby is coming out today."

She wanted to say more, but she was already close to losing control and she was afraid additional words would open the floodgates.

All traces of Isaacs's fatherly image vanished.

Sternly, he said, "Mrs. McCormick, you are emotional and irrational. This fixation you have regarding death makes you a threat to yourself and your unborn child. Now, I've tried to be patient. I've tried to reason with you. But you persist in being irrational, leaving me no choice but to confirm Dr. Boscacci's recommendation of a psych consult. I warn you: If you persist in this unreasonable behavior, or attempt to leave this hospital before a psychological evaluation can be administered, we will be forced to restrain you physically to keep you from harming yourself or your unborn child. Do I make myself clear? As for you . . ." He pointed a sausage-fat finger at Josh. "Either leave these premises, or I will have you forcibly removed."

It was a hit-and-run threat. Isaacs was out the door before either Cheryl or Josh could respond.

For a time, neither of them spoke. Having hope handed to them and then jerked back like some kind of bad practical joke left them numb.

"Maybe I should . . . ," Josh said.

"Please don't go," Cheryl said. She pulled his hand against her cheek. Her tears fell on it.

"I was going to say that maybe I should check on Stacy. But I can see from here, she's still asleep."

Josh Leven sat down in the chair beside Cheryl's bed.

CHAPTER FORTY-FIVE

5:30 a.m. (PST)
The red digital numbers on the hotel radio clock read 7:30 a.m.
Sydney turned its face to the wall. The two-hour differential gave
her heart a start every time she looked at it.

According to her watch, Hunz had three hours and seventeen
minutes to live.

Sydney told herself not to look at her watch so frequently. She
couldn't help it. But with each time check, she died a little herself.

She was alone in the room. Hunz had retreated to the bedroom.
He said he needed to do some things, make some calls. Sydney
didn't pry. Not because she'd known him for such a short time—it
was amazing how quickly you could get to know someone when you
share a crisis—but because of the shortness of time. A man with
only hours to live should be allowed to call the shots. Lyle Vandeveer had welcomed company; Hunz wanted to be alone.

He took his cell phone into the bedroom with him, and Billy's
Bible. Sydney had circled a verse on Lony's tract and inserted it into
the Bible like a bookmark. Before closing the door he mentioned he
wanted to touch base with EuroNet, to see if they had any more
leads. He'd already told them of his Death Watch, and they had
arranged to carry a live feed from the American network.

He'd also told Sydney there were a couple of people he wanted
to call.

Before I die.

He didn't say those last three words. The inevitable didn't have
a voice. It didn't need one.

Though she didn't say anything to him, Sydney hoped one of Hunz's calls would be placed to his father. And she couldn't help but wonder if he'd call his old girlfriend. Married or not, she'd want to know, wouldn't she?

Meanwhile, Sydney occupied her time by taking care of business. A conference call with Sol and Helen ruled out the possibility of an on-the-air report regarding the Billy Peppers incident.

As Sol put it, "The suicide of a religious fruitcake isn't newsworthy. And the sooner people forget his request to speak to a reporter from our station, the better. We don't want viewers associating us with that kind of religious fringe element."

He came to his conclusion based on the videotape of Billy's fall—both Sol and Helen had seen it—and Sydney's account of what took place on the roof.

Sydney didn't tell them what she and Hunz alone had seen. It bothered her that she didn't tell them. But every time she played out the telling in her mind, it sounded like something out of a Ray Bradbury science fiction novel.

Besides, if she linked Hunz to some kind of angelic appearance now, she was afraid they might think twice about putting him on the air in a couple of hours. They might conclude he was mentally or emotionally unstable. Better to say nothing for now, though she didn't feel good about it.

It fell upon Sydney to make the final arrangements with WBBT, the network affiliate in Chicago, for a film crew. A woman with a soothing voice confirmed that the crew would arrive an hour before airtime. She sounded more like a receptionist for a mortuary than a news station. She said they were sending a makeup person too.

The combination of voice and mention of makeup spawned an image in Sydney's mind of an open coffin with the corpse wearing a thick layer of cosmetics, as they often do. It takes a lot of effort to make death presentable. Sydney couldn't shake the feeling the network was so worried about the appearance of the soon-to-be-dead that they were sending a mortuary cosmetician to ensure that Hunz would be presentable.

Brushing aside the thought like a cobweb, Sydney gave the woman at the station the hotel room number.

The arrangements made, there was little for her to do but wait.

She stared at the closed bedroom door. A part of her knew it was best to respect Hunz's wishes. But there was another part of her that wanted to go in there, to do something, to say something that would ease his suffering.

Defying herself, Sydney looked at her watch. She couldn't help herself. She remembered doing the same thing sitting next to Lyle . . .

We celebrated too soon!

Going to the phone, Sydney called the front desk. She asked for the exact time, to the second. The desk clerk gave it to her.

"What's your source?" she asked.

"Excuse me?"

"What instrument are you using? Is it accurate?"

"We have a clock in the lobby, ma'am."

"Not good enough. I need the exact time. Get me the naval observatory."

"Ma'am?"

It took some explaining, and then longer for the desk clerk to find a phone number, but eventually he gave her the phone number for time, the National Institute of Standards and Technology.

She placed the call. Just as she'd feared. Her watch was a minute and four seconds fast.

Correcting the digital readout of the minute was easy enough, but she didn't know how to adjust for the errant four seconds. She called the automated time number three more times, just to make sure her watch wasn't gaining or losing seconds.

The four-second differential held.

Hunz's official death watch time was now 8:47 a.m. and four seconds.

Sydney's heart was racing.

At first it seemed absurd that it would be. She'd set her watch hundreds of times before without anxiety, but add death to the operation and everything changed.

A phrase came to mind.

When time shall be no more.

She didn't know why it came to mind, or from where. A hymn? The Bible? She couldn't remember. She did know, however, that it was a phrase she associated in some way with church.

When time shall be no more.

Poor watchmakers. Eternity will put them out of business. But then, who would want to keep time in paradise? And for those not in paradise, where time would drag insufferably, they wouldn't want to be reminded constantly of the time, would they?

"For an eternity," Sydney said aloud.

Another thought came to mind. Another link to something she'd heard in church.

Do not be afraid of those who kill the body but cannot kill the soul. Rather, be afraid of the One who can destroy both soul and body in hell . . .

"For eternity," Sydney said again.

She was certain that was in the Bible somewhere. But where? Hunz needed to see that verse too. But where to begin looking?

All men die, Sydney.

Suddenly, she understood what Billy had been trying to tell her. It was not what happened at 8:47 a.m. and four seconds that was important, but what happened after, when time was no more.

All this outcry over Death Watch. It was absurd, wasn't it? All the media attention. All the panic. Nations scrambling for an answer, a solution.

All men die.

Do not be afraid of those who kill the body. Fear the One who can destroy both body and soul.

Why the outrage over something that threatens the part of man that grows old and decays? Where was the outrage over the threat against the part of man that is timeless?

I'll tell you what's nuts. Believing in a supernatural God and not believing in the supernatural.

Sydney went to the table by the window. She stared out at a world that was being tricked, diverted into placing too much emphasis on the wrong death.

Then she did something she'd been too busy to do for years.

Sydney prayed.

CHAPTER
FORTY-SIX

With two hours and forty-four minutes remaining on Hunz Von-ner's life clock, at 6:03 a.m., Sydney turned on the television.

Death Watch dominated the airwaves. Reruns of *Family Ties* and *Cheers* were preempted by special reports featuring terrorism specialists who gave updates on the latest developments—which meant they rehashed old news—and psychologists who advised parents how to talk to their children about death and terrorists.

In the bottom right-hand corner of every station in every region of the country, the Homeland Securities Awareness system indicated the nation was now on Level Four, the highest alert. Terrorist attack was imminent.

A news segment aired on WBBT. The morning anchor, a middle-aged brunette, looked more like some kid's mother than a media professional. However, she had a warmth and sincerity that came across nicely, and to Sydney, it was obvious why the station had hired her. People tended to adopt news personalities into their families, and this woman had "understanding friend" written all over her.

Reports of death watch—related deaths are coming in from all over the world.

Sydney had turned the television on too late to get the woman's name.

In Italy, a young couple, both nineteen years old, committed suicide by jumping from the fifth floor of the Leonardi Edera Hotel in historic Rome. The police found a note in their room in which they compared themselves to Romeo and Juliet. The young Romeo was a death watch recipient with less than an hour to live. His Juliet wrote, "I refuse to live in a world without my true love."

The news anchor paused, moved with motherly emotion for the young lovers.

And closer to home, in Peoria, Illinois, veteran storyteller Homer Blakely, a nationally acclaimed, award-winning storyteller, fell dead just as he was completing his story, "Terror at the Top of the Stairs." Blakely, a regular at the Chinquapin Folk Music and Storytelling Festival, which is held annually at Camp Wokanda, was performing at the Ghost Story Concert. According to eyewitness reports, he was just about to reveal the terror that lurked at the top of the stairs of his childhood home when he fell over dead. A death watch notice was found in his pocket.

Meanwhile, around the world, reports attributed to the death watch terror continue to escalate at staggering proportions, prompting several countries to declare themselves under attack, while here at home, the president has scheduled a national address for this evening. It is believed he will at that time explain the rationale behind raising the Homeland Security Awareness system from Level Three to Level Four, the highest level possible, indicating severe conditions. This will be the first time in our nation's history the risk level has been set at Level Four.

And finally, here in Chicago, another first. Visiting international newscaster Hunz Vonner, on assignment from EuroNet news, will broadcast a live death watch Special Event from the Hilton Hotel at O'Hare International Airport. Vonner, a death watch victim, will share the thoughts of a dying man as the clock counts off the final minutes of his life. This WBBT Special Event will be the first live broadcast of a death watch death aired on national television. Here, on WBBT at 10:00 a.m.

The newscaster pursed her lips with distaste before handing the news to the weatherman. Sydney knew how she felt.

"It'll make a splash," she said flatly, turning the television off.

6:50 a.m.
One hour, fifty-seven minutes remaining.

Sydney sat on the French sofa staring at the bedroom door. She hadn't heard a sound come from the other side in the last thirty minutes.

Hunz's muffled voice had fallen silent. Earlier she could hear him talking, not clear enough to make out what he was saying, but the pattern of speech and pausing suggested he was on the phone.

Every now and then he'd laugh. Sometimes his tone was conciliatory. Somber. Then his tone would change, indicating another call, another person. Sydney found herself wondering who was on the other end of the line with each change, sort of a mix-and-match game, pairing voice tone with the people Hunz had told her about.

She chastised herself for listening, but she couldn't stop herself. At one point she thought he was talking to his old girlfriend, but she couldn't be sure. It started out lighthearted, turned to melancholy, then almost apologetic.

On a previous call, he bordered on anger. His father? A coworker? A friend? Hunz never mentioned any of his friends. Probably like her, he didn't have many outside the industry. Contacts, for the most part. Sources. People you could spend an enjoyable evening with, but not anyone you would consider a friend.

And now the other side of the door had fallen silent. Sydney ached to cross the room and knock on it.

Just to see if he was all right.

But the strength of her desire was far greater than mere casual concern. It bordered on compulsion.

She wanted to talk to him before the camera crew arrived, to tell him about the Scripture verse she'd remembered, the one about not fearing the one who could kill the body, but fearing the One who could kill the soul.

She wanted to make sure he understood about the second death.

That phrase came to her often now, unboxed for the occasion from somewhere in the attic of her mind. Probably from a sermon she'd heard. She wanted to warn him of the greater danger.

All men die, Sydney.

She knew the truth of that now. Billy was right. All this death watch hoopla was a clever diversion from the real threat.

All men die.

Yet look at all the time and effort and money and resources that go into postponing death, postponing the inevitable. Compare that to how few resources go into warning about the second death. The one that counts. Everyone was so concerned about the pop quiz, they weren't preparing for the final exam.

Sydney stood, crossed the suite to the bedroom door, and lifted a hand to knock. Gently. More of a suggestion of a knock than a real knock.

But before her knuckle hit wood, she heard Hunz's voice from the other side.

"Helmut! Hunz . . . Ja . . ." Then he began rattling off German sentences, none of which Sydney understood.

She lowered her hand and retreated to the sofa.

CHAPTER FORTY-SEVEN

The WBBT crew arrived while the bedroom door was still closed, 7:30 a.m. according to Sydney's watch.

One hour, seventeen minutes remained.

There were three of them. Phil, the cameraman. Dorian, the soundman. And Joanna, to do the makeup.

Dorian, a round-faced, good-natured African American in a Hawaiian shirt, seemed to be the one in charge. He made the introductions and asked Sydney where to set up. She asked them to wait a moment and knocked on the bedroom door.

It swung open midknock. Hunz had obviously heard the crew come in. He was all business, pointing and giving instructions without so much as a glance at Sydney.

She stood off to one side while the soundman and cameraman turned the area surrounding the French sofa into a ministudio. They worked quietly, efficiently, hospital quiet, on the verge of mortuary quiet. They spoke in low tones.

"Mr. Vonner, if you'll sit over here."

Joanna, a thirtyish woman with auburn hair and fire-engine red nails, pulled out one of the chairs at the table by the window. Hunz sat. She fitted him with a tissue collar and opened up a good-sized tackle box of cosmetic goodies. She grabbed a white wedge latex sponge from a bag. Next she sorted through disks of foundation.

Hunz sat motionless. He stared straight ahead at nothing, the way Sydney remembered her father sitting in the barber's chair.

"You have nice coloring," Joanna said. "Do you know what shade—"

"Suntone," Hunz said.

Joanna found the right makeup disk and began with his cheeks.

Hunz appeared calm. Had this been any other broadcast, Sydney would have equated his quiet mood to a baseball pitcher's game face. It wasn't unusual for a broadcaster to withdraw just before airing, using the time to arrange his thoughts and put himself in performance mode.

But this wasn't a normal broadcast.

And Hunz had to have things on his mind other than how he was going to come across on camera.

"Are you all right?" Sydney asked.

Joanna glanced at her, as if wondering whether asking such a question of a dying man was acceptable etiquette.

"You'll need to do Sydney too," Hunz said to Joanna. "She'll be on camera with me."

Clearly, he didn't want to talk about it. Maybe he didn't want to talk about it in front of strangers. Either way, Sydney got the message.

It was 7:49 a.m.

Hunz had less than an hour to live.

CHAPTER FORTY-EIGHT

The news program featuring Hunz Vonner's death began at 8:00 a.m. Pacific Time, 10:00 a.m. local time, though the studio was not scheduled to send it live to Hunz until a quarter past the hour.

"Countdown to Death" was the title the network settled on. At the top of the hour, the team in the hotel room was performing sound checks and making last-minute adjustments to the lighting.

Sydney and Hunz stood in front of the French sofa.

"There will be three cuts to us, the first at 10:15, the second at 10:25, and the last at 10:40," Hunz said. "At that time we'll take it to the end."

Sydney nodded.

"The first cut, right after I introduce myself, you introduce yourself. That's all you need to do."

She nodded again.

"You don't have to do anything else until the third cut. I'll start out, take it for as long as I can, then . . ." He gave her a half grin. "Well, then you're on."

You're on. Simple as that. I'll be lying dead on the floor at your feet; you take it from there. Did he know what he was asking her to do?

"What do I say?" she asked.

"A good reporter writes his own copy. Just wrap it up and send it back to the studio."

Just wrap it up and send it back to the studio. Simple. Piece of cake. Easy as pie. Walk in the park.

Sydney really didn't want to do this. She *really* did not want to do this.

10:15 a.m., local time.

Sydney heard two voices in her earphone, the WBBT morning news team. A prepared clip documenting the sudden appearance of Death Watch two days ago and its vicious rampage around the populated world had just ended. The anchors were segueing from the clip to the live feed at the Hilton Hotel.

"This morning we have with us one of our own, a veteran newscaster, himself a death watch victim."

That was Hunz's cue.

Portable tungsten lights made seeing anything beyond five feet impossible. The three-person crew moved like spirits behind the cameras.

Holding a microphone and looking every bit the professional, Hunz gazed into the camera lens and said, "This is Hunz Vonner . . ."

He trailed off.

Sydney had her own microphone. That would change with the third segment when she alone would hold a microphone. Apparently, the studio execs had discussed this at great length before dispatching the crew. It was their opinion that when Hunz died, it would look unprofessional for him to drop the microphone. Sydney would hold it for him.

". . . and Sydney St. James," Sydney said to the camera audience.

Hunz said, "We're coming to you live from the Hilton Hotel at O'Hare International Airport, Chicago, Illinois." He took a breath. "Victor Hugo wrote, 'All men are condemned to death with indefinitely suspended sentences.' And while that was true in Victor Hugo's world, a new world began two days ago when thousands of people had their suspended sentences revoked and the time of their deaths appointed and announced. I'm one of them."

Hunz held up an email printout.

"Nearly forty-eight hours ago, I received notice that I would die at 8:47 a.m., Pacific Standard Time. I'm not the first to receive a death watch notice; many have received notices with an announced time of death earlier than mine. To the best of my knowledge, without exception, they are now dead. Death Watch has proved itself frighteningly accurate. The night before last I witnessed one man's death, a victim of Death Watch. Although he was surrounded by emergency personnel at the time of his death, nothing could be done to save him. Which means I have every right to believe that within"—he checked his watch—"thirty minutes, I will be dead."

Sydney checked her watch too. Thirty-one minutes, fifteen seconds, to be exact.

Hunz continued. "Between now and the appointed time of my death, I will share with you the thoughts of a man who has been abruptly reminded of his own mortality. But, for now, back to the studio."

A teaser to keep the viewing audience tuned in.

The voices in Sydney's earpiece picked it up from there.

"Carol, that must be tough," said the male anchor, "to be suddenly aware of the time of your death, and to know nothing can be done to save you."

"You're right, Hal. And the precision of the timing . . . I've heard that death watch sentences—for that's what they are, aren't they?—are carried out at the exact second. Chilling."

From behind the cameras, a voice: "The Hugo quote was a nice touch," Dorian said.

"Thank you," Hunz replied.

Sydney leaned close. "Hunz? Before we go back on the air, I want to talk to you about . . ."

Hunz fiddled with his earpiece. He took it out and stepped toward the lights. "Excuse me a minute, Sydney. Dorian, can you take a look at this? It was cutting in and out during the last segment."

10:25 a.m., local time.

More prepared clips were aired between the live segments,

recorded segments of world leaders reacting to Death Watch. The Prime Minister of Great Britain said the earth was "on the edge of Armageddon." President Hu Jintao of the People's Republic of China declared the Death Watch—which had hit his country hard—to be a Western plot to overthrow the Chinese government. As evidence, he cited the number of death watch announcements that had been transmitted via modern communication devices: computers, faxes, cell phones. He likened Western technology to the Trojan Horse.

All around the world, combative nations blamed each other for Death Watch, in many cases launching retaliatory strikes.

A second prepackaged segment documented theories of who was behind Death Watch. The theories ranged from Death Watch being a prelude to an alien invasion, to nanobots that had formed an intelligence and declared war on human life-forms.

Hunz and Sydney were standing on their marks—masking tape Xs on the carpet—ready for the next live portion of the show, though Sydney didn't know why she was needed, since Hunz would do all the talking on this segment.

It was Dorian who told her to get into position. Another directive from the powers-that-be? Were they concerned Hunz might keel over before his time, possibly from a heart attack brought on by the anxiety? But then, if that were to happen, couldn't they just cut back to the studio? Maybe they were hoping she'd provide some good old-fashioned female hysterics.

To make a splash.

If that were the case, she could certainly oblige them the way her pulse was racing. She felt like she'd downed a dozen cups of coffee, her nervous system caffeine-charged even though she'd only sipped her latte.

The live feed was passed to Hunz.

"It's difficult to describe to you the range of thoughts and emotions that have crossed my mind in the last forty-eight hours," he said to the camera.

"From thinking it was a prank, or a mistake; to getting angry and desperately wanting to track down whoever was behind this; to the realization that the mortality rate for Death Watch was 100 percent, yet still believing that a solution or cure would be found; finally, to realizing that I was soon to go the way of all men and there was nothing I could do about it."

All men die, Sydney.

But not like this, Sydney thought. Hunz wasn't dying. He was being executed.

Hunz continued. "More times than I care to admit within the last forty-eight hours, the universal cry of the victim has escaped my lips: Why me? What have I done to warrant death? Am I a random victim, someone who walked into the wrong restaurant at the wrong time and sat next to a man with a bomb strapped to his chest? Or was I selected? Marked for death?

"And not just me. What of Lyle Vandeveer of Pasadena, California, who lived long enough to see his wife and daughter die when a commercial air flight plummeted to the ground, only to die while tinkering with his model trains? To whom was he a threat?

"Or Cheryl McCormick, who even now lies in a hospital bed not far from here at Prentice Women's Hospital. A compassionate woman, mother of a beautiful three-year-old daughter, heavy with her second child, hoping to deliver before her time runs out and she dies. A threat to whom? What kind of man would dispatch a death watch notice to Cheryl McCormick? What kind of monster would deny little Stacy and her unborn brother or sister their mother?"

Hunz's voice grew husky with emotion.

Had she been asked, Sydney would have been willing to bet that never once in his career had Hunz Vonner come close to losing control of his emotions on camera. He was close now.

"I am one of thousands of death watch victims," Hunz said. "Together, we cry out with a single voice: Why? To be sentenced to die is one thing. But not knowing why is cruel and inhuman. Every death watch victim lowered to his grave will have one word on his lips. *Why?*"

The show was once again transferred back to the studio.

"Hunz, we have to talk," Sydney said.

He dropped his microphone onto the sofa and pulled out his earpiece. Squaring his shoulders, he looked at her. The weariness he would never show on camera revealed itself now. His eyes sagged. His shoulders slumped.

"Sydney, could we do this later? I'd really like to be alone right now."

It was a plea, not a directive.

"Sure," she said.

It wasn't until he'd crossed the room to the bedroom and closed the door that she realized Hunz Vonner didn't have any "later" left.

CHAPTER FORTY-NINE

He said your name, Mommy!"

"Yes, he did," Cheryl McCormick said, staring at the screen in disbelief.

Stacy sat on Josh's lap as they watched the television in the hospital room. The program went to a commercial following Hunz Vonner's segment. On the screen a white duck attempted to shout the name of an insurance company. His attempts were repeatedly thwarted by various loud noises at an automotive repair center. Stacy thought the duck was funny.

"Can you believe it?" Cheryl said.

"I didn't know," Josh replied.

Josh was in Cheryl's room courtesy of Dora Evans, LPN. Upon learning of Dr. Isaacs's threats, the opinionated hospital worker— who'd lost a son to Death Watch—conspired to keep Josh in the room.

"Kick a good-lookin' hunk like you off my floor? Not on my watch, child," Dora had said.

She kept watch in the hallway for Isaacs's return. Calling the doctor's name was Josh's signal to slip into the closet.

The plan went off without a hitch. Dora called. Josh hid. Isaacs poked his head inside the door, looked around, grunted, and left.

Now, Dora stood in the room, having watched the first segment of "Countdown to Death" with them. According to her, every television in the hospital was tuned to the program.

"You sure you want her watching this?" Dora inclined her head toward Stacy.

"We know Hunz Vonner," Cheryl said solemnly. "We met him last night."

"Hunz, like the ketchup," Stacy said.

Dora and Josh laughed. It lightened the mood.

"Stacy! Where did you hear that?" Cheryl asked.

"Hunz told me. Hunz, like the ketchup."

"Mr. Vonner and Stacy hit it off," Cheryl explained. "He was very good to us. Arranged to get me back here to the hospital on the station's corporate jet."

"Really?" Dora said, surprised. She glanced back at the screen, even though Hunz's image was no longer there. "He doesn't look the type, you know what I'm saying?"

CHAPTER
FIFTY

10:39 a.m., local time.

Sydney stood on her mark, microphone in hand. She stood alone. Hunz had yet to come out of the bedroom with less than a minute before the studio would switch over to them for the final segment. Once they did, Hunz would have seven minutes of time to fill, and to live.

Dorian knocked on the bedroom door a second time.

"Mr. Vonner? Thirty seconds."

He pressed his ear to the door.

"Mr. Vonner?"

Sydney wasn't concerned about Hunz missing his cue. Veteran television newscasters were adept at handling time. It wasn't uncommon for an anchor to emerge from his dressing room—often in a coat and tie and Bermuda shorts and tennis shoes—make his way onto the set, take his place behind the news desk with less than a second to spare, and launch into the first news story without missing a beat.

Sydney glanced at her watch.

It was dead.

A blank gray face stared back at her. No numbers. No time. Nothing. She pushed the buttons on the side, hoping to stir it to life. She got nothing. The battery. It had to be.

All her attempts to have the precise time had been wasted.

"Fifteen seconds," the cameraman said.

"Mr. Vonner?" Dorian said to the door, louder now. Veteran or no veteran, anxiety was creeping into his voice.

"Ready on the set," the cameraman said.

Voices sounded in Sydney's ear. The anchors were preparing to hand the show to Hunz, and he wasn't there.

"No, not ready on the set!" Sydney said.

"Mr. Vonner?" Dorian shouted.

"Try the doorknob!" Joanna suggested.

"I did!" Dorian hissed back at her. "You think I'm stupid?"

"Five seconds," the camera said.

And at the Hilton Hotel at O'Hare International is Hunz Vonner, veteran newscaster and victim of the death watch terror. We're switching live to him, where he has just seven minutes left to live.

"Four, three . . . ," the cameraman was counting down.

Let me remind our viewers that this is the first live network airing of a death watch death. Hunz, are you there?

The cameraman cued Sydney.

"This is Sydney St. James," Sydney said, using her on-the-air voice. "A short time ago, Hunz Vonner retreated into the bedroom, closed the door, and has yet to return."

Sydney? This is Carol. Did he give any indication why he was going into the bedroom, and when he would be coming out?

"Apparently he wanted to be alone for a while, Carol. At the time, he gave no indication he would not appear for this segment as planned."

Hal here, Sydney. Has anyone attempted to communicate with him?

"Yes, Hal. As a matter of fact, at this moment, a member of WBBT is attempting to communicate with him through the door."

Maybe he fell asleep, Hal's voice said, presumably to his coanchor. *Sydney? Do you think we could get a camera shot of the door?*

The bedroom door opened. Sydney couldn't see it, she heard it, along with Dorian chastising Hunz in stage whispers.

"What have you been doing? We're on the air!"

"Hunz Vonner is coming to the set now," Sydney said.

While Hunz fitted his earpiece in his, Hal made a lame on-the-air comment about being glad Hunz didn't die prematurely.

As for Sydney, she was just glad Hunz's arrival was taking the camera off her. She was angry he'd hung her out to dry like that on national television, and if he wasn't about to die in six minutes, she would have wrung his neck.

Now that she was off camera, she motioned to the lights that her watch wasn't working. Joanna appeared from the bright haze. Off to the side, she turned the hotel alarm clock—the one Sydney had turned to the wall—so that Sydney could see it. Sydney nodded in thanks.

10:43 a.m.

"With hard evidence to go on," Hunz said, without apology to the audience that had tuned in to watch him die, "at this point in time, the best I can give you regarding the origin of Death Watch is this reporter's observations.

"First, it's obvious to me there is intelligence behind Death Watch. Whether it's a singular or collective intelligence, there are not enough facts to determine. We do know, however, that the messages are composed and delivered, both in print and audio format, to select persons. We also know that, whether directly or indirectly, the source behind these notices can pinpoint a person's time of death. Do they cause every death? I can't say that with 100 percent certainty. But I do know this: They can determine the time of death, and to know that and to make no attempt to prevent it, in my mind, is equally criminal.

"Second, we know that whoever is behind Death Watch has vast resources. Even with our most sophisticated communication technologies, no one has succeeded in tracing a death watch notice to its point of origin. Yet those who transmit the notices have done so in virtually every country in the world.

"Third, whoever is behind Death Watch has a plan. For reasons unknown, they have remained silent and hidden. Dwelling in the shadows, they strike and retreat before anyone can see them. This darkness in which they dwell is the home of serial killers, stalkers, murderers, and thugs. Hidden and silent, they strike fear in the heart of every being on this planet. For we have yet to see evidence that any of us is protected, that any of us is safe. Maybe this is their plan. To step out of the shadows, to identify themselves, would invite dialogue, and possibly bring an end to their killing."

10:45 a.m.

Two minutes remaining.

Hunz's breathing grew erratic. He blinked several times.

All of a sudden, everyone was shouting at Sydney at once. From the studio, the voices in her ear—

Hunz, are you all right? Sydney, help him out. Get him something. Water, or something. It looks like he's having trouble breathing.

From behind the lights—

"Step closer to him!"

"Grab his arm!"

"He's going, he's going! Sydney, take it!"

Sydney didn't need instruction. She went to Hunz's side. Her microphone lowered, she whispered, "Are you all right? Do you want to sit down?"

"I think so," he whispered back.

"Into the microphone!" Dorian cried. "Speak into the microphone!"

Sydney helped Hunz onto the sofa.

This is ridiculous, she thought. Whose idea was this in the first place? She was a heartbeat away from yelling at the crew to turn off the camera, turn off the lights, and if they didn't, she would.

Seated, Hunz seemed to rally.

He reached for the microphone.

"My final observation—," he said.

"You don't have to do this," Sydney whispered.

He gave her one of those looks—one of those bullheaded, testosterone-charged, male looks—that told her it was something he had to do.

"—is that behind the Death Watch there is cowardice. Everything about it reeks of cowardice. The slinking, chickenhearted, bullying strike-and-run tactics are all the evidence we need to evaluate the true character of whoever is behind Death Watch. I was taught that a true man could look friend or enemy in the eye. That he took responsibility for his actions. That his friends could count on him, and while his enemies may not agree with him, they knew where he stood."

10:46 a.m.

"And so—"

With effort, Hunz stood. Sydney stood with him.

"—as I face the final minute of my life, I choose to stand and face whoever, or whatever, would strike me down and kill me. If there is any manhood in him, or them, I challenge them to come out of the shadows, stand like men, and show their faces."

Hunz lowered his microphone.

He faced the camera resolutely.

Sydney! Say something! This is dead air. Say something!

Sydney pulled the earplug from her ear. It dangled on her shoulder. She could still hear the voices. They sounded far away.

She stood next to Hunz.

"Thirty seconds," Dorian said behind the lights.

Hunz Vonner stood tall. There was no fear. No sign of regret. He didn't tremble. He had the appearance of a man resolved to his fate.

"Fifteen seconds."

"Hunz . . ."

Sydney wanted to say something, but the words weren't there. She wanted to tell him that over the last couple of days, she'd come to admire and respect him, that when she thought of him she'd remember him holding Stacy and the way she clung to his neck like he was her father, that the last few hours they spent together talking at the table had meant so much to her, that . . .

"Ten seconds."

But there wasn't time. There was only time to say—

"Do not be afraid of those who kill the body," she blurted.

Hunz turned to her. Their eyes met in silent communication.

"Five seconds."

"Four."

The verbal countdown made Sydney angry. This wasn't a rocket launch. This was a man's life!

"Three."

"Two."

"One."

Hunz's eyes closed.

No one breathed.

At Prentice Women's Hospital, nurse Dora Evans turned away from the television to Cheryl.

"Do you really want her to see this?" Dora asked.

Stacy's attention was diverted between coloring in her Wonder Woman coloring book and her friend Hunz—like the ketchup—on television.

Josh and Cheryl were both leaning forward as though the news would reach them sooner the closer they got to the television.

"Maybe you should," Cheryl said, with a worried glance at Stacy. "Do you mind?"

"Child, I see people die every day. I don't have to watch it on television."

She scooped up Stacy.

"You like orange juicy, honey? Let's go see if we can find you some."

"Dora? Wait . . . ," Cheryl said, her eyes fixed on the television screen.

The only sound in the hotel suite was the buzz of the lights.

It was one of those moments when time slows and a dozen heart-beats squeeze into a single second.

Hunz was stiff, but upright. No buckling at the knees. No timber like a felled tree.

He opened his eyes.

Cheers went up from behind the lights.

Sydney didn't join them.

She'd learned her lesson with Lyle Vandeveer. She looked at the hotel alarm clock.

10:47 a.m.

But was it accurate?

She waited.

Hunz didn't move. Was he thinking of Lyle Vandeveer too?

Seconds ticked.

A trio of voices from behind the lights urged Hunz to say something.

He didn't. Not for a while.

The voices in Sydney's earpiece chattered against her shoulder. She ignored them.

10:48 a.m.

Hunz was still standing. Still alive.

He looked at Sydney and grinned.

Professionalism, take a hike. She threw her arms around him.

At Prentice Women's Hospital, little Stacy jumped up and down on the bed clapping her hands, though she didn't understand why everyone was happy. Cheryl and Josh hugged and laughed and cried. Nurse Dora brushed a few tears aside herself.

CHAPTER
FIFTY-ONE

Sydney had no idea how long she'd clung to Hunz's neck. She didn't want to think about time right now. All she knew was that she hadn't hugged him long enough.

Voices chattered in her earpiece. Sniffles could be heard behind the lights, presumably Joanna, but it could have been Dorian.

"We're still on the air," Hunz whispered, though he had a grip on Sydney equal to hers. "We're on the air internationally."

The letting go was awkward. Sydney found herself less than inches from the face of a man she'd known for less than two days—but she knew him, didn't she? She knew him better than some men she'd known for years. Still, they'd never touched, not even an accidental brush of a hand, until now.

Her face warm, she stepped back.

Hunz made the quick transition from joyous and amused to his professional broadcaster demeanor. He addressed the camera.

"I'm alive!"

A grin cracked through his hardened professionalism for a moment, but was quickly repaired.

Sydney replaced her earpiece.

What's going on here, Carol? Did he have the Death Watch or didn't he?

Let's hear what he has to say, Hal.

Hunz could hear the voices, too. He ignored them.

Sydney made no attempt to regain her professionalism. She was grinning like a joker, unable to do otherwise.

"I suppose an explanation is in order," Hunz said into the camera. He took a deep breath. "Frankly, I'm still coming to terms with it myself, but . . . here I am. That's something, isn't it?

"Well, I can tell you this much: To the best of my knowledge, I'm the first man to beat the Death Watch. Good news, certainly, for I had pretty much concluded that my life on this earth had come to an end."

He took another deep breath.

"The answer to the mystery behind the terror will surprise many, but not all. It did me. Even now, I find it difficult to believe that, for reasons I cannot explain, I would be the one to prove the solution true, let alone be the bearer of such momentous news. The bottom line is, as of today, no one need ever fear Death Watch again.

"And while I am the first to profit from the solution, the answer came from a source even more unlikely than me. Actually, my colleague, Sydney St. James, deserves credit, for it is she who interviewed the source behind the solution to Death Watch. She then passed the information to me."

He nodded warmly in Sydney's direction.

Another deep breath.

"The key to defeating the Death Watch," he continued, "was delivered by a most unlikely messenger. A modern-day Elijah."

Hunz described the events leading up to Billy Peppers's plunge from the roof of the hotel. To Sydney's surprise, he didn't stop there. Knowing that his words were being broadcast literally around the world, translated into every major language, Hunz described Billy Peppers's fiery translation with a beautiful and accurate description of the angels.

The chattering in his earpiece increased.

Hunz pulled a piece of paper from his coat pocket. "As improbable as all this sounds," he said as he unfolded it, "the death watch attack is a spiritual one; therefore, to neutralize it, we must use spiritual weapons. Just hours ago, I learned the truth. Minutes ago, the truth was confirmed."

Reading from the handwriting on the paper now:

"'For our struggle is not against flesh and blood, but against the rulers, against the authorities, against the powers of this dark world and against the spiritual forces of evil in the heavenly realms.'"

Hunz's voice broke. Until now he'd managed to run ahead of his emotions. They just caught up with him.

Sydney stepped in. "A message that shouldn't come as any surprise," she said. "As Billy Peppers told me, 'It doesn't make sense to believe in a supernatural God and not believe in the supernatural.'"

The camera lights switched off.

"Save it," Dorian said.

For Hunz and Sydney the room went black. It took several blinks before shapes began to appear, and when they did, they were of the news crew packing up the equipment.

"The station pulled the plug," Dorian said.

While the cameraman and Joanna stowed the lights for transport, Dorian took the microphone and the earpieces from Hunz and Sydney and coiled the wires.

"You know, that was pretty low," Dorian muttered. "I mean, handing out tracts at the airport, holding up signs at football games . . . that stuff's annoying, but this? This was low, man."

In the bedroom, Hunz's cell phone rang. He went to answer it. A moment later, Sydney's cell phone rang in her purse. It was Helen. No hello. Just shouting.

Hunz walked out of the bedroom, his hand over the phone. "Sol," he said.

They held separate conversations as the WBBT crew exited quickly without further comment.

They cut them off!" Josh said, jumping out of his chair and pointing at the television screen.

The WBBT anchors appeared on-screen seated behind the studio news desk. Hal and Carol exchanged nervous glances.

"Well, that was embarrassing," Carol said with a self-conscious chuckle.

Hal, a middle-aged man with thick silver hair, spoke directly to the camera.

"On behalf of WBBT and our affiliates, we want to apologize for what you have just witnessed and state for the record that the views expressed on this program do not represent the views of this station or its owners."

Carol nodded her agreement. "Because of past abuses, we have attempted to introduce measures that would allow us to protect our viewers from this kind of unseemly behavior on live TV. However, in this case, a five-second delay has proved inadequate. And, for that, we apologize."

In the hospital room, Josh was beside himself. "Can you believe that?" he cried. "They're apologizing that Hunz didn't die!"

Back to Hal at the studio. "Furthermore, we wish to apologize to all groups who find the content of Mr. Vonner's commentary offensive, particularly our Jewish and Islamic friends."

Carol continued. "Please believe us when we say we were caught completely off guard. Hunz Vonner came to us with impeccable credentials from the EuroNet broadcasting system."

"A highly respected international news source," Hal added. He turned to his coanchor. "I don't know about you, Carol," he said, "but I feel like I've just been bushwhacked."

"Bushwhacked?" Josh shouted at the screen. He turned to Cheryl. "Bushwhacked! Did he just say bushwhacked? I can't believe it."

Using the remote control, Cheryl clicked off the television set. She stared at the blank screen.

She said, "I wonder how Sydney's holding up under all this, poor dear."

Sol wants us back in Los Angeles, ASAP." Hunz flipped his phone closed.

"I've never heard Helen use language like that," Sydney said. "What are we going to do?"

"We should probably do what they say."

"Yeah."

Hunz looked at Sydney. "We're not, are we?"

"I don't know about you," Sydney said, "but I'm not leaving Chicago until I talk to Cheryl and Josh."

CHAPTER FIFTY-TWO

D on't dawdle," Dora said, waving them down the deserted hallway. Sydney, Hunz, and Josh stepped lively, their shoes squeaking on the polished white tile floor of Prentice Women's Hospital.

It was the second time Sydney had stepped foot in the hospital. Both times had been an experience.

Yesterday, not long after Hunz's broadcast, when they walked through the sliding glass hospital doors into the lobby, they were recognized immediately. Over a dozen people populated the lobby, filling out admission forms, waiting for news of loved ones. Some booed when they saw Hunz and Sydney. Others were more articulate with their opinions.

"Shoulda known. Nothin' but a cheap stunt."

"You owe me, man. The station promised us a death."

"Yeah. And what do we get instead? Billy Graham!"

Now, the morning after the broadcast, Sydney made her second entrance into the hospital as an adventurous and sympathetic nurse sneaked them into Cheryl's room.

Dora Evans didn't put much stock in visitors' hours or the rules restricting the number of people allowed in a pregnant woman's room.

"Don't dawdle! Don't dawdle!" she said, with the vigilance of a sheepdog.

"Good morning," Cheryl greeted them from her bed. "Just in time."

The off-duty news trio circled her bed. She held up a hand. Josh seemed to know just what to do. He took it and got a squeeze.

Stacy lay next to her mother in the bed, asleep.

From the door, Dora said, "Keep it down, okay?" She started to leave, then stopped to say, "If this don't beat all. I've seen death watch vigils for terminal patients plenty of times, but this is the first life watch vigil I've ever seen."

She closed the door. The two couples and Stacy were alone.

"Should we wake her?" Sydney asked.

Cheryl lovingly straightened the bangs on her daughter's forehead. "No, let her sleep," she said. Tears came.

"Oh, honey." Sydney took Cheryl's free hand. "Are you scared?"

Cheryl smiled bravely. "A little," she said.

Hunz checked his watch, comparing it to the wall clock.

9:26 a.m.

"Two minutes," Cheryl said. "The time on the letter was 7:28 a.m., but that was Pacific Time."

"Are you ready for this?" Hunz asked.

Cheryl knew what he was asking. They'd had a long talk during his visit yesterday.

"Can a person ever be 100 percent certain?" she asked.

"You have to put your trust in the One doing the rescuing," Hunz replied.

Cheryl nodded. "Then I'm ready."

9:27 a.m.

Cheryl looked up at Sydney. "I don't even want to think about what would have happened if it wasn't for you," she said.

Sydney kissed her hand. "Who would have thought God would use *Wonder Wheel* to bring people together," she said.

Cheryl smiled. She looked at each of them in turn.

"Thank you," she said. "Thank you all for being here."

"Thank Hunz," Sydney said. "He's the one who negotiated an extra night's stay in Chicago with our producer."

"Negotiating is too noble of a word to describe what I did," Hunz said sheepishly. "Making excuses is closer to the truth. It bought us last night and a couple of hours this morning."

"However you arranged it, thank you," Cheryl said.

"Josh, what about you?" Sydney asked.

"It was easy for me." Josh shrugged. "I just told them I had a death watch notice and they placed me on extended leave. New KSMJ policy."

They watched the last thirty seconds tick off in silence, Cheryl holding Josh with one hand, Sydney with the other. Hunz had reached out, consciously or subconsciously, and was touching sleeping Stacy's foot.

9:28 a.m.

Cheryl gasped as the wall clock's red second hand continued its sweep into the morning.

"Welcome back to the living," Hunz said.

Stacy woke.

"Mommy?"

"I'm here, honey," Cheryl said. "I'm here."

The last thing Sydney told Cheryl before leaving the hospital was that she would return in a month to assist in the birth of the baby. Hunz told Cheryl he'd try to arrange to get some time off to look after Stacy. He said she was going to need a playmate to help her adjust to the fact that she would have to share her mommy.

CHAPTER FIFTY-THREE

Hunz, wake up!"

Slicing through the upper atmosphere somewhere over Colorado, the Dassault Falcon streaked toward California and, for Hunz Vonner and Sydney St. James, a day of reckoning at KSJM studio.

"It's Josh at the hospital," Sydney cried.

Hunz sat up, groggy. "Is something wrong?"

"It's Cheryl," Sydney said.

They were two hours into the flight. Hunz had fallen asleep shortly after takeoff. Not having slept much the last two days, he was exhausted. Sydney alternated her time between looking out the window—amazed at how peaceful the world appears at thirty thousand feet—and worrying about the scene that awaited her in Helen Gordon's office. No matter how she played it out in her mind, it was ugly.

The chirp of her cell phone had startled her. Hearing the sound of Josh Leven's voice on the other end startled her even more. With the cell phone in one hand, she shook Hunz awake with the other.

"What is it?" Hunz said, awake now.

"Josh wouldn't say. All he said was that he could only get through this once, so he wanted us both to listen."

In the time it took Sydney to rouse Hunz, a hundred scenarios flashed through Sydney's mind. The one that kept surfacing to the top was Death Watch. Had they mistimed it? Had something gone wrong?

She held the phone between them so that both she and Hunz could listen.

"Josh? Hunz is here now. What happened?"

"It's a girl!" Josh shouted.

"She's not due for another month!" Sydney cried, happy and relieved at the same time.

"The kid didn't want to wait that long," Josh said. "Cheryl went into labor not ten minutes after you walked out the door."

Sydney and Hunz exchanged happy glances.

"Everyone's healthy?" Hunz said.

"Cheryl's fine. The baby's fine. Stacy's fine, though she thinks the baby is some kind of toy doll. I'm the only one who may not survive."

"Well, you gave us quite a scare," Sydney said.

"Did I? Sorry. I guess I'm not very good at this. It's a lot harder than reporting sports scores. I gotta go. Cheryl gave me a whole list of people to call. You were at the top of the list."

"Good luck," Hunz said.

"Yeah, I'm gonna need it. How am I going to do this? I don't know these people..All I can think of is: 'Hi, I'm Josh Leven, sports-caster for KSMJ-TV. You don't know me, but Cheryl just had a baby.'"

"I'm sure you'll think of something," Sydney said.

Slumping back against the plush leather seats, Sydney and Hunz basked in the good news.

"Well, that was unexpected," she said. "I was looking forward to being there for the birth."

"He didn't tell us the baby's name," Hunz said.

"What's the female version of Hunz?"

Either Hunz didn't hear her, or he pretended not to.

"You know, I'm new to all this," he said, "but you have to admit this morning has been amazing. I can't help thinking that God had it planned this way from the beginning."

Sydney listened.

"A mother is saved and that same morning she gives birth to a child, possibly the first child of a death watch survivor in the history of the world," he said.

Sydney smiled. "I'm just glad Cheryl's baby has been born into a world that doesn't have to live in the shadow of Death Watch."

CHAPTER
FIFTY-FOUR

Give me a break!" Sydney cried. "It's three thirty in the afternoon!" Traffic on the Hollywood Freeway was the worst Sydney had ever seen. A tractor trailer had overturned just before Silver Lake Boulevard, blocking three lanes of traffic. Everything was at a standstill as motorists were funneled down an exit ramp, through a five-block maze of city streets, then back onto the freeway.

At least that's what the radio reports said was happening. From Sydney's vantage point, it was a parking lot. Inching was considered progress.

After landing at Los Angeles International Airport, she'd dropped Hunz off at his hotel. He wanted to change clothes before meeting with Sol Rosenthal. Having arranged to meet Helen in her office at 3:30 p.m., Sydney thought she had time to run home and freshen up. The circumstances behind the flight to Chicago hadn't exactly given her time to pack a suitcase. And now, here she was, sitting motionless on the freeway when she was supposed to be in her assignment editor's office.

She had no other option than to pick up her cell phone and dial the station. It was a call she dreaded making. Punching the speed-dial number for the station, she held the phone to her ear. It was dead. She checked the display. Dead. She pushed the ON button. The display flashed just long enough to see an empty battery icon. She hadn't had time to pack, and neither had she had time to charge her phone.

In frustration, Sydney St. James banged the steering wheel with the palm of her hand.

It was after four o'clock by the time Sydney reached the station. As she hurried past the receptionist—who silently warned her with a shake of the head that what she was walking into wasn't good—Sydney looked around, hoping to see Hunz. Just knowing he was nearby would provide a measure of comfort. Instead, she ran into Cori Zinn.

"What did you do to Josh?" Cori shouted at her.

"Cori, I don't have time for this. I'm late for a—"

"He flies off to Chicago with some pregnant woman—"

"Cori, really, I don't have time—"

"—calls the station using the death watch ruse as an excuse to spend more time with her—"

"Cori, listen to me."

"—and then, he calls me a couple of hours ago all excited to tell me he's at the hospital helping this woman deliver her baby!"

Sydney smiled. She couldn't help herself.

"I blame you for this!" Cori shouted. "You turned him against me! You brainwashed him by introducing him to that Chicago bimbo!"

Helen stepped out of her office. She made eye contact with Sydney.

"As delightful as our conversations always are," Sydney said, stepping around Cori, "I'm afraid we will have to pick up later."

Only when Cori saw Helen did she let Sydney pass.

"This isn't over between you and me," Cori hissed.

Helen disappeared into her office. Sydney followed.

"Our meeting was at three thirty," Helen said.

Sydney closed the door behind her. "Helen, I tried calling. My cell's dead. There's an accident on the freeway. A tractor trailer."

Even as she spoke, Sydney hated the sound of what she was saying.

There are no excuses in journalism. Professor Puckett. Journalism 101.

Helen wasn't listening. She arranged stacks of file folders on her desk.

Not knowing whether to stand or sit, Sydney opted for standing.

Helen busied herself awhile longer. The phone rang. She took the call.

"A press release will be sent out tomorrow morning," she said. "We'll announce it on the air tonight . . . Yes, C-O-R-I . . . just one R . . . That's right, five years . . . No, she's filled in, but she's never been a prime-time coanchor before . . . Fort Worth . . . yes."

Helen hung up. Several minutes of awkward silence passed, long enough for Sydney to get angry that the station would reward Cori Zinn with a promotion after all the things she'd pulled.

"I thought you were smarter than this, Sydney," Helen said.

Sydney said nothing.

"You know, they're blaming you."

Blaming me? For what? Why was Helen being so cryptic?

Since she didn't understand this conversation, Sydney decided to launch one of her own.

"Helen, we know how to defeat Death Watch!" she said. "Hunz was just the first. Cheryl McCormick—remember Cheryl? The pregnant contestant on *Wonder Wheel?*—this morning, Cheryl confirmed—"

"The way network executives see it," Helen said, cutting her off, "it isn't Hunz. He doesn't have the background for this kind of stunt. You do. Midwestern Protestant roots. Church attender at an evangelical—"

"Helen, listen to me! We know how to stop the deaths! I know it sounds crazy, but—"

"Here's how they see it: The two of you, going off together the way you did. A romantic affair. He becomes infatuated with you. You tell him nothing can come of it because of your religious faith. He says he's willing to convert for you."

"Helen, listen to me!"

"Sydney, you're fired."

"What?"

It wasn't as though Sydney didn't see it coming. It was one of the scenarios she'd imagined at thirty thousand feet. But imagining it and hearing it were two different things.

"Of course, the union will protest," Helen said. "They'll say a person's personal religious beliefs are not grounds for dismissal. The station will counter that you were well aware of the rules against proselytizing. I'm confident we'll work out some kind of settlement."

Helen spoke as though the settlement had already been worked out.

Sydney leaned forward on Helen's desk.

"Don't do this, Helen. You've got to listen to me! We know how to stop Death Watch!"

Helen looked at her with deadly earnest eyes.

"I went out on a limb for you, Sydney," she said. "Perhaps I was assuming too much. Even if I were to overlook all this religious mumbo jumbo, your actions these past two days have been unprofessional and irresponsible. Sydney, if you want to save the world, you'll have to do it on your own time."

Hunz was waiting for Sydney when she came out of Helen's office. She didn't see him at first. He was off in the distance, standing next to a monitor playing a *Gilligan's Island* episode. Mary Ann and Ginger were putting on a stage production for the castaways.

Sydney wondered if they had *Gilligan's Island* in Germany, then wondered what the German actors thought of the state of American television script writing as they dubbed over the voices.

As she walked toward Hunz, Sydney noticed the Homeland Security Awareness system symbol in the bottom corner. In contrast to the canned laughter of the sitcom, it was still set on Level Four.

Had anyone taken Hunz's broadcast seriously?

Hunz heard her coming. He turned. "Are you all right?" he asked. "Sol told me."

Sydney made a casual gesture with her hand. She pretended it didn't hurt, but it did, despite the fact that she was still pretty much numb from the shock.

"What are you going to do?" he asked.

"I don't know. I haven't had a lot of time to consider my options. I wanted time off to go back to Evanston. Guess I got my wish. How about you? Did Sol banish you from the KSMJ kingdom?"

Hunz smiled. It wasn't a real smile. "In essence. He's sending me back to Germany. Said he was disappointed in me."

"Seems to be the theme of the day around here," Sydney said.

They ambled to Command Central and lingered over the huge conference table, quiet now.

"What does EuroNet have to say about all this?" Sydney asked.

"They're heated. Particularly because it aired shortly before six o'clock in the evening."

"That's right, the time difference."

"They're upset that Sol is angry. They say I've given EuroNet a black eye."

Hunz spoke in a low tone. Sydney could tell this was hard on him too. And getting harder. She didn't want to ask the next question.

"When do you fly back?" she said.

"I don't. I quit."

"Hunz!"

"I promised Cheryl I'd help out with Stacy."

Sydney couldn't believe what she'd just heard. Did Hunz Vonner, internationally recognized newscaster for EuroNet, really just say he was quitting his job to take up babysitting? He even shuffled his feet like a little boy when he said it! Stacy McCormick had really done a number on him.

"What about your career?" Sydney asked.

Hunz became deadly earnest.

"Sydney, we know how to stop Death Watch. How can I continue broadcasting descriptions of death watch tragedies when I know how to prevent them? How can I report the latest theories about who is behind the terror when I know who it is and how to stop him!"

"We do know, don't we?" Sydney said excitedly. "But they won't let us broadcast it."

"We'll just have to find other ways to get the word out."

"Even so, Hunz . . . your career . . ."

"Sydney, knowing what I know, how can I possibly keep silent?"

We want to hear from you. Please send your comments about this book to us in care of zreview@zondervan.com. Thank you.

GRAND RAPIDS, MICHIGAN 49530 USA

WWW.ZONDERVAN.COM